ANOTHER
JUSTIFIED
SINNER

SOPHIE HOPESMITH

ANOTHER JUSTIFIED SINNER

SOPHIE HOPESMITH

dead ink

dead ink

The right of Sophie Hopesmith to be identified as the author of this work has been asserted by her in accordance with the Copyright, Designs and Patents Act 1988.

First published in Great Britain in 2017 by Dead Ink, an imprint of Cinder House Publishing Limited.

Paperback ISBN 9781911585015
Hardback ISBN 9781911585008

Printed and bound in Great Britain by Clays Ltd, St Ives plc.

www.deadinkbooks.com

For James, for hope

'An exaltation of spirit lifted me, as it were, far above the earth and the sinful creatures crawling on its surface; and I deemed myself as an eagle among the children of men, soaring on high, and looking down with pity and contempt on the grovelling creatures below.'

James Hogg
The Private Memoirs and Confessions of a Justified Sinner

Part One
Black

Chapter One

I woke up to a ghost masturbating in my face. Darkness sucked in deeper darkness. This kind of ringing in the ears. Then an off-white, spectral, ethereal thing – like a splash of paint before a paintbrush gives form. Her eyes were screwed up incredibly tight, but I could still see the amber flash of fire in her eyes, I could still tell it was her. And she moaned very slightly and started to cum; amorphousness pushed against the bed frame, an underworld howl, and I could feel the vibrations of a contracting pussy...

Hours later, it was breakfast. I pottered about my kitchen, doing all the ordinary things that someone does in the morning. Somebody who goes to work and has to be in first thing, who leads an office existence in a rich, western city. I would brush my teeth, I would shower quickly, cock my leg and unleash a fart. A quick dab of aftershave, a quick cup of coffee – never finished. Sometimes a slice of toast or maybe some cornflakes – but seldom. And somewhere between all this glutinous triteness, and my reaching the tube, I had a sudden and startling and brain-jabbing thought: why was she masturbating? Why wasn't she tossing me off? Why wasn't she fucking me senseless? Why wasn't I holding her and stroking her and suckling her breasts, and telling her I loved her, and telling her I wanted her back? Who else would conjure up a dead former love in a beatific burst of 4am fantasy and have her so apart, so detached, so self-sufficiently fingering? What a loser. What a mug. To be emasculated by your own subconscious, by your own despair. I picked up a newspaper to calm myself down, but my hands were trembling and my eyes got sore. And I wept.

The colours that morning were sensational. It was the beginning of May, and things were unfurling and unfolding with a quiet intensity. There was a burgeoning, a blast, some beckoning of fingers. The sound of dawn reaching fever pitch: this roar of relief at the death of the winter, its entrails slung up in the sun-rising sky. Every blossom of a flower, every bounce of a butterfly, every buzz of a bee, could be heard in mass exhalation, like some victory wheeze.

When I turned to her, she was tangled up in sun motes, her hair dancing against the pillow as she coughed her way back to life. I had a sudden instinct to kiss her, to touch her, to squeeze her hand. To say I was sorry, even though I wasn't sorry at all. To forget all the arguing and the bickering and go back to something bigger and better: the in-jokes and quotes, conspiratorial chuckles, lovingly cooked lasagne, the smell of her perfume, my arms around her waist. But then her eyes flickered open and consciousness entered, and I was seized with a hatred so fierce, so overwhelming and crude, that I had to leave the room immediately and try to wash it down the sink.

Downstairs, she was in the kitchen with the kettle switched on, some inane radio DJ chirruping in the background like an unwelcome visitor. She liked that kind of stuff: she said it made her feel 'cheery', set her up for the day.

Her lips parted open, she went to say something. I shook my head. 'Don't.'

Her eyes watered up. 'Do you want me to leave? Just tell me if you want me to leave.'

'What, the flat?'

'Yes.'

'For good?'

'Yes, that's what I meant.' She snorted loudly, unattractively – there was obviously an ocean of snotty tears in that long, gentle throat of hers.

I had no time for martyrdom. I raised my voice a notch. I tried to sound pissed off and angry in the coldest, I-don't-care way I knew how. 'There are contracts, Nancy. There are fucking contracts!' Now my voice had risen too far. I tried to harness it, tame it – but it was a wild horse galloping away, with stampeding hooves and the dust in its nostrils. 'Or do you want to fuck things up for Jamie and George, too?'

Then she broke down completely. She said she was sorry. She said she would help sort another flatmate. But she didn't want to leave. She wanted to work things out. She loved me still, she needed me. It had only been a kiss. A stupid, senseless, inconsequential kiss. She was drunk, she was lonely, I had been so distant lately, so terribly distant. And she bit her lip in that way she did, when she was scared and panicked. And she looked up at me with those big amber eyes, and she blinked back the tears and she had never looked more beautiful.

That's when I really hated her. That's when I actually despised her. I can't remember all the things I said because I was twenty-two and it seems a long time ago. But somehow, her beauty and her vulnerability and her female power made me all the more incensed. How dare she shift things on to me, how dare she suggest I was to blame? Her actions had led to this consequence;

her actions had knotted my intestines with thick, heavy rope.

So I shouted and raged and I threw something – I think. Maybe I even went to strike her, maybe she ducked beneath the curtains and yelped and pleaded forgiveness. Maybe I looked at her spongy, perfect body and I wanted to wring it dry, I wanted to squeeze out all the virtue and love and I wanted to exhaust her, to crumble it, for her to feel the shock of my temper, to be beaten down and crying and trembling from all the testosterone.

It is hard to explain. It was like one of those old clichés. A blind rage that broke my body. I was not in control. I wasn't myself. I yelled at her, 'I hate you, I hate you,' as she ran up the driveway, as she was shrieking hysterically, as she shot into that scrap-heap car, and I saw her back out of the driveway with her make up in chaos, with the tears streaming down and her banging the wheel – all the time, biting and chewing that full lip of hers.

'I hate her, I hate her,' I screamed, and I unplugged the toaster and I hurled it at the wall, and I chucked plates on the floor, and the crashing and banging and breaking were the sounds of some powerful symphony. They calmed me down, brought me succour, like I was physically prising apart the hormones that surged through my body. And afterwards, I didn't scream or break things anymore. Instead, I was rocking with my knees up to my chest, and I was thinking back on her, and how much I had loved her – once upon a time. And it seemed to me that she had destroyed all my potential, that she had ruined my life. I remember saying out loud, with a deft smile on my lips: 'I hope she fucks off and dies. I want her to die. I want her out of my life.'

It's an odd thing when it happens. Like one of those police dramas or films, the kind you've seen a million times before – so many times that they cease to feel real when the moment comes. A knock on a door that already seems significant, to carry weight, that seems to echo in a particular way, a way that singles it out from a postman's knock or the doorbell buzz of a chugger.

Anyway, before all that, my fists were shaking, there was a surge of adrenalin. I called into work and said I didn't feel well. I hung up and gazed out of the window. The sky was such a neon, lambent blue that it looked sort of glazed. I poured a few cups of coffee, but it didn't steady my nerves. I opened my laptop and surfed. I downloaded some porn in a spot of childish rebellion, but my heart wasn't in it, so I tabbed back to the BBC with all the usual war and genocide.

When the buzz happened, there was – looking back – a very small part of me that already knew, that had watched this bit already; fast-forwarded to the end. I sidled up to the door with contrived carefreeness. I think I even stretched back and sighed, maybe yawned, maybe not; but I remember pulling my dressing gown tighter, too tight, and I could feel the constriction.

Even as I opened the door, my heartbeat was accelerating and I had twitching legs. Even as there was just a glimpse of light, a distant sun that throbbed and singed and turned its head ever so closer towards us. Even as there was nothing but a whip of wind in my face and the sound of school runs and a shuffle of somebody's feet on the doormat. Even as the door handle lay cold and inert in my hands and my hands robotically, mechanically, tugged and twisted, and the exit turned into an entrance.

There were no words. There were no gestures. Just the sight of two police, a man and a woman. A hat in his hands. Yes, I remember the hat. All it seemed to signify – condolences, regret, respect, remorse. It lay in his hands at a crooked angle and he held it, lightly, pathetically, with his eyes blinking quickly, betraying embarrassments. Then the woman cleared her throat.

Sometimes people ask me, maybe morbidly, maybe kindly, exactly what they said that day: how they phrased it, the words they chose. But the thing is, I can't remember. I only remember that moment, as if in tableau, as if in dumb show. As if nothing else ever happened, and we are still there now on that step, silently staring: the horrors of life all mixed up with banality.

But enough about her. This story isn't her's, after all. Let's talk some more about me, and let's start somewhere near the beginning. For I was a naive child, a wretched child. The sort of child who believed in Father Christmas until I was in double digits. I hugged too much, I clasped too much. How did all those other five-year-olds get to that age and act so worldly wise, so slick and severe? It seems remarkable now, when I see the lines of children march up to the school gates. They look so sweet and innocent, with their rolled-up socks and banter and leap frogs and satchels; it seems remarkable to me now that, unknown to the adults, there lurks an 'in crowd' and 'out crowd', a strict enforcement of rules, a cruel criteria of coolness – just like the grown ups, only without self-restraint.

I wasn't cool, I wasn't slick. And I had some major setbacks. I was fat, for a start. Not obese, mind, or anything reaching that level, but a little pudgier than the norm, and it wafted around me like some terrible fart. Girls with little ringlets and clear, crystal eyes, who smelled sweet and synthetic like they'd rolled around in popcorn; these girls openly sneered and poked my belly and let names tumble out: horrific, monstrous names, which they chanted like witches. If they could, they'd have dragged me to the back of the playground and sliced me open, with a gleeful skip-rope over my tumbling guts; humming nursery rhymes about Tommy Tucker singing for his supper no more.

Oh, and I was bright. I wasn't clever like an Einstein or a brain surgeon or a rocket scientist or any of those other clichés of genius. I was certainly no child prodigy and no teacher ever gave my parents the 'special talk' about my gifts. But what I had, which I quickly noticed most people lacked, was this powerful, burning, yearning, screaming, churning drive to learn. And part of the package was a ferocious conviction, an ability to sit still and listen, and really try to remember, to be determined to know. The other kids were mostly restless and bored and looking ruefully out of the window at the small rectangular strip of lawn that to them resembled heaven, a release from facts and figures and numbers and words. I was the one who found the specks of light in those things.

Don't get me wrong, I'm not bigging myself up. Like I said, I wasn't particularly know-it-all, and these things sure didn't come easy. It wasn't as if I just had to sit there and get the knowledge sucked in by osmosis. It wasn't as if I were ever in the top one per cent, or had a startling revelation, or I ever truly, truly conceived of something original. But I had the staying power. I wanted to win at something, and so I chose that. It was stubbornness, I guess. My eyes on the long game, the long road to power. I never felt young, even when I was young. I always felt like somebody old but immature for their age.

So I devoured everything in front of me, took the path that led to straight Grade As and a decent education and a better quality of life. And if I had… What? A different character, a different upbringing, a more traumatic birth? If I hadn't been breastfed? No, wait a minute, I wasn't breastfed. OK, if I hadn't been fat? Yes! If I hadn't been fat, they might have accepted me straightaway, I might have kissed a girl at kiss chase, I might not have looked so stupid with those stupid freckles that clustered about my nose. I might have stared at the playground too, with a premature lust, and a longing to escape the confines of learnedness. I might have flung the alphabet book to the floor and decided to be a different man, a different person. The trail in front of me would have shifted somewhat and I would have lost my footing for a moment, but only a moment – and then carried on, never to know the difference, never to pay any attention to these facts that have given me form.

Oh, who knows. Maybe it wasn't being fat. I don't really know what made me, but I do know that I can feel the five-year-old still in me, and I can feel the adult me huddling in that five-year-old freak. We are most definitely one, and I can feel his shyness, his innocence, so painfully, that I have a pain in my side, even now, just talking about it; I mean – can you believe that? His mannerisms, his speech – though the voice is a little higher, of course. The way he swept his floppy fringe to the side. The way his feet looked too big, precursors to their future size 12s. The way he made up stories about the stars at night when he huddled beneath his bedcovers; carving characters from constellations. The way he often slipped his hand into his mummy's purse. The way he hid things around the house just so he could watch people look and then save the day by 'finding' them, by taking away the panic. The way he often told tales on his brother – and his parents always believed his side, always. The way he saw his father once, wrapping up the presents, and drinking sherry with his mum, but he so wanted to believe, that he willed the memory away, and only recalled it, later, much later, when he was walking down a cobbled street at university, and the snow toppled down, and carollers accosted him for money, and he suddenly wanted to give them his debit card, he wanted to get down on his knees, and he wanted to sob, gratefully, mournfully, winching up their white robes and kissing their ankles.

'No time for daydreaming!'

'Oh fuck off,' I muttered. And I punched something into my phone, to try to look convincing.

'You fuck yourself when your clients go shove their hardwood pulp up your arse.'

'Yeah, yeah.' I flashed him a smile as he thwacked me on the back.

This is how we speak around here, this is our dialogue,

our wonderful way with words. All we do is yell and holler and then lurk autistically in corners and mumble streams of incomprehension to people across the world.

Some of the older employees here remember the days before online trading platforms, when they got to stand in the pits and arb rather wildly, palms facing outwards, palms facing inwards, bobbing heads impatiently to demonstrate blocks of ten. (In case you don't know, 'to arb' is to hand signal. It was a kind of a code in this world of commodity exchange. Now we're through with all that, and all we have left are sneers and explosive expletives, and we blow each other up with this weird smile on our faces, like a mask we wear constantly.)

Sometimes I stand at my desk like it is a pit, pretending I am in an amphitheatre in Ancient Rome, orating on philosophy, love, democracy, wisdom. Except our values have changed and, just like the Romans, we are tumbling towards excess and our rule is nearly at an end. This time there is no hidden poison, no half-concealed dagger. We are both murderer and victim. Now I stand at my personal pit and I am yelling out 'Sell, sell, sell!' and someone else is calling out 'Buy, buy, buy!' and there is a new kind of beauty in this open outcry, there is something harmonious and whole, like a negative and a positive coming together and forming something new. Except now we have a global cancelling out. Zero. Nothing.

For this is a world of illusion, and it is no wonder it hooked me instantly, it lured me in, it sought me out. I was drawn to this world of commerce and commodity, where future contracts get stacked up like giant houses of cards. And I remember my first break as a floor trader, when I made a massive windfall on wheat, and I didn't think about the prices of the goods in the grocery stores, of the farmer who tilled the land, no, nor even the client. I thought of myself and the profit now stockpiling, the money that enmired my feet. I wanted a lifetime of flash little flats, wads of cash, penthouse apartments and convertible cars. I felt like I was snapping the neck of every little brat who had ever mocked me. It was a fist shake in revenge. A maniacal laugh, for what got me here was a foray into falsehood, an understanding of untruth.

At first I thought I had made her up, too. She was beautiful, though I'm not sure if she really was, it is hard to be objective. But she definitely had a way of voice, the way her voice would dip and dive and drip caramel all over you. Her legs were long and slender, she went in and out in all the right places, as they say. And she had this terrific laugh. She would put her hand up to her mouth and it would tumble out in fits and bursts, as if she were desperate to stifle it, but never quite could. And, most importantly of all, she was into me. She mistook my fear for confidence, she miscalculated me as solid and dependable because I was doing an economics and finance degree, and I seldom got pissed like the rest, and I always woke up for the 9.15 lectures.

She was American. She spoke with disgust at the Americans, at the way they sucked the world dry, how they depleted everyone of everything. I didn't have the heart to tell her that she was dressed top to toe in sweatshop clothes and eating pizza in a pizza chain and, besides, things weren't really so different here. In fact, we were all the better for it. I loved all the chains, especially the coffee ones: their familiar muzak, so typically jazz, and the waft of over-extracted beans, the identikit chairs and unobtrusive wall panels. And, to tell you the truth, I'd never given any of it much thought. But I wanted to sleep with her, and her lips were all rouged, like they were ripe for clamping my dick. And it was making me hard just watching her, so casually slurping at her wine, like I knew she might later be slurping at me. And so I leaned forwards, I nodded sympathetically, and I said what a tragedy it was, what an absolute *tragedy* – or did I mean travesty? – and when I leaned forwards, she leaned forwards too, and her breasts were shoved up against the table, looking soft, round and fuckable. I pushed the dough balls to one side and I kissed her.

I had more clout as a couple. I seemed to gather in weight and influence and sphere. Soon I had planets orbiting around me, all eager to be my friend because they were Nancy's friends, too. We were like that star couple in the Hollywood films. The one that everyone stares at and whispers about, like they command some cosmic power. We balanced each other perfectly: there was something for everyone. We were the greatest accessory that anyone could have.

I didn't think it would last forever. I was very cold about it at first, and I bet I sound cold writing about it now. I was just a nineteen-year-old boy looking to get laid. And I got laid. Oh yes. But I also fell in love, pretty hard as it happens, and it seems utterly pointless denying that now. I guess love is interdependency; when you realise that being without the other leaves you shocked and wheezing, as if you've been chest-struck.

I knew things must be pretty serious when I took her home to meet my mum, in the second year. I had never brought back any girl to meet my mum. OK, that was probably because there weren't any other girls. But, if there had been, I wouldn't have led them down that garden path, as it were.

My mum was a frail, meagre, feeble woman who let everyone walk all over her. My brother wasn't there that night, thank god; he was out with his friends. We conversed in unspoken words about how she would cope once he was gone, too. I could make out the conversation in her head by the way her eyebrows were dancing and the veins in her forehead throbbed. She seemed to have no eyelashes. She never laughed but only smiled, and even this looked an effort. It was a dinner of silence.

Mum went to bed first, although Nancy and I were guests,

of a sort, and when she had gone, there was such complete, impenetrable sadness that Nancy had an asthma attack. She blamed the cats, but I knew it wasn't them, that it must be the sadness that clogged up the sink, that rattled the pans, that stuck tablecloths to the table and whistled the kettle. I felt contaminated by it, heady and gutted: and rather than stay the night, we decided to leave a note for my mum and left by the last train back. Nancy was sighing and yawning and looking confused, but I knew I couldn't be there, I couldn't bear to see those photos turned against the wall, I couldn't bear to see his shoes still on the shoe rack.

I saw that sadness in the mirror on the day Nancy died. I don't know why, but I was trying to be sensible, I was trying to keep it together. My flatmates went out, they weren't sure what to do, but I said I wanted to be on my own.

I watched them walk out of the flat. They were walking so slowly, like they'd never be able to walk fast again. Their backs were cowed. They were grieving themselves, their eyes red and hollow, a realisation that this was the start of connections being eroded one by one; and they would never win this battle, for life and death are irreparably linked (in fact, the same thing), and the pair shall always prove victor.

But I can bring her back to life just by telling you this. The happiest memory. God, that is hard – what's the happiest memory? Our first holiday, together; yes, that must be it. When I worked in some office reception, and she waitressed a bit, and her folks clubbed together and sent a contribution from Seattle. We had never felt so giggly and grown up, so conspiratorial and free. An entire life of going on holidays with parents, with family, and now we were a unit of two, a little family of our own: booking tickets, taking planes, making decisions, snapping photos. She sat next to the pool, and her feet were swinging. Such colours in the sky. The sun set into an inscrutable horizon.

Another Justified Sinner

The hotel lights stammered on, all twinkly and magical. The sound of people inside, a susurration of Spanish. The thick scent of jasmine and fried sardines.

Chapter Two

Here's the thing: I always fail the psychometric tests that they give you in interviews. I say my favourite colour is white and my favourite number is zero. But they lap it up, dazzled. For now I represent a challenge; an affront. 'We need a maverick,' said Finnegan. 'Someone who thinks outside the box,' he said. But outside the box is space, nothingness, void. I got too far outside the box. I just floated from day to day.

One day it was Sunday, and I went to work. I had no qualms about working on a Sunday; in fact, I relished it. I liked the way the streets were quiet and empty and there was only the occasional tourist or pissed-up reveller on the 'walk of shame' home. There was an eerie solace to everything, and you could even hear birdsong through the thrum of the buses. I listened to it as I made my way through meandering alleyways and passed quaint, dark pubs with panelled-wood rooms; then the tall, striking buildings; the modern and archaic; gargoyles and plinths peering up at one-hundred-metre daggers of glass.

And I liked the way the smugness started from my belly and ended up in a zipper-like grin on my face. I liked how the boss looked up and assessed me, with a little flicker of surprise – the tremulous nod of approval. All the time I was there, even if I just wanked into a spreadsheet, I would feel virtuous and brilliant and top dog and top drawer.

'It's a fucking Sunday,' I thought, as I stood in the office and surveyed my city. 'It's fucking Sunday and I'm here.'

They'd only recently given me the job. Through a sheer fluke, as it happens. I had been at a party, full of dicks and whack jobs. One of Nancy's friends had thrown it – someone who was born into money and would die out of money, probably a heart attack while reclining in a rooftop spa pool.

Anyway, Nancy was desperate to get us talking; she was desperate to turn our luck around. I was just doing administrative temp stuff, then. So she wheeled and dealed and coquettishly teased him. There was lots of hair flicking and eye fluttering and laughing at miniscule jokes and softly wetting her lips. I could see it all happening, and I tried not to care, tried to see it as a compliment.

'This is Matthew Rickshaw,' she said, her pupils big and unfathomable. 'He works in the city.'

She made it sound like a magical city, like the Emerald City, come-meet-the-fucking-wizard city. It was a different city to my own; threadbare and worn, full of holes and impurities.

But it turns out it really is who you know. Matt set me up with Finnegan Fishman, which led to my climb through the world of commodities exchange and dancing figures. But it also led to Matt kissing my girlfriend. It led to my girlfriend being dead. Life can be funny like that. It can go ahead and pass moral sentence all by itself.

But it's not all bad. Because I've excelled in this job. At work,

I show guile. I am relaxed and extrovert, I have a spring in my step and a sparkle in my eye. To be a good commodities broker, you need zing, pizzazz, the gift of the gab. I have all this and more. 'Ability to negotiate' was on the job description. I thought about how the untruths just slip off my tongue, and I signed up straightaway. Lies can be a good thing. Lying can buy you snazzy clothes, a tropical beach, a pretty girl on your arm. Lies can give you success.

It's a shame that Nancy didn't see it that way. When we left university, we struggled, but she seemed to revel in it, at first – it conformed to the story in her head. She loved renting the tiny flat in zone 6, with slits for windows and a half-size bath. She loved eating beans on toast and watching box sets in pyjamas. She sometimes got a bit down that she couldn't find work as an actress, but that wasn't fuelled by a desire to pay bills, it was a desire to fan an inner flame. She'd come from auditions with her eyes sad and droopy and a kind of atrophy in her limbs. 'I didn't get it,' she'd say, but even these four words were an effort. She never got it. She never got the parts and she never quite got that maybe she just didn't have 'it'. She skulked in corridors, waiting for auditions, refusing to give up her dream. There was the odd am-dram – sorry, 'fringe' – production, a photo shoot in a magazine (I think it was for shoes). She got some minor model work. At least I knew she wasn't sucking cocks.

The sad thing is that she was actually a brilliant actress. I would get tingles watching her practise her lines in the mirror. The way she looked at her reflection, the way she'd change the expression, even the animus in her eyes... I would see her and this reflection as two different people, and it made me panic. It worried me to see how she could inhabit these characters; the way her face could fall so easily into those feelings. It was the opposite to me: I'm a terrible actor with fiction, but a brilliant actor at real life. I always seem to get the best lines.

So I thought she'd cheer up when I started trading – and, for a while, she did. But there were long hours to put in and parties to have and contacts to network. On her side, there were too many dinners for one and too many one-way conversations. I couldn't buy her approval, although I tried hard. It was strange, sometimes, to come back very late and see her curled up asleep in one of my old sweaters. It was like she was cheating on me with an old version of myself, one that didn't exist anymore. How can you not change, endlessly, countlessly, time and again? Every second, millions of cells in the body are replaced with new ones. Every little experience changes and adapts the brain. So how can we stay the same person? Why was the sweater scrunched up in her hands, why was she loving the form I had made a ghost? It had shrunk in the wash; it now fitted her, not me.

But it's me who sees ghosts, now. She always did laugh the loudest.

You see, Nancy's death left a missingness in the world: like the imprint of your shoe in mud or that rush of air as somebody passes. It feels like she should still be here, that maybe she might come back, that all the signs suggest it.

Her cupboard, for example: in those early days, before the funeral. Her dresses and cardigans still messily lined up, belts heaped up on a shelf, shoes slotted in underneath, like mollusc shells: things that looked waiting, expectant, ready for the right-sized body to fill them. Looking through the clothes, I had memories of her wearing them: that one was Cornwall, this one was the National Gallery. That yellow dress she had teamed up with a straw hat, as we swept over Hyde Park, the sun beating down on our bodies, our noses getting pink, a lazy Sunday stretched before us. I saw there were still grass stains on the hem, and that is when I lost it.

Everything was marked by absence. Everywhere were shapes and indentations. Intangibles turned tangible and spoken words slammed into walls; banged into cupboards like kinetic particles of heat. Mirrors reflected what wasn't and rooms grew gaps – gaps grew on gaps – like cancer of the hole. The kettle shrieked her name, the curtains fell like hair. Silence clung to clothes and hissed in the ears like a body deflating. Numerous people called round to see me and, although sympathetic and cooing and making all the right noises, they didn't seem to notice that anything was different in the flat. The paintings hung on the wall and there was this hint of perfume in the air and that coffee book was open on exactly the same page. They drank from glasses once held by presence, once bought by form: absence trapped between the fingers, a sniff of skin once kissed and held. Nobody noticed, nobody but me, who had to pick up that invisible body and hide it away.

I did this by moving out. I did it very quickly, so I wouldn't turn into a forever griever like my mum. I had a conversation with our flatmates Jamie and George about who might take over the room, how I might break out of the contract. They listened to what I had to say and nodded uneasily. Trying to smile but not smile too much. Unsure when to make a joke, whether they should speak softly around me. They were upset too, catastrophically upset (I heard them weeping sometimes through the walls); but they knew my grief must be worse and this frightened them. We were British, we were blokes, we were crap at this sort of thing. Nobody knew the codes, the etiquette, the conduct. Nobody teaches you that. Something had snapped between us. They would never treat me the same again.

Jamie and George were friends from university. They were one of the first planets to orbit around me and Nancy. They were both in Nancy's drama class. Jamie was gay and in love with George who was in love with Nancy, who had just fallen in love with me. It was complicated. But it worked. We existed in harmony through some crooked commensalism.

What I'm saying is – the system worked fine. Nobody wanted to rock the boat and risk losing contact with the object of their desire. It must have been painful for Jamie and George at times, but they came to accept it. And, anyway, even they would admit that the cult of Marcus and Nancy was exhilarating. We just carried charisma, like a mist of cologne or the heat of fire. We went well together. We added up to more than the sum of our parts. But I've told you this already… I mustn't keep saying it. It's just that those were the happiest days of my life. You must have had them, too. They're usually when you're young. Proper young. You feel heady and invincible. All the songs sound louder, all the colours are brighter, and life is a list of 'first things' that you can't wait to discover.

#

I wanted to punish God for Nancy's death, so I decided to break the commandments in order. The first one is kind of lame, truth be told. 'You shall have no other gods before Me.' Well, this is the 21st century and I can fucking idolatrise until kingdom come. What don't I label a god? I worship at the altars of naked women in magazines, of waitresses who bring me tasty food, of movie men who say all the best lines. Fuck it, I even made Nancy a goddess, for a bit, in those early days. I read between her lines and I genuflected at her breasts and I supped at her pussy until we transubstantiated into cum. You get the drift.

The second one is ridiculous, something about making yourself a carved image, a likeness of heaven – idolatry, I guess. So, anyway, I went out to the shops and I bought anything I could lay my hands on: awful posters, crucifixes, some pisstake cartoons. And I bowed down to them in mock worship, I asked God to enter into my emptiness and fill it with something, anything, just fill it up and reseal it. Then I took everything into the side garden, and I struck a match on it all, and just watched it incinerate.

I was trying to break a commandment a day, but some are too easy. So while I watched everything burn, I struck off number three, and I spat out God's name and I cursed him or her or it or whatever the fuck is in heaven. I took his name in vain and I delighted in the old-fashioned thrill of retorting 'Oh god', 'For heaven's sake': all of that. When the flames died down, I looked up into the stars and saw things twinkling down at me that were billions of years old, that were already dead. And I wanted to be up there, in the swirls and whirls of the outer galaxies. Perhaps up there is an advanced planet with an extraordinary telescope that you can point at Earth and you will see the past pulsing, your history reanimate, the lights of her eyes all still lit up and dancing.

I remember they told me that in Physics GCSE. Fifteen years old. The teacher, Mr Lennon, jabbing furiously at the board, trying to whip us into a frenzy. He always tried so hard to excite us, to get us interested in the subject. How his heart must have sunk when he looked around the class and saw a boy yawning into his fist, a girl passing a note to her friend, the sound of bubblegum smacking against somebody's chin, a glazed eye peering up at the time, willing it to strike lunch o'clock. But there was also me in that class, and I sat up a bit straighter when he told me the bit about the stars. It was like fiction was fact and I didn't know what to believe or disbelieve. My lies could be credible. My life was anything I said it was. The world was malleable and shifting.

I saw that the note was passing over to me. 'Marcus', it said on the front. It was covered in hearts. I looked up and saw Charlotte winding her long blonde tresses around her finger. She blew me a kiss from sticky lipsticked lips.

I could scarcely believe it. But then, the stars were actually dead and yet present, and time travel was possible, and reality was unreal. Maybe Charlotte fancied me. I had lost a little weight. I had stolen Jackson's jacket. I unfolded the note and there was the punch line: 'you thick ugly purvurt [sic]. I wouldn't fancy you in a million years.' Then half the class exploded into laughter and Mr Lennon stopped teaching us facts and started waving his arms about, trying to conduct our behaviour. It was atonal as fuck.

Jackson had left school by then, but he had a girlfriend in my year. He was standing by the school gates when I left that day; smoking a cigarette, trying to look like Michael Hutchence before the sex noose stuff.

I tried to shrink, to camouflage, to turn invisible, but he spotted me at once. 'That's my jacket!' he barked, and pulled me by the collar. 'That's my fucking jacket!'

'I didn't know,' I stuttered. My policy was always to deny everything, even when all the evidence was stacked against me. Even if I could plant the tiniest seed of doubt in their minds, the possibility of my innocence, I called that a victory.

'How could you not know? You little shit! I've been looking for that jacket everywhere.'

'Mum put it in my bedroom,' I lied. 'I thought she'd gotten it for me or something. She must have mixed up the washing.'

He released his grip on me but looked unsure. 'I didn't put it out in the wash. Jackets don't get washed.'

'Maybe Mum thinks they do. Maybe she dry-cleaned it. I don't know. You'll have to ask Mum. All I know is that it ended up in my bedroom. I mean it, Jackson. Leave it out.'

But by then he was distracted and walking away. Kitty had landed on the asphalt runway, her skirt hitched up, the sunnies on, her hair flicked back. She flashed a billion-watt smile at Jackson and they sort of melted together, their flesh tangled up and disgusting.

It wasn't long after that that I joined the church group at school. Maybe it was the thought of Jackson's dick in Kitty's underage cunt. (I often heard them going at it in their bedroom.) Maybe it was the constant rejection from the girls. Maybe it was what Mr Lennon had said about stars. Suddenly the world opened up to me, like a glorious flower, and I was heady from the scent. I saw mystery, glorious and blissful, radiate from everything around me. And in that mystery I saw a source, ineffable and potent, and I decided it was God.

The church group were also the only people who were nice to me. Once I started to approach them, they always sought me out at lunch times and assemblies, offering me bites of ciabatta, friendly slaps on the back, enthusiastic talk about timetables. And revelation and temptation and original sin. But that was by the by. Mostly it was just solidarity and camaraderie. I would be lying if I told you that they were fascinating, stimulating people. On the whole, they were all the stereotypes you can imagine: serious and quiet and mousey and dulled. But they had smiles for me and came from tidy homes where lunch was full of sundried tomatoes and balsamic glaze. They spoke in twisted facts, and it was so nice to hear my language. We'd converse about floods that cascaded over the world and killed every living thing (except the 50,000 animals that managed to fit inside Noah's boat). We enthused about people who lived for days within whales and the magic trick of turning water to wine. Our faces would go quite pink when we told these stories, and our voices would drop to mere breath, like our soul was already leaving our bodies. Sometimes, I admit, I would get tears in my eyes. The thought of so much love, so much hope, so much endlessness.

I would replay scenes in my mind of my death. My enemies at school: their howling and their wailing, this dramatic sense of guilt. A couple even kill themselves. One is a girl from afar, who has always been a bit in love with me, but hasn't been able to say.

And then there is Jackson, his hand beating his chest, repeating over and over: 'I never told him how much I loved him; I never told him how much I loved him.' And the jacket gets tossed on top of the casket, the pockets sucking up soil. 'Keep it forever,' he says. And then he retreats to the background, where my mother and grandmother stand, their bodies darting with grief. 'He was always my favourite,' my mother whispers into Nana's ear. 'My beautiful boy.'

And then there is the best bit. The momentous, majestic, almighty bit. The bit where my spirit shimmers out of my body and out through the casket and looks down on these sorry folk and then ascends through the clouds. Up, up, I go – then suddenly a whoosh and acceleration and a tumble and flare. Then things are mottled and vague and indefinite. Things are more thoughts than things. Nothing is confined or restricted or actual. And there's this parental sensation, this overwhelming worship. I'm in the arms of my creator, the one who approves me. The angels play at harps. It's a 'welcome home' party and everyone in heaven is invited.

I wish I had believed in God and Jesus and everlasting love when I was fourteen. It came a year too late. Because, when I was fourteen, my dad died. One minute he was driving home from work, singing along to the radio; the next he was crumpled into a lamppost, his brain skewered with shards of glass. It was just before Christmas, which might explain why I didn't want to celebrate Jesus at the time.

On Christmas Day, my mum went to bed with a migraine. We were put into a taxi and sent to my nana's, where we pretended to be happy. Her toyboy carved us some turkey and we put party hats on our heads. Except Jackson wouldn't do it – his sorrow soared into anger, he smashed up the bedroom and drank all the bottles of brandy. He jumped on his bike with his face mulled red. No-one could find him, but my nana didn't want to worry my mum, so she didn't tell her anything. Instead, she went back to the table and pulled a cracker with me. I read out the joke, and we all fell about laughing at how terrible it was; and Toyboy Tony made me say it again, as he didn't quite get it. And I did all of this, and I somehow performed it quite brilliantly. Sometimes a fantasy is easier, the pretence is a comfort. I didn't have that distraction at night, when I switched out the lights, and I saw my dad's face in the darkness. The radiator pipes gurgled and the floorboards groaned. Even the house was releasing its breath, was unleashing its sadness, now that no-one could see. So we both cried together, and my hand stroked the wall like it was somebody's face.

After the first month, things started to change. I got to understand the phrase that life 'moves on'. I really could feel this rapid conveyor belt that I had to stay on top of, that I had to hold on to. It was sink or swim. Drop off or survive. So I let go of Dad until I could barely remember his face. When I tried to picture it, it was usually a memory of a photo, or else it was pixelated, with none of the detail. He was getting left further and further behind. He had dropped off the belt.

I was young enough that the whole thing was swept up into an overarching narrative. The accident didn't feel real, so I wrote it into an epic story in my head: triumph over adversity, endurance and valour. A sob story, no less. But Jackson took it worse than me. And my mother, the worst of all. My mother was never, ever the same – and I hated her for it.

Maybe that's why I wanted to punish God so badly when Nancy died. Because he had done the same thing to me twice. He had given me something I loved and that loved me back and then he had destroyed it in exactly the same way. What could be a clearer message than that? It was a vindictive act, an act of swollen power. I sort of pictured him as a Super Accountant: performing miracle formulae in spreadsheets as he reckoned the grand total of sins.

Or maybe like a beardier Alan Sugar: the no-nonsense work-harder who didn't take any crap. 'You're fired,' he'd say, as he pushed the less savvy into Hell. 'You're fired,' he'd say, casually kicking folks from the game. Argh, and after all I had done for him: the sore knees on pew cushions, shrapnel tossed in the tin, the fervent preaching of gospel. The best days of my life – all given to serve the Big Boss in the Sky.

But there were other days, you know, there were ones he didn't get, before it all went wrong. I remember when dad took me to the horses. I was eleven, so Jackson was fourteen; this meant that he was getting into hanging out at shopping malls and bowling alleys and trying to peer up teenage skirts. So Jackson wasn't coming. It was just me and my dad.

Dad wore a suit. It was a throwback pastel blue from his prime. His tie was a little too long and he tucked it into his trousers. The hair was slicked back, with an excess of gel, and he reeked of chemical sandalwood. 'Come on, son,' he said, and pushed me out of the door with his hand on my head.

There was a sense of occasion about everything, the way there is at ceremonies or festivities, Christmas or weddings. Dad pulled up besides the bank and very gruffly said, 'Wait here.' It seemed like an eternity that I sat there, playing around with the dials of the radio, blinking up at the sunshine, watching women push their pushchairs past, the frantic dance of shoppers shopping. But time did indeed pass, like all time must, and eventually he was back beside me, solemnly flicking through a wad of notes with an enchanted, faraway look on his face.

'You see this?' he said; lowering himself a little, to make sure he was staring me right in the eyes.

'Yes.'

'It's money, isn't it?'

'Yep.'

'And you know how we get this money?'

I knew better than to roll my eyes in front of him, but I did think, jeez, Dad, I'm eleven, not five. But I copied his gravity and nodded emphatically. 'You and Mum make it.'

'We do indeed, son. Now, listen to me carefully. You better listen. You hear? Right: money is a precious, precious thing, and not to be thrown away unless you can afford it. What Daddy has done is save up very hard so he could have this little outing with his boy. The same way we save up for a holiday every now and then. It just so happens that Dad likes to relax, he *needs* to relax, and he finds going to the horses relaxing, you see? So he's been saving for a while, keeping his money, the money he makes and takes out from the bank, you know? He's been doing that so he could have this next outing, and he could take his two sons. Now it's a pity that Jackson isn't here, but *you're* here, Marcus, and that makes this a little dad and son outing, right? So we're going to have fun with this money, but I want you to know that I saved it up properly, that I'm not spending money I can't afford to spend. You hear?'

It was a longwinded message but I gave him another solemn nod, the kind that might fool him into believing that he'd given the speech of a Churchill or King. I would give him anything, anything he wanted; I just wanted to be his favourite son, like this, sitting next to him in the car, with the wind whizzing through my hair and making my eyes water up.

When I think about it now, that wad of cash – so formally held aloft – was about a hundred quid. I'm pretty sure it was a pile of ten pound notes. I mean, that's the way I remember it. But in his hands it had the significance of millions. It represented freedom and fun and adventure and 'relaxing'. It represented a rare day out between father and son.

The races lived up to this speech: it was a spectacle on a scale never hitherto seen. There were women with sculptures on their heads, elaborate bows and nettings, lips heavily rouged, their heels a good two inches higher than normal. A lot of the men wore suits, like my dad, and many of them bought champagne, including my dad, who purchased a glass, just the one, and then drank it very slowly. He sat down on the grass, beckoned me over, and let me have a sip of it. It tasted like bubble bath and I wanted to spit it out, but I saw the look of expectation on his face, that reverent, trance-like gleam. I had a sense that this was a glimpse into some distant, other world that he longed to be part of, so I returned his appreciative look, and he chuckled loudly and ruffled my hair.

The day reminded me of pantomime. Every Christmas we would get dolled up and go to the local theatre for the once-a-year treat. There was always some washed-up celebrity in the title role, usually a full-on-top soap star or a one-hit wonder. I always wanted to get the programme but my mum always said it was too much money. I would enjoy the red velvet seats against my arms and the buzz of expectation just before the curtain began to lift. To me, it was the most exciting thing that there could possibly be, sitting there, amongst all those people, all seeing and believing in the same storyline, all knowing the same lines, the same 'Look behind yous' and the 'Oh no you didn'ts'. It was comforting to buy into this together and watch people play the parts they always played, with their heroes and villains and the happily ever after: so delayed, so tremulous, and yet so sweetly inevitable when it happened, such a relief that yet again it had happened, and exactly as we'd hoped it.

So these people around me were all dressed up too, all head to toe in their fancy garb, their special occasion clothes. And they seemed to speak in this strange, private language of numbers and figures and the passing of currency. I didn't know the script yet, but I enjoyed watching them say it, especially my father. He turned to me.

'What shall we bet on, boy?'

'What do you mean?'

'What horse!' He laughed. 'That's a list of horse names, there. You see it? They're going to run against each other, and if we pick the right horse, we win some money. And I'm going to place about a third of this money' – he waved the wad in front of me again – 'on this race. So who's it going to be, son?'

'They've got some funny names, Dad.'

'Yes, they've got a good sense of humour, these jocks and trainers.'

'Are they really called this?'

'Yes, son. Come on, Marcus, before the race starts...'

'Ha ha, I like that one.'

'What one?'

'Hoof Hearted.'

He studied the note very carefully. 'You see those numbers, son? They're the odds. What I mean is – that there is the likelihood of a horse winning. And that's 30 to 1, so they're pretty low odds. He's not going to win, son. If he wins, he'll win us a lot of money, but it's a gamble; because if he loses, and he probably will, we'll lose all our money. You see?'

I did see. And I thought that my best chance of seeming commonsensical and keen was to pick the horse with the second-highest odds of winning (the highest would be too obvious). My dad smiled at my choice, and said, 'Yes, that's my gut, too.' And we went over to the booth and we paid together.

Just like the pantomime, the happily ever after arrived to some rapturous hollers and whistles and roars of applause. I was pleased, especially when my dad picked me up and spun me round laughing. Yes, I had known it had to happen, but that didn't devalue the happiness. There is a kind of deliciousness in knowing a formula and watching it happen, again and again, this eternal alliance of hunger and satiety. The only problem is that films and stories can make you think it happens like that all the time.

But I had never seen my dad look so happy. Not even when the princess got the prince and the ugly sisters were sent away and the bad guys put in prison. I watched as money magicked into being and the paper quadrupled in his hands. And to think that was it – just paper. Whole lives lived in deference to paper, in fear of paper, in thrall to paper. How could the trees have turned into this?

My mother and father met when they were both very young. He was apparently 'Not like the others', not like the 'boys', as my mum would spit. My dad, by contrast, was always a 'man'. He bought her flowers on their very first date. I pictured him with slicked back hair, like he wore it at the racetracks. He probably tucked his tie in then, too. My mum didn't really mention what he wore, but she said that he listened like a gentleman, didn't 'try anything on', although I didn't get her meaning. 'He had rough hands but the softest voice.' That was always the final statement, and her lips would part and her hands splay open, as if to say, 'What?' What could she have possibly done, other than fall in love with him? He had rough hands but the softest voice! For heaven's sake. Who wouldn't have fallen in love?

This was the most passionate I ever heard her. She was always flitting in and out of things, my mum, never holding on, never fully there – except when it came to Dad. One time she was a receptionist at the doctor's surgery; for a while, she worked in Littlewoods, on the front desk, customer services, so it happens. There was even talk of her becoming Assistant Shop Manager, until the incident with the clothes hanger. But her biggest stint was as a dinner lady, when Jackson and I were at primary school. So many embarrassing moments whenever I saw her, standing there, with greasy hair in a net and baggy grey overalls. She never seemed to serve pudding; she always dished out plastic peas and shapeless mash.

Dan Fletcher's mum also worked at the school, but she was a teacher and wore colourful beads and always spoke with a titter. Mrs Fletcher taught us about rock cake and planets and food chains. She was an omnivore, she said, because she ate both plants and animals. Some creatures are prey, others are predators, and some can be both to different things. It all depends on where you are in the food chain. (I thought of mum, then, as we snaked around the frosty hall in our lunchtime screeches, and mum scooped up cabbage that stank of old bin liners and kept her eye forever on the clock.)

Mrs Fletcher said that food is energy, and energy constantly moves from one thing to another. It never gets lost. So the bigger things eat smaller things – but everything eats something. It doesn't really matter who gets the biggest bit of food in the end, you just need the energy flowing, you just need to keep the system in place. (I thought of mum, then, as I shuffled along in the queue and those eyes swivelled to me, the ladle lifting in greeting, the happy recognition in her eyes, and I just looked away, felt food tip and ooze on the plate, kept moving forwards, forwards, forwards.)

Mum and Dad were grafters. They were both from working class families with aspirations. They wanted to work hard, do well, find a way out of this mire and mud. And my dad was a listener, he was a gentle and educated man, but he still had to plaster and decorate and come home with specks of paint in his hair. 'He had rough hands but the softest voice.' Those rough hands could strap her in like a seatbelt on those cold, lonely nights that are made for enduring.

One winter, I remember it, we were particularly cold, frozen down to the bone. You could see the ice on the pane, and wind blowing through cracks so it shivered the curtains, they very visibly moved. Jackson and I spent more and more time round friends' houses, where there was warmth and even heat, and you could stand with your back against the radiators. Back home, we'd slip on the jumpers and Dad would give us hot water bottles to hug.

Mum wasn't doing very much at all back then, she was just there in the background, nothing much to do with her time. We didn't know why, nobody ever mentioned the why. I still remember that dressing gown, all starched and fusty, as she sagged on the sofa. She flicked through magazines, ate pot noodles, sometimes looked at the TV, mostly stared at something I could not make out. Oh yes, she liked to watch films, romantic comedies but also the kitchen grit. She loved Charlton Heston: his solid, bullet-shaped body and the ire in his eyes. On better days, Mum cleaned around our feet and chatted to friends on the phone, people who never hung around long but always seemed important at the time.

Finally, the dressing gown would slip off and the clothes would return. Another job would be found – for a while, at least. And then Mum and Dad would be back around the table, sorting out paperwork, doing their sums, always worrying about money, always fretting, always trying to make the ends meet. If the ends didn't meet up, then the circle wouldn't complete, and then you'd have chaos.

I would go to the toilet in the middle of the night – always very quickly, in case I woke up the monster in my wardrobe – and see the lights on in the hallway downstairs. I'd stay still for a moment and listen to their low, hushed voices, always sounding a little stern, a little sad and disappointed. I felt this awful, unbearable weight of adulthood. This dark, shadowy outline of things that lay before and beyond me. I could feel it slither up the stairs and slip around my ankles and hiss in my face. When Dad died, I thought to myself – at least he doesn't have to worry anymore. At least there is that.

Chapter Three

As the commandments got harder, I knew I had to keep screwing with them for Nancy's sake. We'd been madly in love, in our way. So when it said 'Honour your mother and father', there was a careful plan put in place.

I caught a train to Croydon. I walked to the graveyard nearby. And when I was sure that no-one else was around, I pissed on Daddy's grave. I never knew it until then, but it's pretty hard to piss when you're crying.

There was an awful feeling in my stomach, my throat was raw and clawed at, the sky rumbled with malcontent. But I had to punish God, I had to get even; I wanted to make him angry, I wanted to stop him feeling so powerful, so invincible, so omnipotent, so great.

This was a God who didn't listen to prayers, who didn't intervene, who didn't stop things from happening. Go on, try it: in your hour of need, call up to the sky, scream until hoarse, repeat 'Show yourself, show yourself', over and over, until there is blood in your throat. Your God will not show himself.

Who knew what such a God had done with my daddy? My Dad could be burning or frozen or drifting in timelessness or dimensionally stuck. This God could be using his soul as a plaything, the way a cat toys with a mouse.

I slunk out of the graveyard, passed a young lady with flowers, her face shaking from strain. I walked down the long, suburban road, the occasional car humming by with a haze of headlight. There is something poignant and sinister about walking the streets of your childhood when they are no longer your home. You see dead versions of yourself everywhere that you look. The air reeks of decay.

I rang my mum's doorbell and felt her fear straightaway. She always looked frightened when the doorbell rang. She didn't get many guests. I saw a shiver of colour through the frosted glass. It was the shape of the dressing gown.

'Who is it?'

'It's me.'

'Marcus?'

'Yes.'

'Oh goodness.' She opened the door, her face startled and flushed. 'I wasn't—'

'I know. It's a surprise, isn't it? Let me in, it's freezing.'

We sat in the kitchen with its tatty units and the dishes piled up in the sink. The TV was left on in the living room. It blared out and seemed to mock our silences, our inability to speak. She mumbled something about a surprise (again). She offered me a cup of tea. I accepted.

While the kettle was boiling, she pottered about. She selected the mugs, very carefully, inspecting for cracks. She placed them down and foraged in the fridge, found the milk, shut the door. She sorted through her post – placed some envelopes to the side, put some others in recycling. She even fed the cats. She did everything but talk to me.

I don't know if she could tell that something was wrong, that something was to come. After all, I didn't make a habit of surprise visits. I barely got in contact – I left all of that to Jackson. We didn't have the easiest relationship, and she wasn't much of a conversationalist. A psychiatrist would have diagnosed her as something or other – but she wasn't one to make a fuss. She wasn't one to commit suicide either, so there was a mood of resignation in the house, of just wanting to get through it. If you watch enough TV and do enough pottering, a life can be lived out fairly quickly.

I mean, it didn't seem too long ago that this cowed thing was in our front porch, saying 'Of course, Father Christmas doesn't exist, of course he doesn't; the whole thing's a fairy tale', and then bursting into tears and shaking a hand at me, trying to push me away from her, scuttle back into the sitting room with its comforts and static hiss of electrics.

I can picture dashing up to my room to tip a pocket money jar full of one pennies, two pennies, into a plastic bag. It was very heavy but I carried it down carefully and into the room where she sat.

'Mummy, if Father Christmas doesn't exist, then I can help you buy presents.'

The bag tilted towards her, bulging with brown copper steel.

Her gaze eddied down me and sunk. She was clawing and mauling this mound of fabric in front of her, like a witch stirring a cauldron.

'What's that, Mummy?'

'Just some clothes, Marcus.'

'For who, Mummy?'

'For me, Marcus.'

'But I thought we didn't have any money.'

'It's a secret, Marcus.'

'A secret?'

'Please don't tell your daddy.'

I didn't understand, wasn't sure what she meant. I fondled the clothes – blues and reds, silks and linens – but now she was blowing kisses all over my face, and the tears and snot were tumbling over her face, and her face rubbed on mine.

But then there was an almighty snort, a sealing of the trapdoor. She held me away, at arm's length, and said in a whisper: 'Just go away, Marcus. Go up to your room.'

'Why?'

'Leave Mummy alone and go.' She was bundling the clothes back into a bag, she threw my spare change into it too, sealing it up at the top and shovelling it under the settee. While she did this, she mumbled: 'When you're bigger, you'll understand. Father Christmas doesn't exist, lots of things don't exist and aren't what you want them to be. You can try and try but there's no happy ending for most of us, there's nothing to rescue you like in films. Leave Mummy alone now. Go up to your room.' She looked up. 'Go!'

I was so lost in this memory that when she came back with the tea, I almost didn't do it. My instinct was to lie and beguile, to turn people to my side, not against it. But I had to break the commandment. I had to be honest.

'Mum.'

'Yes.'

'I popped round for a reason.'

Unexpectedly, she jumped in. 'Is it because of Nancy?' My mum didn't know what to do with this probable pain, so her sentence was clumsy.

'Kind of. I guess. Well, there's a link, but it's not for you to worry about.'

She nodded, wrapped her hands around the mug: the British

equivalent of taking the brace position.

I took a deep breath and cut to the chase.

'You're a terrible mother.'

I watched her reaction but she didn't move. Not a millimetre. Her hands were still around the mug, still poised in mid-air. The only thing that maybe changed was her eyes lost some focus; they swivelled to the left of me.

So I started the well-rehearsed speech.

'You left Dad to do everything when we were growing up. And when Dad died, you didn't console us enough. You just left me to myself. You buried yourself in your grief and you should have made yourself strong for us. You should have done, and you know it. Even if you have a problem, I don't know, you should have done it. After all, you were the parent and we were just kids still. You're broken, pathetic, you do nothing but watch TV and look through old photos. You're always crying. You're on benefits for no good reason I can see, you're up to your eyeballs in debt. You're always talking about Dad. You're stuck in the past and you're an embarrassment, to be honest. And I've got to say, I don't like you. You've never inspired me, you've not spurred me on. I'm not sure what I inherited from you. I'm not even sure I love you. I'm telling you all this so it sears into your brain and you remember it forever: your son doesn't like you or love you. You failed. I don't want to see you again.'

I don't know why, but I thought I should give her the benefit of a reaction. So I stayed sitting down, staring straight into her eyes, which finally settled back on me, although the hoods were heavy. And time condensed. All points coexist, all times coexist. Time does not pass; we pass. I passed through every moment together we'd ever had and were still to have. All these versions of us, these Russian dolls.

'I agree with everything you just said,' she said, finally. 'All of it.' I respected her more than ever at that moment. But then the mug was put down, and I could see her hands shaking. 'Please give me another chance,' she rasped. 'Please, honey. Please. I'm not right. Oh goodness, I've not been right for years. I mean it when I say it. Please just help me get through this.' I rolled my eyes and rolled out of the house.

The next day, I killed something.

After moving out of that place with Jamie and George, I'd hauled myself into a tiny one-bed flat in a derelict suburb of sirens and job centres. I shared it with a silent Antipodean who was always hungover and seldom around. He would sometimes leave passive aggressive notes or I'd spot the foil husk of a devoured ready meal. That was pretty much it.

Tonight, he was out (as usual) and I was having an internal debate. I couldn't kill a human, could I? That wasn't in my nature – and I certainly didn't want to end up in prison. That would give a definite advantage to God.

But I had my new neighbours' pond at the back of my mind, and it was easier than I thought to go through with it. Every terrible act starts with a terrible first step. After that, everything whooshes out in a torrent, and you simply go with the flow. So the first step was sloshing weedkiller down the mouths of those koi. And then I was scooping out one of the wriggly slabs and letting it thrash on my hand with its puckering lips and the gills all dried up like steel wool. People eat cod and chips, grilled kipper, tinned tuna – you get what I'm saying?

Well, I couldn't commit adultery, as I wasn't even dating at the time. So I slept with a married woman that I met in a bar. She was quite a lot older, and she had a moustache, but her face looked sort of desperate, and I wanted to sin. When she was sleeping, I found her mobile phone and I sent a photo to everybody in her contacts. I had to assume that her husband was in there. She wore a big wedding ring.

Not long after this, I stole something from a shop:

surprisingly easy. I deliberately picked a large high-street store, but a very small item. It didn't even set off the alarm. The only heart attack moment was when I slipped the item into my bag: I was sure that a camera would pick it up and the security guards come whisk me away. My plan was this: fill a basket with a bit of this and that. Check out the items but casually squirrel just one from basket to bag. That way, people assume you're not a thief, as you're paying for mostly everything. Worse-case scenario, and the alarms go off, or an attendant takes you to one side, you claim it was an innocent mistake; you thought the checkout girl had swiped it through. As I left the store, I felt a triumphant pulse of adrenalin, like I'd just got off a fairground ride.

'You shall not bear false witness', I read. I didn't know what it meant, so I looked it up, and most scholars interpret it as lying. I had to laugh at that one: something I had done so effortlessly for so many years – my entire life, in fact. But I decided to opt for a massive lie to be on the safe side. I phoned up social services and told them that I had seen a child touched inappropriately through my neighbour's window. I imagined that they would have to investigate the claim, but would quickly realise that it wasn't true. This put my mind at rest.

On the tenth and final day, the upstairs neighbour came about the pond. She looked distraught. She said they'd just come back from a holiday. Someone said they had spotted me outside in the communal garden – was I absolutely sure that I hadn't seen anything untoward?

'Afraid not,' I said, looking as sympathetic and concerned as I could muster. 'You know, my best friend at school used to keep these types of fish. There are diseases that can spread really rapidly. They once had a whole tank of fish that just floated right up to the top. One morning, they came down, and they were all floating like that, with these white spots all over them.'

'Thank you,' she said. 'You're probably right. We had

somebody feeding them while we were away. I don't know if maybe they over-fed them... Or underfed them. It might just be one of those things. Anyway, I'm Helen, by the way.'

'Nice to meet you, Helen.' We shook hands. 'I'm just sad that it's under these circumstances.'

'Oh, we were really fond of those fish and we paid a bit for them, but of course we'll get over it. I mean, I know it sounds silly, and I know they were fish, but we had even given them names. Sounds a bit ridiculous, doesn't it?'

'Not at all.'

'No, I know I'm overreacting. That's what Jack – my boyfriend – keeps saying. Anyway, I won't waste any more of your time.'

I smiled, amiably.

'It's really nice to meet you. I always think it's so important to get to know your neighbours. It's too easy in London to live on top of each other and never even speak a word.'

I laughed. 'It's true!'

'And this area's gone a bit downhill, I must admit. We had some awful tenants living here before you. Always playing loud music, doing drugs, having parties – all that kind of thing. So it's really good to meet you, Marcus. You'll have to pop over soon, next time we do drinks. The guys next door often come along. Sarah and Dan.'

'Well, that would be wonderful. I look forward to it.'

When she was gone, I thought about the final commandment: never coveting a neighbour's goods. Frankly, I didn't. Above me was that hysterical fish lady and her boyfriend, next door was the family with the young kid... I guess I envied the fact that they owned a house. I thought about starting a fire but I feared that might be too easily traced back to me. Like I said, I didn't want to go to prison. Besides, I kept thinking about something happening to the child, and that did make me feel a bit bothered. I suppose even sinners have limits. It's just a matter of drawing your lines.

But, in the end, it was such an anticlimax to sit there, thinking the odd jealous thought. Not much of a raised fist to God, not much of a two-fingered salute. But there it was. I sat and I coveted and I chuckled at the ease of it, how naturally it came.

They say the most extraordinary things of God: in Christianity, they say that he sent a son down to us, that he sacrificed a son, that this son died for our sins.

Well, how could such a God not know what would happen to Nancy, what would come to befall her? This God stood by and he let it happen, he was motionless and frozen, he sat and watched and yet he dares to judge us. He dares to condemn! I wanted to commit so much sin that he had to send down another son, and another, and that these sons would die too, in even greater pain, in even graver torment, until the earth caved to its core with celestial sorrow.

You see, Nancy jumped into my mind at the oddest times. I would be washing up and I could swear that her arms snuck up around me. At the cinema, I would get angry if someone sat next to me because I was saving the seat for her. But usually, what came to mind were those final few seconds. What was she seeing, smelling, tasting, thinking?

Just imagine it. The bump of the road beneath you, all that grit and granite. Those houses and people and the cars that you pass. All the lives you don't know, all the lives you won't know.

Thirty miles per hour. Slower than a peregrine or antelope or cheetah or swift. But still fast enough to hear an engine thrum and the metal shake. The world whizzed by in a second, like it never existed. The wheel in your hands, your feet on the pedals, the grunt of the gear stick. A loud noise – spinning – a howling bang as you slam wham bam into that concrete wall.

Just decimated junk – just cinders and black. Your eyes misting up like the windscreen. Then a final exhaust breath.

A person can drive themselves crazy with visions like this. To some extent, I had to kill her all over again with such formidable thoughts. The feelings around it were so heavy and opaque. It takes enormous strength not to suffocate in the folds.

Part of this concerted effort, this superhuman will, this murder of memory, was to stop punishing God. To let it go. God and I were even: he knew I was angry, I had let my feelings be known. I had desecrated his commandments – some of which I had even enjoyed – but enough was enough.

I knew God would forgive me because I still believed. In fact, 'belief' was a ridiculous word. I didn't 'believe' in a God, I simply knew there was a God; the way the sky is blue or the month is January. Yet it was a tricky thing, as it wasn't a belief but it wasn't a fact. It existed beyond the physical laws of the universe, incontrovertible but unprovable. We needed another word for this state, otherwise we were just debating semantics, just trading in sophistry. At least, that was my two cents.

So I knew there was a God and our status was still 'in a relationship'. I prayed to him nightly and we often spoke in my head. But the dynamics had shifted. It was abusive now. I felt his grip on me tighten, the bellow of his reprimands shake every hair on my body. I was the victim of galactic abuse – and there's no charity or shelter that can help you with that.

Sometimes the thought of him could drive me mad. I would sense him staring at me, inspecting me, like a specimen on a Petri dish. The most terrible thing was the inability to escape him. You could close the curtains but he was still in the room. You could turn off the lights but he was more essence than presence. You could crawl under the duvet but he was lying next to you. He could always see you, hear you, read your innermost thoughts. There was nowhere to hide and nothing could be hidden. For

God is all-knowing and everywhere – but not omnibenevolent.

You see, God is a primordial force of timelessness and reckoning; born from a beginningless past and outliving the infinite present. He creates to destroy. To exist is to suffer. The problem of evil is actually the problem of good. Our lives are a great struggle with cessation; an uprising against decay. But even pleasure is just bait that will lead us to pain. When we worship the thing that made us, we supplicate to an almighty vice. Why do we always assume that this being is a hero? There are no good guys and bad guys, just shades of grey, and some more grey than the others. And this was the greyest, at the top of the food chain; digesting our life force and burping out life forms.

But still I prayed. I read scripture and carried a favourite passage in my wallet. I sensed his shadow and let it fuse with me. I would rather be on his side than against it. I revered his power, I respected his scope.

My reasoning took some sketching out but eventually boiled down to this: that earth was a kind of hell, and when we died, we would either pass into oblivion or God would sentence us an afterlife. I figured if God was crooked, he would appreciate the sliver of evil inside me – the fact that I'd acknowledged it, the fact that I let it bear out. I might even be rewarded – with what, I didn't know. Maybe oblivion was the reward. Maybe I would get a well-deserved exit from the game. Maybe I would be absorbed into the cosmic continuum. Maybe I would turn into God.

I was in a new game now. There were new rules to abide by. Sin was celebrated – for good was void of value and changed nothing of any consequence. The fact I had figured this out gave me enormous confidence. I felt selected, chosen, predisposed – the mark of knowing on my forehead. Everything I did was suffused with this secret elation.

I didn't really believe in a single religion anymore. In that sense, I was liberated. I considered all creeds equal, and was content to let their centuries of wisdom pass right through me. But I also saw their tremendous folly, and felt superior to them all. What wasted lives these holy humans lived. What terrible misguidance had sucked them under.

I wished for Nancy to die that day – and she did. It was as easy as that. Just close your eyes and wish for evil. That incident gave me the go-ahead for further wrongdoing. God had repaid the dark tinder inside me and now I must turn everything into flames. Or something to that melodramatic effect.

It was not long after this that I rose up the career ranks. Nancy had been dead a year, and I threw myself deeper and deeper into the job she hated. I had started off in a fairly administrative, clerical role – basically making the coffees, sitting in on meetings. It was almost an internship, the money was so low. But they recompensed my patience with a step up to Desk Assistant (more on the marketing side). I had to look at market reports, prospect for new clients in potential growth areas... Basically, I got to carry paper around and feel important. I was only twenty-three and I already wore cufflinks. Life was good.

My boss was the man I mentioned earlier: a chap called Finnegan Fishman. He wore garish ties and smoked himself hoarse. He would clap thunderously when he got too excited. He took me under his wing and steered me towards the appropriate exams. I had no sense of this wing being anything but protective. But, of course, flies have wings. Wasps have wings. Big, biting creepies like giant stag beetles have wings. If you are offered a wing, it doesn't mean you should take it.

For under a wing is total darkness. I couldn't see any route out of my life. Who wouldn't accept guidance from a man with an alliterative name? Who still smoked from a pipe? Who regaled the bars with tall stories about Fleet Street and the Wharf?

'Marcus,' he said, patting my knee like I was ten years old. 'I see potential in you. You've got drive, you've got guts. You've got the right mix of instinct and analytical what-not. Now, don't get complacent. You've got to aim high. You're on your own now, but one day you'll have a wife, and some kids, and they will like nice things, and they will deserve the very best of life – of course they will. The very best of life means getting the good food, the sun on your back, the clearest sea that stretches out for miles. Yes, we have to work; yes, we have to put in the hours; but the alternative is not working so hard and not getting the best. To me, and I hope to you, that is a poor shadow of a life, a life only half lived. Think of all the things that such a person will never have tasted! All those sights across the globe that this person shan't see! Of course: enjoy your job, make your job your passion; but never fool yourself into thinking you've got enough. Never stop wanting to make it. Never stop wanting to succeed.'

There was something about me that attracted older men with a parched throat for money. I still ached for my father, still felt his absence in lots of life's little things. No wonder I swallowed up every word of Finnegan Fishman's. No wonder that I got that thirst. That thirst got so bad that my tongue hung out of my mouth most of the time, I had to learn to keep my mouth shut. But in the meantime I moved out of that second flat, out of that tiny place full of childish things and the silent Antipodean, and found somewhere of my own: a beige flat in a gated community, on the edges of Balham. I could pretend it was the turret of my own private castle, and watch the commoners walk past.

'But will you be all right?' asked Jamie, in that worried way of his.

'Of course,' I said, beckoning the waiter, ordering another bottle of wine.

I had suggested dinner at this local restaurant – some little eatery that everyone was going gaga about. *Time Out* had wanked all over it.

Usually we'd just go to the pub, so the occasion was already a little odd and contrived. Jamie looked awkward, George looked embarrassed. I didn't care in the least: the sole point of the excursion was to show off all my new money; to let them know that everything was fine, that I was fine, that life was fine. More than fine.

The waiter came over with the bottle: instinctively poured me a taster. I liked that. I took a sip and nodded. I bloody loved that nod. The authority of it, the erotic charge. I didn't even know what I was nodding about, truth be known. I knew nothing about wine and still don't.

'It's fine.' I took a swig of the red. No sips for me.

'But won't it be weird on your own? Have you thought about maybe–'

'It's fine,' I dismissed.

My vocabulary was failing me. Maybe it was the wine. Maybe it was the situation. I felt uncomfortable every time Nancy was mentioned. I didn't like to talk about her. It was like constantly having to explain away a disability: how you lost your leg, the age when your sight went, that sixth digit on your hand. Over and over and over again. It was exhausting, to be blunt.

Anyway. Trying to avoid this, I gestured about me. 'What a great restaurant, eh? It's got some buzz, that's for sure.'

'It's got some buzz?' George scoffed into his bread and olive oil. 'What are you on about?'

That irritated me. 'You know exactly what I mean.'

He rolled his eyes.

'You know, it's got a good atmosphere. There's ambience, conversation, laughter. A sense that the night is young.'

'It's a place "to be seen", you mean. It reeks of Just for Men in here. Or do I mean "Just for Old Men", the way they're all leching after these young blondes. You know, in the way that should get them on the sex offenders' register.'

'So?'

'So, it's not my kind of "buzz". And I can't believe it's yours, either. I mean... When you said you wanted to meet up, I thought we'd be going somewhere...real.'

'So, Marcus,' came a pleading tone from Jamie, trying to break the tension. 'Are you really sure you want to do this? Live alone?'

'Wouldn't you want to? I've always wanted to. The only reason I didn't before is I didn't have the money. And that really isn't a problem now. Give me one good thing about flat sharing that is better than living by yourself.'

'Well... We always had a laugh, didn't we? When we were flat sharing?'

'Did we?'

'I have to admit, I thought maybe you'd move back in with us. You know, get the gang back together. Eventually. I mean... Is it anything we've done?'

'God, no. This isn't about you.' This was getting close to the realm of emotions and hand wringing.

'You're absolutely positive?'

'Fucking hell, Jamie; yes!' I slammed down the wine glass and it cracked as effortlessly as an egg. When I looked down, my hand was holding a jagged flute. The wine was sloshed across the table and down most of my shirt. Zigzags of glass shot into a mishmash pile.

Some people looked over; some stared; some pointed. I tried to redirect the red heat that slid over my body. The waiter dabbed at my shirt, my trousers. He was brushing glass into a dustpan. Slowly, the room reverted to its original state. How sensitive the equilibrium, I thought. How near the surface the social tension.

When he left, I gave my attention back to Jamie and George. My bestest, truest friends. My university buddies. Now they both seemed so distant that I needed a telescope. Jamie, staring at his fidgeting hands. George, biting his lip, looking sullenly into some middle distance. I realised that they had both changed too, in the years I had known them. The world of work chips away at you, turns you a different shape. Jamie was ever more liberal and artsy; George was increasingly football and scorn. And I was progressively...

'Let's get the lobster,' I said. And I closed the menu in a definitive yet nonchalant way: a pretty hard move to master.

'Lobster?' George's eyes were back on me. 'Gosh, what do you think? Just one? Might as well get ten, since they're so cheap.'

'I've never had lobster,' whittled Jamie, a look of desperation in his eyes, the glee of martyrdom. He could still rescue this conversation! 'I bet it's amazing. It's what they always order in the movies, isn't it? "I'm having the lobster." When they want to impress someone or someone is paying.'

'Well,' I said, sensing a perfect segue. 'That's true. I'm paying.'

'Oh, Marcus,' sighed Jamie. 'That's very kind but I can't let you pay for me.'

George was more combative: 'You're not going to pay for me. This isn't a date. If I want lobster, I can pay for it myself.'

'I want to do it. I really want to do it. For my friends.'

'For your ego.'

'George,' hissed Jamie. 'He's trying to be nice.'

'And also because I can,' I grinned. Then I leant forward so they could see the diamond glint in my eyes. 'I can afford it.'

'Ooo-weeee.' Sarcasm from George.

'You know,' I said, pouring myself another glass of wine, now feeling recovered from my mishap. 'I'm seriously sensing some antagonism, George. Is it because, if I leave for good, you're basically living with a gay guy?'

'Marc, I'm more than my sexuality, you know. And besides, it is possible, you know, for a straight guy and a gay guy to live together. It's not exactly a big thing anymore. It's not the 1950s.'

Jamie cleared his throat. 'Yes. Exactly.'

'And also, since when did you become such a walking fucking cliché? The big wanker banker who likes to roll around in massive piles of cash. *"Oh, please, please let me have more cash, I can't get enough of the cash!"* Jesus. It's embarrassing, mate, I tell you. Embarrassing.'

'Look, I don't really give a monkeys if you think I'm a cliché. For what it's worth, I think stereotypes get a bad press, they help us make sense of the world, it's natural. It's normal. We all have our parts. So if you want to see me as a cliché, that's fine by me. I can be your stock-and-shares character, how's that for a joke?'

'Well, here's another one for you, mate: "All that glitters is not gold."'

'That's not even a joke,' I said, shrugging the weight off my shoulders and really getting into my stride. 'And anyway, you've all got your golds. *You* like your food too much, *you* watch too much shit TV. It's all just a load of rubbish. It's all glittering gold that don't mean a shit – but it's fun, isn't it? So what's the problem? Eh? Just roll around in the shit and wait for it to all rot away.'

'Wow. Eloquent. And you don't think you're losing it? Wow.'

I waved my hand. 'Anyway, I hope you weren't really expecting me to come back one day and fill that room, guys.'

'No shortage of people looking for rooms in London, mate.'

Silence.

Jamie put his head in his hands, he couldn't let it go. 'Things have been so odd since Nancy passed.'

'Died, Jamie – you can say died.' He made it sound like she'd gotten her fucking A-levels.

'We were all so close, and now everything's different. It's not been right for ages. It's been over a year now – it was the anniversary the other week and none of us even said a word to each other. Something's changed. Who knows, maybe we always needed Nancy to glue us together. Anyway, what I'm saying is—'

'You make it sound like we're together, Jamie. "It's not her, it's us." I'm not interested, all right? Get over it...'

'Well, I was thinking that maybe you would actually benefit from a different house, meet some different people, and stuff. Not that Australian guy, that wasn't quite right. He was never there. But maybe some other group, a few more people, something a bit more sociable. I mean, I know that we're probably not the people to help you right now because of our connection to Nancy. But I'm just worried about you spending so much time on your own. And you don't see your mates anymore, and you're always working... I'm worried you're – not coping. I'm worried you're going to crash at some point, and it would be good for you to live with people who could see that and avoid that and be there for you. That's all.'

I laughed. I actually snorted. It was a loud, obscene laugh – the sort of laugh that shows teeth. 'Are you kidding me? I don't need your sympathy, Jamie. I just want to buy you lobster and get you the fuck out of my life.'

'You're being a total dick.' George was up and standing now, the entire restaurant swivelled towards him. 'Why are you acting like Michael fucking Winner?' He was stabbing his finger through the random reference and into my personal space. 'Grief isn't an excuse for turning into a cunt.'

And at that point we were asked to leave. I never got to buy George and Jamie that lobster. A shame, as I doubt they will ever get offered it again, and they certainly will not buy it. I had fully intended to get them one each. For swagger, but also for swansong.

So we parted on difficult terms, and we knew that the scene had finality. I had lost all my friends from university. I had not kept any friends from school. There were one or two people on social media – there was the odd 'status like' or MySpace comment. But even this I let slide, as these people were The Christians, and I felt no link to that kind of faith anymore. It had eroded away.

Inevitably, my social life was swallowed up by workmates: whether wining and dining clients or competitive binge drinking into early hours. Not everyone in the company was part of this social group: there was a selection of family men or older men or men who skulked through different walks of life. And sometimes women, too, with ceiling glass matted into their hair. Outrageous, isn't it? These people worked with money and yet they weren't all scum. Some were decent, nice-enough folk who were just trying to get by, make little love nests, push through to the future, playing the long game to win that sweet-as retirement.

But in my Friday Drinks Club was Harry, my mentor – a private school toff of the old-school variety. He boasted about the Bullingdon Club. He liked most nights to end up in the hands of a prostitute. He was thirty-eight and married with three kids.

Finnegan was occasionally there, although he always left at an appropriate hour, to conserve the requisite aura of mystery.

Philip was thirty, a confirmed bachelor and suspected poof. He would overdo the lechery to try and dispel our suspicions. In fact, his whole shtick was one of fitting in, of trying to emulate others. I couldn't complain though – we were cut from the same kind of cloth.

And then there was Ben. He was closer to my age – just a little bit older. Twenty-four, twenty-five, something like that at the time. He wore an inordinate amount of gel in his hair. It made me think of my dad. Anyway, Ben was very quiet, very reserved, with unnerving eyes of blue steel. He was the one you could imagine skinning a cat or chewing off a stranger's ear. The one who would one day be in the news for terrible, wicked, indecent acts. (Well – people bet on either him or me.)

There were, of course, no women. Not on our nights out. Boys will be boys. Banter, banter. Off the leash. That's just how it is. Get over it.

Anyway. Our behaviour was completely acceptable to each other. We got used to a certain level of drink, a certain level of drugs, a certain level of sex and shallowness and pride. We didn't get *American Psycho* on each other's asses. We didn't rape and butcher women. We just…floated. In this cold miasma. Indifferent to everything.

A night that sticks out in my mind? Nothing that was full-on Vegas or worthy of newsprint. Possibly the Friday night that carried on into the early hours of Sunday. We were trying to find after-parties to the after-parties. Soon the after-parties became the parties. I was still wearing Friday's suit, flecked through with specks of vomit. I had sex with some girl in the alleyway. We had to do it standing up, which I always hate. It's exciting for the first thirty seconds and then it becomes a real drag, keeping a girl up like that, having to hold her and fuck her. This one wasn't a lithe, petite thing, either. It was knackering. The sweat pooled down my back.

When I rejoined the group in some soulless basement bar, Harry was flat out on a stretcher. He'd OD-d on the pills. I don't know if he had too much water or too little water or what. There was froth over his mouth, and Phil told me he'd fitted. I have to admit, it was grisly. I'd never seen a man so grey. As grey as a tombstone. It lifted your skin up. You felt the breath of death run down you.

'We have to tell Claire,' said Phil. His fingers yanked back and forth through his hair, all agitated and shit.

'Who's Claire?'

'His wife, Marcus!'

'OK, fucking hell, I'm sorry, I didn't know her name.'

'But you knew he had a wife.'

'Of course I knew he had a fucking wife. I just didn't know her name. Fuck me, how long's he been like this?'

'I really don't know. Fifteen, twenty minutes? The ambulance came pretty quick. Oh Jesus, the fits were scary, man. He went blue, he wasn't breathing. It scared the hell out of me.'

I looked around. 'Where's Ben?'

'He did a runner when the fits started.' Phil saw my face and shook his head. 'No, not because he freaked out. Because of the pills. He'd taken pills too. They're going to get the police involved. I don't know how far it will go. But it would look bad for work, if two employees were caught doing it. Wouldn't it?'

I thanked the stars above that I hadn't done pills this time. Phil and I had stuck to alcohol. Phil always stuck to alcohol. And I was in a weary, despondent mood and could face a hangover better than a comedown. 'How do they know it was pills?'

'I had to tell them. They asked all kinds of questions. What he took, how much he took, when he took them.'

'Do you think they'll…'

'It's just doing, not dealing, so I don't know, man. But Jesus Christ on a bike, it doesn't look good for work, now does it?'

We looked up and the ambulance man was standing there, a stern and disgusted face. 'Can I break this up?' he asked. 'Your friend's in a bad way. He needs a hospital. Some tests and check-ups.'

'Right.'

'Either of you coming with him?'

We looked at each another. It was a long and lingering battle not to give in first; as sharp and complex as any chess game.

'I will,' sighed Phil, readjusting his glasses, his eyes grey and frosty. 'I'll go with him.' He had revealed greater moral fibre than me, and was ashamed of his colossal weakness.

The ambulance man said: 'Was he showing any symptoms

leading up to the attack, like chest pain, breathing problems...'

'Yes,' said Phil. 'Yes, all of that.'

'OK, well, let's talk some more at the hospital. We can also contact the next of kin.'

I met Phil's eyes. We both knew this would end in carnage. The relief surged through me, such wonderful uplift.

In the end, they didn't even call the police. Seems it's not so common for the medical lot to do this, especially if there wasn't a fatality or they didn't find a stash of drugs and needles in your keeping. I don't know, maybe Phil sucked up to them – he was always very good at playing the upstanding citizen, although deep down he was surely as cold and heartless as the rest of us.

Harry's wife found out though. Apparently she was numb with shock, her skin so porcelain, you could see right through it. But she was in love with her life: the cars, the house, the live-in nanny. She shut her mouth and let the tears roll back. She sat next to the hospital bed and stroked his hand. Although she must have wanted to shout: 'You idiot! You cock! Having an overdose at thirty-fucking-eight! Married with three kids! What the fuck were you thinking?' She'd not seen him since 8am Friday, and he hadn't phoned her, not even a text. This wasn't even unusual. She told Phil all her worries, all her vexations. He told me this later with wide, excited eyes, swerving on to the topic of her giant tits. Whatever, mate – you know she's not your type.

But anyway. When you get buddies from work, you validate yourself. You start to believe that everyone is like you: they work to the same aims, use the same buzzwords, live by the same principles. You exist in a cocoon, in this reckless echo chamber that rings on and on into emptiness. Before you know it, you are one and the same: *an organisation.*

That year, on my birthday, I booked the day off work. But I didn't know what to do with it. I did the crossword over coffee – it was just like my commute, only the scenery didn't move.

Then I showered and dressed. While in the shower, I tried not to think about what I was going to do with the day. I shaved extra carefully and then stared in the mirror for a very long time.

If you stare for a long time in the mirror, odd things start to happen. Your face goes unbearably strange – like when you look at a word too long and it doesn't seem spelled right. I couldn't see a complete word in my face anymore, I could only see letters. Ears. How bizarre were the ears! The mole to the top of my temple. Features: ugly and misshapen. Stare a bit longer and the boundaries go fluid. I could see my face like a woman's – imagine it with long hair and lipstick and a buxom chest. I could see my face black. I could see my face with chins doubling up all the way down to my knees. I could see my face as any other face and it no longer was my own.

My phone rang. There was a pang of relief in my lungs, like it might be work. It was urgent, they needed me in, they were dreadfully sorry, *that's just how it is in our line of business*. I patted my face clean and strolled over, renewed purpose in my stride.

It was Jackson. When his voice cut into earshot, the day deflated over me.

We hadn't spoken for well over a year – since I confronted Mum and gave her up. My birthday must have triggered some strange solidarity, some forlorn loyalty... The date must have been sitting in him like a tumour. He must have been feeling the push of it, the growth of it. He must have sweated the night away – to wake up with this burden inside him. It was 9am and already he'd called.

I cannot remember all of the things we discussed there and then. I only remember half listening as I watched an unseasonal blue bottle flying round in circles. It crashed against the windows. Then it roared around the room. Its defiance grew more and more frenetic; its buzz became a scream. It didn't even know what it wanted anymore. The smell of the outside had drifted away into never-wasness. Towards the end of the phone call, it stopped; settled on the remains of my croissant, in joyful wait of putrefaction. So I drowned it in jam.

Jackson was a mix of emotions. There was sadness there, and embarrassment, disapproval, love. Mostly he was furious at me for what I had done to his mother. I agreed to meet with him to talk it out.

Anyway, later that week. It was a bitterly cold day, the sort of day when you wrap yourself in as many layers as possible to try to forget the sheer brutality of nature. You still want to pretend that life is oh-so-civilised, with its radiators and central heating and boiling kettles and hot running water. You want to forget that if the frost-bitten ground tied you down, hypothermia would mash you in minutes.

Jackson was sitting at the table when I arrived. It was in a pub, one of those gastropubs where they hike up the prices and serve you ale in goblets. Décor was wooden and inoffensive but with 'manly' touches, like black chrome chairs. Jackson was snacking on posh pork scratchings and avoiding eye contact.

It was awkward at first. Of course it was. Jackson could barely look at me. I couldn't wipe the grin off my face. For there he was, my big brother, the one who came first: pitiful and failed and drunk as a skunk. I enjoyed being in this new position of power, looking down on that figure hunched over his food, hands scurrying to and fro like trotters. This man was as bad as his mother, really. He is three years older, don't forget, which is a lifetime when you're younger. I remember that ride on his bike on Christmas Day. The tyre screech on wet pavement as he left us all to our misery and didn't help us to hide it.

'I've met a girl,' he told me, later into our talk. 'She's amazing.'
'Seriously?'
'Yeah. Her name's Lisa. I might marry her.'
'What makes you think she's the one?'

He shrugged. 'Just instinct. Isn't it? You get an instinct.'

'And she's amazing.'

'Yeah, like I said. She's a great girl.'

There was a pause. He excused himself to go smoke. I could see him through the big glass window, pacing and fidgeting, his brows hooded and hangdog.

When he came back, he spoke more about his life. But his heart wasn't in it. I assumed he was jealous. He hated not being the popular big brother, the alpha male. Sure, in our house, my parents had always believed me over him, always favoured me, if you like. I was the youngest, that's just how it goes. But outside, in the real world, he had all the girls and he had all the fun. He jeered at me, sneered at me. For years, I envied him: his quitting of school, the parades down the high street, the screech of secondhand Ford Fiesta wheels. Now I already earned so much more than his pitiful salary. He was scraping by as a welder apprentice. He was back to living at home. No wonder he had to keep talking about Lisa – it was the only thing he could still beat me on. She was lovely and nubile and loving and alive.

The food arrived. Something about this caused Jackson to cut to the chase. Maybe the meat gave him power.

'We need to talk about Mum. You haven't been in touch for over a year, and she's getting frail.'

'She's not in her 80s, Jackson.'

'But her heart's not good. The docs told her so.'

'Well, she needs to get out more. Do some exercise.'

'You know that won't happen.'

'Very much so.'

'Look, she's devastated, Marc. About what you said.'

'I meant every word.'

Jackson's eyes narrowed, but I carried on eating. I made a big point of eating at a steady speed, chewing my chips very carefully. I kept my face even.

'I don't get it.'

'What?'

'Her and Dad worked their whole lives for us. They sacrificed things for us.'

'Nobody asked them to.'

'You would have done, I promise you. If they'd stopped doing it. If we'd been thrown on the streets. If we'd been chucked into care. You would have done.'

I couldn't help myself. 'And what makes you suddenly the golden child, this perfect son? Hey?' He had riled me.

'I'm not. I got into trouble for a bit, I'm the first to admit it. But I'm trying to start over. I honestly am.'

'Are you now?'

'Yeah. Look, I'm sorry if I was a twat when we were younger, but I had my own shit to sort out. I was just a kid, let's face it. We both were. You can't hold it against me.'

'And is this where Lisa comes in? With the "starting over"?'

He met me in the eye then, his pupils constricted until they were slits. 'Yeah.'

'I see.'

'What do you see?'

'You.'

'Look, I got guilty around your birthday, OK? I didn't like the idea of nobody phoning you. I stopped Mum from contacting you, but I didn't like it. It felt wrong. I felt bad, if I'm honest.'

'You really didn't have to.'

'Well, yeah, I can see that, can't I? You don't seem worried about Mum at all.'

I exaggerated a yawn. 'I needed parents when I was a kid,' I sighed. 'I don't exactly need them now. I'm doing pretty good for myself.'

'Can't you just call her? Say you're sorry. She's going out of her mind, Marc. Her depression's getting worse. Every day and shit. I'm worried she's going to do something. I'm not going to lie.'

'I thought you said it was her heart.'

'I'm not making this up, Marc!'

'There is nothing between us but genes,' I laughed, holding my hands up, pushing the plate to the side of me. 'I feel nothing at all for her.'

Then Jackson said this: 'You're a heartless bastard then, and I don't want you as my brother and I don't want to see you again.'

And the weirdest thing is, he didn't storm out like George, he didn't create a scene. We just sat there in absolute silence, while he finished his food and I finished my pint. And when it was all gone, we both stood up and left together, but we walked out in opposite directions.

It was that summer we had the 7/7 bombs. Blood sprayed the whole tube, like it was all now the red line. The world filled with terror, whether real or contrived. I didn't take a position either way. God might be on the side of the terrorists, for all I knew. Or maybe he approved of both: they both made monstrousness, they both dealt with death. Body bags tugged from the planes. Faces whipped by tears. I saw it all on the news. More consequences of the whole Iraq fuck-up. How humans must surpass anything that God deemed possible, with our inexhaustible ways to cause suffering. How delighted he must be with us. What beauty he must see before him – since the necessary is beautiful. And somewhere in time, we humans must live out these terrors again and again.

Still, I didn't bother myself with politics or current affairs. I was out every night, pubbing and clubbing, a constant conveyor belt of women. I was living the dream! I got to grope every kind of breast: small ones, big ones, flat ones, inverted nipples, dark nipples, pale things with the veins stuck out. These women were all different in bed, all had their own ways of cumming. Some were totally cool with me not phoning them back. Some got really upset: called my mobile incessantly, somehow found me online and sent me angry, puerile little messages until I had to block and report them and hope I'd never bump into them again.

There was this one girl in a bar, I admit; her name was Chloe. We shouted over the music for hours, she gave off this pulse and I just had to have her, there was some kind of pull, some instant connection. I starting seeing these visions of marriage and babies and turning my crusty leaf over. (I forgot her number, so it happens – too drunk to save it into the phone. I should have bumped into her by now, I thought those were the rules of the romcom. Funny, how she just vanished in a population of 63 million. Well, fuck you, Kismet.)

There were one or two I dated for a while, when I kind of missed company, although I abided by rules. I would never let them love me. I wouldn't let them stay more than a night at a time. I would never cook them a meal, or have them cook for me. We would go out to restaurants or bars, where we could show ourselves off, but never on 'date' type things like the cinema or bowling. We wouldn't curl up on the sofa, I wouldn't let them see me in pyjamas. I hoped to god I wouldn't see them in theirs. And I'd never meet their best friend or family. Eventually, one or both of us would grow tired of the whole charade, and then that would be that.

Gradually, I had reached a point where I shunned all meaningful contact with another human being. It was terribly easy to do and terribly easy to sustain. It is easier to be a loner than ever before. Everyone left me alone. Nobody bugged me for intimacy, nobody asked any questions. In this day and age, they just presume you've got a syndrome. Everyone is labelled and boxed up and tied up with a bow. They just let you get on with it. They just look away.

Chapter
Four

I don't know if it's just me who gets this, but when I am sick, I give off a scent like parsley. And all the stress at work was making me stink like tabbouleh. Even the air was compression. I could feel it sliding towards me, ready to crush from all sides: an invisible foe.

The obvious thing was to go and visit my father.

The walk from the station was clogged with the usual detritus: regret, sadness, anger, hurt. I had to kick my way through those streets. It was hard to keep going. I was also terrified that I'd see my mother, even though I knew she wouldn't be awake this early, let alone out of the house. I'm not even sure why such a frail woman scared me; her lips receding into her face like cliff erosion, the lids of her eyes all hooded and craggy.

Constantly looking over my shoulder, my fingers uncontrollably itchy. They just scratched at themselves inside the baggy coat pockets. I was getting nervous about touching the earth, I guess. Then, as the gates approached, I nearly buckled. Whatever was left of him, if there was anything at all, wasn't inside that plot. Yet when I walked through the gates, it was like walking into his arms.

I could barely see the way to the stone, my eyes were so blurred up with tears. Again, this ferocious itching, now spreading its way up my arms, my neck, the little patch behind my ear. My skin revolting, trying to tear itself off from the bones.

I got to the headstone. It's a plain rectangle of granite, just a few sandblasted words; nothing of interest or controversy. Just the tragic promise of the en dash, jammed between two immovable dates. A prisoner of time.

I got down on my knees and lifted up clumps of earth, letting the soil tumble between my fingers. Maybe he was in there somewhere. Cells and microbes giving nutrients back to the earth.

The cemetery smelt sweet and wonderful. Often graveyards are the most fecund places: so much blossom and nectar that it can make you feel heady. The air was thick with pollen, I could hear the wing dance of a hoverfly. Gentle sun poured down like a morning shower, waking everything up from a long winter slumber. It didn't smell of my piss anymore.

Jesus claimed that it was easier for a camel to go through the eye of a needle than a rich man to enter the Kingdom of God. Well, my father was never rich. He coveted money and always thought of it, from waking to sleeping. But he never had much of it, for all of his dreams and schemes and betting on horses. He was in constant pursuit of it – or perhaps *he* was pursued. He was always running away from some new and terrible threat. But it was coursing right through him, it was thick in his skeleton. Our tree is a long line of losers stretching back to the primitive: lobotomies, bankruptcy, incest and slums.

I did not know if I believed in God at that moment. But I

still hoped for my father to be in that kingdom. The angels on harps. Wispy, gossamer clouds. A great cosmic land of plenitude. A place where the horse that won was always yours, despite the odds: where odds did not exist.

I cried myself hoarse. The manly, guttural kind. Tears that come out as grunts and short expiring spurts. When it was over, I dug around the headstone and wedged fifty-pound notes into the soil. I knew they would discolour and rot, but I thought it would put a smile on his face, wherever that face might be. All that money turning to compost, mixed in with the particles. It would forever be part of him now. He could finally stop running.

Only a couple of months before my dad died, we had another 'special' outing that sticks affectionately in my mind. I had just started a new year at school. Shortly before this, there had been conversations about whether I should be moved up a year, since I was doing so well. I think my form tutor was a little perplexed by my parents. She was probably expecting some pushy lawyers or hardnosed business executives. Surely my comprehensive – and Jackson – should have prepared her for the reality, but I could see that it hadn't. The academic contrast between me and my parents was so enormous that it was evidently a gulf. Their faces were furrowed and harassed, scraps of fear in their eyes, as Mrs Clement informed them that I was doing very well indeed. In fact, I was top of the class in most subjects.

Once again, I need to remind you that I was no genius or prodigy or virtuoso. I was simply steadfast and diligent. But teachers seldom distinguish. They see only in 'grade-a-vision'. If you tick those curriculum boxes, then you must be excelling. You have to know the facts, not necessarily apply them: and certainly not stretch them or test them or question them.

But my father was visibly shaken by this meeting. In fact, it was he who insisted that I stick to my year. 'All his friends are in that year,' he said, his head shaking faintly, his eyes closed for a moment, confronting an alternate reality. Not my mother nor dear Mrs Clement dared interrupt at that point – to point out that I didn't have any friends, whatsoever.

That very weekend, my father took me to one side. 'We're having a day out today,' he laughed. 'A real special treat.' But the tone was a little off, and I think he knew it. I was nearly fourteen, not four. I was starting to pull away from my dad, from the flotsam and jetsam of childhood.

He was taking me to an art gallery. 'Proper art. Proper pictures of proper people. You know, the traditional kind. None of this misconceptual crap.' I have no idea if the phrase was a joke or misnomer. To this day, I don't know what he was trying to prove. It might have been puffing out peacock feathers or showing your best poker face: *you mustn't get too big for my boots*. He was still the father, the boss. He was just as clever and cultured. Understand?

Or maybe it wasn't that at all. There was no sizing up of manhood, no reassertion of patriarchy. This was about re-educating so he could reconnect with his son – who clearly had different interests now to horse racing or pint drinking or watching The Generation Game. This was about stretching out a hand and trying to feel his way through my territory.

I hope it was the former. Because if it was the latter, it severely misfired. I wasn't interested in art! There was no future or leverage in art. I wanted to get the grades that got me laid. I wanted to work my way up to such a height that I could see the peers around me fall into the moat and drown. If I wanted fantasy, I had it in my head, in spades.

But I went along with it because it was a day out and Dad was paying. It was guaranteed to involve something stodgy and carb-laden, like pizza or doughnuts. My dad would pretend this a secret treat for me, but it was always an excuse for his own predilection, away from the hectoring tones of Mum. I waited for this moment with fervent glee – and was quite happy to strain through all the artwork to get there.

But what a lot of artwork. Tate Britain is big: monstrously big. Room after room of hanging pictures. I was happily distracted at first. I gawped at the high ceilings, the frescoes, the latticed cornices. But soon it grew tiresome. I was in covert battle with my father: we both felt obliged to read every tiny script of text on the wall, as if swotting for a quiz at the end.

The room was full of bodies like ours that just stood and stared. Deluded people, who seemed to believe that this room contained answers. As far as I could tell, you were simply looking at the faces of artists and nothing more: as bewildering and literal as a normal face. You could read what you liked into it, but you'd never really know. People were looking for depth but it was still only surface.

My father stopped opposite every painting, just for a second or two. It was a gesture of courtesy. A carefully timed show of respect and (he hoped) intellectual judgement.

But there was one where he lingered. I counted to three seconds and then found myself counting to ten, fifteen, thirty, a minute! A whole minute he stood there, oblivious of the shuffling behind him, the soft push-back of spectacles.

'You all right, Dad?'

'Yes, son.'

'You recognise this one?'

'Nope. Never seen it before in my life.'

I wanted to ask him more questions. I wanted to know why he had stopped. But then the feet moved on, and I scurried along to keep in his wake, let his direction guide me.

And yet. When I think of that moment, I become frantic with a yearning to place the picture. I cannot remember a single detail. I was looking at his face so hard that I didn't really look at the painting at all. This fact made me sad for a long, long time

– but I've finally forgiven myself. For maybe I was looking at the right thing all along?

Yes, I buried myself in facts and figures at school, but I always had this secret world of make believe. I've told so many lies that some have turned into truths. It's possible that Dad had his own secret world, too – and, just for a moment, he saw its reflection in the canvas.

There are other things, as well, when I think of it. Mum and Dad were always telling me that maybe the moon landings didn't happen, maybe AIDS was manmade, maybe the world was ruled by a secret lizard elite. They had so little power and persuasion, perhaps it made them feel better to doubt the credibility of experts. Indeed, there was no truth except your own. You could justify anything. You could make anything real. You just didn't know, did you?

I've always had this power. Even as a child, all my wishes came true. That's how I recall it. You see, I'm the man who can hold up planes. The first time I got on a plane – with Nancy, to Spain – I had to concentrate very hard to keep that can of shaking metal stuck up in the sky. It was just me and my thoughts and that furrowed brow, stopping the plane from diving into a fireball. By the time we landed, I was completely worn out.

So, I got struck in the face by a thought. The world is my invention. That's how the accident happened. Because *I asked for it to happen.* Nancy and I fought that morning. Her face was trembling. On the way out, she dropped her keys. She could barely start the engine. I was alone in that kitchen, I was swelling with rage. I thought to myself – maybe I said it out loud: 'I hope she fucks off and dies. I want her to die. I want her out of my life.'

The only woman I've ever felt soppy for was Nancy. That's probably because she arrived on my terms. As soon as I saw her, I wanted her. But before I even saw her, I asked for her.

Another Justified Sinner

I didn't mess around much with girls at school: a couple of suck jobs if they were wasted at a party; the substandard thrust of teenage sex, that one time only. On the way to uni, I looked out of the window and I knew I was ready, I knew I wanted a girlfriend. The physicals were sketchy, but I'd always had a thing for blondes. I liked an athletic figure: pert breasts and sturdy calves. I wanted her to laugh at my jokes. She'd think I was brainy and brilliant. She wouldn't question my lies. She'd keep me company, but know when silence was better.

I saw Nancy on stage. Someone on my corridor, who I don't even remember, told me they'd get me into the wrap party. I couldn't stand drama and English and all that wallowing world. But this guy promised me beer stacked up to the ceiling and a forest of cunt. ('Those theatre girls are gagging for it.') So off I went.

The play was impossible to understand. A 'greek tragedy', I believe. I dozed off several times. It was a lot of wailing and shouting and histrionics. *Nobody speaks like this in real life*, I thought. But then I wondered why this moment was any less real than the next, and I started to watch it like it was actually happening. That made it pretty awesome. Foetuses sewn into thighs and people changed into snakes. Wild, frenetic dancing, the stage pulsating with strobes. And there was Nancy, her hair hanging loose and her eyes thick with kohl; carrying the head of her son, in the throes of possession. She wore a long white tunic, all stained with fake blood.

'You were amazing,' I said. All the audience had gone. It was just the actors and crew, first-year theatre studies, a pervy tutor with a thick russet beard. The chairs were stacked up at the back of the room, there was an impromptu dance floor. People were throwing themselves around, arms in the air, their feet kicking and twitching. Alcohol covered the ground. There was some audible singing. I was slimy with sweat.

'Oh yeah?' she smiled. She'd changed into some jeans and a vest top, but kept on her stage make up. She looked like Barbie-turned-zombie. It was sexy as fuck.

'Seriously. You were wonderful out there. I'm genuinely scared of you now.'

'Yeah?' She laughed. 'No, you don't need to worry. There won't be any sacrifices tonight. Well, maybe my dignity.'

'What's that?'

'I plan on getting *hammered*.'

'Yeah?'

'Yeah. I've been working on this all term. I'm beat. I need to seriously let loose tonight.'

'Hey, I've always wondered. What's your accent?'

'American. Can't you tell?'

'Yes, but whereabouts?'

'West coast. Well, Arizona originally, and then California when I was about ten. But my folks have just moved to Seattle now, which is, like, *a lot colder.*'

'Oh right. What was Arizona like?'

'Lots of rocks. Lots of sunshine.'

There was a pause – an engorged pause, almost violent. It was beautiful. She was beautiful. We just smiled at each other's eyes, kept slurping our drinks. When she reached the end of her glass, I went to get another. When I got back, she was dancing, rubbing her back on a guy's back. Her arms were outstretched, she knew all the words. I didn't even feel jealous. I was happy to watch her, this lulling feeling in my stomach: I'd found her, I'd gotten her. She was everything I'd wanted, plus some surprises thrown in.

We spoke a bit more that night, but nothing happened. Life became a chess game: strategic moves plotted out several goes in advance. I discovered all her hangouts. I became buddies with Jamie, who was doing her course and in the debating society with me. I got invited to all her parties. I found out all the things she liked and didn't, and moulded myself in their image.

When we got to the date in the pizza restaurant, I knew the timing was right. I kissed her and she gasped a little, then put her hands on my face, and I scrunched up her hair in my fingers. My tongue twitched against her wet and gummy mouth. I nibbled at her upper lip. We were oblivious of everything, all the other customers, the food, the knives and forks – everything. I felt her body slacken in my hold. I knew she was mine forever.

Those moments, lying in bed, our bodies slotted so neatly together. When the morning was just morning, before the day got old and died like everything else. I played my fingers on her back. Our stomachs lifted and fell in unison.

'Nothing is a coincidence when it comes to us,' I said.

She looked up from my chest: frowned, crinkled nose. 'What do you mean?'

'I was always going to be at that play. You were always going to act in it.'

'Do you really believe that?'

'It's not about belief. It's a knowing.'

'Do other people have that too, then?'

'No. It's my world. It's my rules.'

'And my world too, I hope?'

'Yes. Our world,' I said – but I wasn't sure of that part. She was made for me, not me for her.

'So other people just serve our purpose, like puppets?'

I was uncomfortable to admit this. I wasn't going to. The 'yes' slipped out of me. I was too relaxed, too trancelike. But she must have thought I was joking – being deadpan. She burst out laughing, put her hand over her mouth in that way she always did. So I laughed along, too.

She added: 'In drama, we study motifs. An idea or symbol that keeps coming up in a play, over and over, and it's shouting to tell you something.'

I said: 'What's that got to do with anything?'

'You said nothing is a coincidence. Maybe there were signs in your childhood that you'd meet someone like me. Maybe every life has motifs, you just have to make sure you spend time deciphering them. Wouldn't that be cool?'

I didn't know what to say about that, so I just said: 'Yeah, that's a nice idea.' But that very night, I put a notebook aside, called it the 'Book of Coincidences & Synchronicities'. Ever since, I have scrawled down every possible coincidence, every repetitious thing that may conceal some grander meaning. But I've never made head nor tail of any of it. But wasn't that just such a Nancy thing to say?

In the cemetery, I thought about Nancy's grave. They'd flown her body back to California. She was buried next to her grandparents, in the family plot near the coast. You could just about make out the sea and smell the salt in the air. I tried to picture it very hard: picture laying down flowers, picture kissing the framed photo of our graduation ball.

Cosmic ordering should come with a warning. To coin a cliché – you have to be careful what you wish for. If you become too attuned to the universe, it can hang on your every word – you don't even have to write your wishes down. You can just have an innocent thought, a throwaway thought. Like wishing someone dead.

But cosmic ordering is too full of holes and paradox, I mused. Why didn't my wish for her to die conflict with somebody else's for her to live? If everyone is one, why didn't the power of entirety overrule me? Nobody else would have wanted Nancy dead. She didn't make enemies. She was kind and considerate, if sometimes caught up in her dramas. Am I really more connected to the cosmos? Am I really that powerful? Am I really to blame…?

I started to wonder if maybe I was God. Maybe I created the

world, the universe, the everything and the nothing. Maybe I had just forgotten. Maybe I had self-inflicted amnesia. Maybe I created the world and realised that I had forged everlasting pain and suffering. In punishment, I sent myself down in human form. I was destined to live over and over: never self-actualising enough that I could harness my powers and break free; wondering if I was God but always forgetting again, in the furnace of death.

I became so convinced that the world was of my own making, that I decided to have fun with it, to see what would happen. When I got back from the cemetery, I gave my brother a nudge. We hadn't spoken since that time in the gastropub – about a year earlier. We had defriended on Facebook and I wasn't even sure if he still used his old number. Anyway – when I texted him, a message pinged back almost instantly.

Soon the texts were flying back and forth. After about a day, I asked if I could call him. There was a longer pause that time. But then he messaged back to say that yes, I could.

On the phone, he told me about how he was now a qualified welder and that business was going well. He was engaged to Lisa, they were due to get married next spring. They were currently looking for somewhere to rent, so he could get out of Mum's.

'I'd love to meet her.'

'Who? Mum?' Audible delight in his voice.

Awkward silence. Awkward cough. 'No, I mean Lisa.'

'Oh, right. OK.'

'She's going to be my sister-in-law, isn't she? I'd like to meet her. And see you again.'

'Marc, it's great talking and everything. I've not liked having this grudge. It just isn't right to me. We're brothers. But, look: I'm not sure…'

'Why?'

'Well, basically; it just feels wrong to see you when you won't see Mum and all that. Like a betrayal or something. And last time we met—'

'I'm sorry for last time. I am. Listen, just the once, all right? Let's meet just the once. I know I'm not getting an invite to the wedding. It would be nice to just meet her, and see you; just the once, that's all. Just to see you. The two of you together. Well, before you get married. That's all. I'm not saying anything else, expecting anything else. That's it.'

It's amazing how quickly he relented. I guess a brother always finds it in his heart to forgive.

I had the plan half-baked in my head, but it wasn't until I actually saw Lisa in the bar that I knew that I had to have her. She had long golden hair, and bore a passing resemblance to Nancy. She was a deep toffee tan and there were freckles on her shoulders. Her lips were wet with gloss. She extended a hand to me and said, 'I can't believe I'm meeting the little brother.' She seemed a bit nervous and her accent was Essex.

There was no God but me. All those years of worry and prayer, and to suddenly know this fact! I was exempt from punishment. This was a world without consequence, a world of my making and choosing. All I had to do was be more careful what I wished for. I was wishing for a woman, and it had to be Jackson's. It had to be her.

You see, I'd always wanted a brother. I needed a brother. Something was wrong with Mum, clearly. A curtain had dropped down over her spirit and no light could get through. Jackson should have said something, he should have sorted it out. He was already working when Dad died – he should have chipped in with some money.

And then there was Kitty. Oh, Kitty, Kitty, Kitty. How I gazed at that girl in every class. It all started when she thanked me for passing a compass. She must have said it absentmindedly, forgetting she was supposed to detest me like everyone else. I don't know. She said it automatically, sweetly, the trace of a smile left up on her lips. 'Thank you.' That was all it took for pages of feelings about Kitty. I scrawled her name obsessively, over and over, in exercise books. I thought of her body when I wanked, as quietly as I could, leaking onto the tissue and caressing the folds as if they were bits of her. Then that bastard found the book and tore everything down.

'Fancy that skirt, do you?'

I glowered at him.

'OK, "fancy" isn't good enough. Am I right?' He paused, violently. 'Is it love?'

I went at him, instinct, lashing out like an animal. But he tossed me back without effort and my head hit the wall. Tears flew into my eyes, and I hated myself then, I really honestly did. I vowed to change everything, to muddle it all: to get fitter and leaner and the hell out of that hellhole. Of course he got Kitty, made sure of it, afterwards, although he said it just happened, no hard feelings, whatever. But I kept my word, didn't I?

That's why that night with Jackson was such a success. I was in it for the long game. I played the role of charmer; I wanted Jackson to think I'd changed. So I had one monologue that was particularly tender and poignant. And I could feel the charge between me and Lisa. She was tossing her hair back, her hand slipped between her thighs. When Jackson went to the toilet, I sat very close to her and asked a million questions: probing her, poking her. Making her feel like she was the most fascinating woman in the world, like I could hardly believe the sheer fact of her.

When we all parted, Jackson had a doubt in his eyes, like he might want us to resurrect our brotherhood. As Lisa stepped out, I held him back and said: 'It's for the best, Jackson. I agree that it would upset Mum and this is between me and her, it's got nothing to do with you. Let's just be glad we had tonight. And maybe we can get together at some point in the future, maybe when you are married.'

He smiled, and looked the most sincere I had ever seen him. 'I'd like that, Marc.'

Three weeks later, Lisa left him.

She was so easy to drag away. It was odd: you wouldn't think they'd been dating for almost two years. All it took were a few smitten texts for us to meet up in a bar and have a smashed-up kiss, full of guts and guilt. She tried to stay away after that, feeling all shameful and vexed, but I got her back with some hushed, sweaty phone calls where we said things like, 'We shouldn't', 'We can't'; which only made it hotter. Then a few dirty photos, and we were meeting up once again, for dinner. She told me about her life, herself. I gave very little away but I was always topping up the glass, nodding with gusto, making sure our hands kept touching. Whatever her interests, I said I enjoyed them, too. Whatever opinion she held, I said it was brilliant. I told her how wonderful she was in so many wonderful ways, and I said *of course* I didn't want to do anything to hurt my brother, *of course* – but who could deny this, who could earth this charge?

Maybe it was because she knew I was richer. Maybe it was because I was younger and (now) better looking. Maybe it was because their relationship had reached that over-familiar, turgid stage, which even the distractions of wedding planning could not save.

Not long after that, she moved in with me. I persuaded her to. I seduced her completely. From the things she told me, even in those brief conversations, I knew her self-esteem was slight, that she was easy to manipulate. So I said that her family were a bad influence, that she needed only me. Told her to quit her job as a cashier, that I would look after her, keep her safe, secure. I had enough money, she didn't have to work. She could figure stuff out.

Sure, there were a few early obstacles. Like when Jackson called round and punched me straight in the face. I'd never been hit by a sobbing man before. I replied very calmly that if he did it again, I would call the police to lock him up – and that would break our mother's heart. This was undoubtedly bullshit, but it gave him the fear; and he backed away with his eyeballs all shot through with blood.

It turned out that Lisa wasn't a bit like Nancy. After we fucked a few times, she actually grew pretty tiresome. The novelty of the situation was ebbing away. For we had nothing to talk about, nothing to laugh about. I stopped asking her questions. I treated her like a slave. I started to punish her – because she wasn't Nancy, because she'd been so easy to flatter, just because I could. I would shout at her, hit her, leave her hanging until the early hours, not knowing where I was. Yet the most maddening thing was she never shouted back, never retaliated, never told me I was a bastard. She was completely obsessed. She told me she loved me in less than two months. And she said it like she meant it: the colour drained from her face, that golden hair now straw-like and matted. She would do anything for me: *anything*. I don't think a man had ever driven her so crazy. Something chemical had gone off like a bomb.

As I withdrew from her, she withdrew from food. At first, it was the odd skipped meal. Then it became starvation. I don't know if this had always been inside her, although she said it had, and from an early age. All I know is that her face got hollows and craters and lines and looked like the pockmarked howl of the moon. Her upper arms were thinner than her lower arms. There was no colour to her lips. She would sit there and not even speak to me. All I could hear were the rumblings and gurglings in her stomach. When they were noisiest, she would involuntarily smile.

Well, I wasn't going to throw her out. I liked having her

around, in the background, wanting me. We somehow co-existed like this for a year. But one time she wrapped her arms around my neck and begged me to kiss her, to touch her. She hadn't done that for a while. So I said to her I couldn't, not with the way she looked.

She gasped and the tears sprang to her eyes and her face contorted. She ran to the bathroom and locked herself in.

'You disgust me,' I shouted. 'I can't stand the sight of you.' Of course, I meant skeletal – but it was only later that I realised she might think I meant fat. Well, it was what she wanted to hear, wasn't it? That was her make believe. She was stuck in her own little world, and I knew what that felt like. Sometimes it's easier if people play along, rather than try to wake you up.

Her health deteriorated further after that. She refused to eat anything. It got so bad that she wouldn't even touch liquids, and after a day or so of that, she finally went for an ambulance. I was at work, and her parents called me, the fury and agony shredding their throats. Her heart was very weak. They had forced her on a drip. I said I would visit, but I didn't, of course I didn't, the situation had me in hives. I dropped off her things at the hospital, in neatly packed suitcases, and legged it out of there. I changed my phone number, so her parents would stop calling. I changed the locks, so they couldn't get into the building. It was over.

At night, I would think about Lisa, and how I should feel something. I'm capable of emotions. Look at Nancy. I loved her like crazy. And this time, I did feel something abstract, but it wasn't really pity or guilt, more a burning, surging innerness. An energy, with the lens zooming in. It took an hour of staring up at the ceiling to figure out that it was anger. I didn't even know why I was angry. I tried for an hour to understand the reasons, but I got overwhelmed in the generals and, pretty soon, I gave up.

Well, none of that mattered; a distraction soon came. Credit got crunchy and harder to swallow. Not that it seemed to mean much, at first. The system is set up so it should hurt us the least. So we continued to binge on expensive food and burn it away at expensive gyms. We ranted about reality TV, rather than act out our storylines. We lived for the weekend but then recalled nothing at all from the blowout of boozing and drugs. We hid from the headlines and buckled down in our habits. We did what we always did. We were invulnerable – weren't we?

Chapter
Five

One day, we watched the big financial institutions just topple down, like a new 9/11. We saw pale people stumble from the Lehman Brothers' building, a laptop in one hand and office mug in the other. The world was all shaken up. Like a believer on the deathbed who suddenly blinks at oblivion and wonders 'What if?' Housing bubbles popped. Outputs popped. Eyeballs popped right out of people's heads.

The recession swept over the UK like a pyroclastic flow. We got burned by the heat. In early 2009, the UK was officially in the slump, although it had looked that way for months. The banks were begging for their life. House prices got shot. People lost jobs. We suddenly went on 'staycations' and grabbed at Groupon codes. Everything was depressed.

Shops lurched into administration: MFI, Dolcis, our Woolworths who art in heaven. Cue the pictures in papers of pitiful people stockpiling a final Pick 'n' Mix like they were scooping the hem of the Turin Shroud. Nobody believed this was happening. There had been nearly two decades of continuous growth. It felt like growth would just go on forever. But when cells grow out of control and invade other tissues, that's when you get cancer.

And yet, just before the recession, there was a global peak in food price. I read in *The Economist* that the spot price of food was at its highest since 1845, when the records began. Business was booming at Fishman & Sons.

A few years earlier, Goldman Sachs had created a food index. It meant that all the commodities could be grouped and measured together, like stocks. This made the assets so much easier to grasp for your average non-specialist. It widened the client pool, basically. On top of that, other rules and regulations were loosened too, which made it more desirable for other banks and bodies. Private investors were just clamouring to add commodities to their portfolio: the icing on the cake, the *pièce de résistance*. Our clients gobbled up cheap land around the world: millions of square miles at a time.

Food and farmland are fantastic things to invest in; even better when times are bad. Although the global food price dipped a bit at the start of the recession, it soon hiked up again. The greater the investment, the higher the prices – and the more clients feel a need to invest. The price generates its own demand. Since agriculturals were a big part of our skillset, the firm simply flourished at the time. Finnegan was ecstatic. I got promoted. Finally: a trader.

I didn't feel bad about it. It was just supply and demand. Anyway, we needed the speculators. High prices drive innovation. But let's not mince our words: there was obviously a tricky in-between period. A few million extra went hungry. There were food riots in North Africa, Asia, the Middle East. All of this is true and unfortunate. But I knew the money would – in the end

– go into food production and help drive the cost down. It was all in the system. And who knew what was behind the rising cost of food? It could be down to oil, weather, biofuels, diet. We'd never know. And until we did, here was a fantastic situation to exploit and invest in. It was, we told our clients, one of those rare and precious things: a win-win business deal.

I mean, the situation was farcical. The UK was at its lowest ebb in years: on its knees and crawling through razorsharp debt. But here I was, making more money than I had ever seen in my life. Every time a grain contract reached its expiry date, I rubbed my hands in anticipation of an absolute mint.

I celebrated with a final Pick 'n' Mix. I'll admit it: the tears sprung into my eyes. A scene from childhood: shoving a gelatine ring over some scowling girl's finger. Her biting it off and chewing it in her mouth, her eyes burning with hatred and her lips all dyed pink from the food colouring. Then another: me dropping candy cola bottles into Mum's Bacardi – pure sheepish glee on my face. Yes, every bite was a saccharine hit of nostalgia. For – despite the world food price – the UK was now leering at superfoods and antioxidants, blueberries and smoothies. We were trying to live forever, trying to outlast all this shit. That bright shovel of sugar was a hangover from some other time.

Well, I allowed myself a final flourish, after the saccharine feast. It was a birthday present, you see. So I moved out of rental and bought my own digs: somewhere even closer to the centre, can you believe. Oh, it was a no-brainer: I was always worrying about retribution from Lisa's family. There had been the odd hour of angry intercom buzzing. Some hate mail in the post. Some threats from a half-brother I didn't even know she had. In every possible way, the move made sense. It was wonderful.

I sat in the living room, surrounded by boxes. I said: 'Well done, Marcus. You did good.' My voice had a bit of an echo, some reverb in it. A bit baggy and loud. I liked it. I opened a bottle of *Salon* champagne and drank it all. I went round the luxury flat and clinked my glass with the cooker, the bath, the windows, the bedframe... 'Cheers.' 'Cheers.' 'Cheers.' 'Cheers.' I sat on the floor with my head against some half-emptied box, fell asleep as the drink roared in my head, sloshed about in my stomach. My dreams were fitful.

I was happy to wake up, as life was good. Ridiculously good. The sort of good you see in the movies, that you think couldn't possibly happen that way: it's too unlikely, too contrived. Everything gleamed with the sheen of high-definition TV. My time was now. The timing was great. I felt like punching the air every time I stepped into the office. Everything was good until my brother found me.

Apparently, I had been tricky to find. He'd looked online, but my email and work number weren't there. He couldn't get past the security at reception. I never really found out why. Then he tried me at the old place, but of course I'd moved on, not stupid enough to leave a forwarding address. He tried my mobile, but I had long changed numbers. He looked on Facebook, but a short while earlier, I had decided to leave it. He even tried those websites where you pay to see people's registered addresses, even the famous ones – but I wasn't there, either. Just when he was close to giving up, he had a quick search on Twitter and found me.

I don't even know why I was on Twitter. I was just dabbling, I suppose; following other grain traders, keeping an eye on my clients, fishing out others. Its take-up had been pretty slow to build, but now people were starting to talk about it. There were a few celebrities on there who regularly filled out the news columns just through these tweets. It looked like you could bypass the old press and now file your media release in 140 characters. It looked like it was getting to the point where it was actually bad business *not* to be on there and managing your reputation and brand and contriving an image. I made sure I followed *The Financial Times*, *The Economist*, journalists and businesspeople who thought like I did and would give me retweets. I enjoyed living in this world. Other views did not exist. If they did, I blocked them. It was nice like that.

I was happiest when crafting a carefully cultivated image: an avatar. I traded in virtual food, food I would never actually see or touch or till, future food that didn't even exist yet. So it sort of made sense to trade with virtual personalities, most of whom I would never meet or know, personas that were all somebody's fiction. It was a game.

But like a fool, I was easy to find. Jackson set up an account and started to tweet me messages, over and over. *How can I call u? Its urgent.* And *How can I contact u? We got to speak.* Finally, *Its about mum. We got to speak. Its urgent. I mean it.*

I was about to block him when I saw that final message and something churned up inside me, like my insides were shoved in a food processor. Everything fell into itself. There was something thick in the air, something that slowed me down. I could not move my hands to type. I breathed in treacle.

I followed Jackson and DMed him my email. Within minutes, a message was bold in the inbox. *Hi Marcus. First off this isn't about Lisa or anything like that. You dont need to worry about that. But this is something id like to talk to you on the phone about. Not email. Ring me. Jackson.* He left a number underneath (although I still had it in my phone, I confess) and I stared at it for a while, trying to absorb every digit, trying to drum up the confidence. Since leaving school, I had never lacked confidence. I always seized a moment without any self-analysis or doubt. But now I felt brittle and monstrously weak. My hands were shaking. I picked up the phone and put it down. Several times. I went to make a cup of coffee. I watched the kettle rumble. I watched the steam billow up to the sky. Back at the sofa, with the cup in my hand, I punched in a few numbers. Then cancelled. A couple of times I was only two digits from a dialling tone. Then I did it, and the phone was ringing, and I was too startled to hang up. I clasped the phone to my ear, tenterhooked.

When Jackson answered, the words fell out of his mouth much the way I imagined them. Our mother had died. She had died in one of the ways Jackson had foreseen – but deep thanks, it had not been suicide. Her heart gave out. She must have been washing up, or cleaning, since she was discovered by Jackson still wearing the marigolds. The place was spotless. He gave that detail: 'The place was spotless.'

Unfortunately, it was an unseasonably warm March. Daffodils had long broken free from the mud. So her place was already stunk through. Well – she'd been dead for two full days, you see. Jackson hadn't heard from her. He was worried. So he turned up at the house; the two cats mewing outside, all wild and teeth. He had to break down the side door to get at her, her body was there straightaway. Apparently she wasn't smiling or frowning or looking at peace or anything at all. She was just expressionless. Like she'd been caught totally unawares, in the midst of a daydream. Her flame blown out: just like that. Except he didn't say it like that, did he? He said: 'One second you're living, and the next you're dead.' I started to cry.

'Marc?'

'Oh fuck,' I sobbed. My face contorted. I smeared the snot with my hand. 'Oh fuck. Fucking hell. Fuck, fuck.'

'Marc?' Now he sounded paranoid. Like I was toying with him; an elaborate game.

'Jackson, she was *young*. She was too fucking young.'

'Look, I know. Her heart–'

'But wasn't she on medication? Weren't they fucking sorting that out?'

'They were still testing the medication, trying to find the

right dose. They hadn't quite sorted it. They thought she might need an op. She was trying to back out of it. And then there was her seroxipram...'

'Her *what*?'

'Her anti-depressants. For depression and anxiety and stuff like that, basically.'

'Right. I see.'

'They always said there was a risk with the heart: irregularity or something. They said it was a very small risk, but... she should never have been on it. I think she was addicted. I think she might have gone over the dose...'

'Oh fuck.' I tried to stop the sobs but my whole body was shaking. I was shaking like it was twenty degrees below freezing.

'Anyway. The funeral's tomorrow. I know this is last minute, but I've been trying to find you for days.'

My body reeled. 'OK.'

I heard a sharp intake of breath. 'I don't want you to think I forgive you. Because you're my brother, but I don't. I don't even think of you as a brother anymore. You are dead to me. You hear? Dead to me. Deader than Mum could ever be.' He swallowed, hard.

I didn't reply.

'But Mum would have wanted you there tomorrow, basically. Even now, just a couple of weeks ago, she was talking about you. Talking about you as a boy. Talking about you and Dad. Just talking and talking about you, on and on and on. She knew you were doing well, she knew you were "successful". I didn't tell her about you and Lisa. She just knew the good stuff. She was proud of you. She loved you. She always thought you'd patch things up. She never gave up on you. But I have. I have. We're done. All right?'

'Yes. I know.'

'So I'm just telling you this so you'll come to the funeral.

Yeah?'

'Yes, I'm going to come. Of course I'll come.' I couldn't even process things mentally, there was just this gush of feelings inside, I was drowning in it, suffocating.

He sounded a little taken aback. 'Right. All right, then.' Pause. 'Because you were harder to persuade before. But I guess she wasn't dead then. She'd have preferred a visit when she was alive even better, you know that, don't you? Fucking twat.'

I took it. I just held on to the phone and took it. Crying. Wailing like a banshee. I don't even know where it came from. It wasn't normal.

'God, you're a fucking bastard. I would love to just smack my fist into your face. I would love to fucking *annihilate* you. You twat. Ughhhh.' He grunted. I heard a bang. Maybe he punched a wall. He was still grunting a bit. A mix of crying and grunting. All I did was listen. Just held the phone and listened.

We both calmed enough that he could give me the name and address of the church. He didn't need to do that. I knew the church, all right. It was where Jackson and I had been christened. My dad's funeral had been there. All night, I stared at the ceiling with every cell in me numb, and braced myself for the stink of that church.

It was a fucking awful church. It didn't have much of a congregation. Just a few old people, hanging on for dear life – the priest waiting for their will in the collection box. The vicar was loud and obnoxious. He always tried to slide stupid jokes into things. His parables didn't make any sense. The building was falling apart. The wood was rotten. The stained glass was scratched and all covered in bird crap.

I noticed this when I sat down on the pew, right near the back, where I was firmly directed. Of course, I wasn't doing a reading. Nor was I apparently 'family', who sit at the front. Jackson read out something, I don't remember what. My aunt

Tilda, who I'd not seen for years, gave a poem. She said it was one of my mum's favourites. I had no idea. She said that Mum had loved it since she was a little girl. I had no idea about that, either. I didn't even know Mum liked poetry. I could scarcely believe she had been a girl.

I got out my phone and noted down the title and poet. A few people turned round and gave me withering looks. I recognised one as a cousin, now long grown up. Another was an older lady. I didn't know who she was. Anyway, her look was livid. It only occurred to me later that maybe it looked like I was texting or booking a holiday or checking the football scores. I had a status in this family. I was the black sheep. I was evil incarnate.

The funeral was pretty insignificant. There was nothing really of Mum in it; or it least it felt that way to me. She wasn't in the hymns or the prayers or the casket. She was in me. Yes, surely I was one of the few true receptacles? She wasn't in that urn they were going to put her in: charred bits of bone and marrow. Just physicals. The strewn shell of a tortoise or snail. Like loving a puppet but never reaching for the hand underneath.

I walked to the car very upright and stiff like I was the urn, like I might accidentally spill pieces of Mum that I would never get back.

What was inside those pieces? What did I know of her? Her favourite musician, her favourite film star, the endless iterations of telly soaps, all the births and the deaths. A smile at the woman's weeklies. Her famous roast potatoes. The synthetic smell of lemon. The tears, the shivers, the impassive, cling-filmed face. That bloody dressing gown. Her love of Dad, her love of us. What else was I carrying around?

I didn't go to the reception. It was in our old house, and Jackson had made it abundantly clear that I wouldn't be welcome. Lots of the family said so: I was a disgrace, a disappointment, a dickhead, to be frank. Jackson had spared Mum the detail, but he hadn't spared anyone else. Everyone knew about Lisa, he said. Everyone knew about what I had said to Mum that day. About how I blamed her for everything, for things that didn't even make sense – when she had never done anything wrong, hadn't even remarried, *and she could have, you know, she bloody could have.*

We were not a large family. Dad was an only child. Our grandfather was alive, somewhere, in a home, but I had no idea where. Nana and Gramps on Dad's side: dead. Toyboy Tony, whereabouts unknown. There was Aunt Tilda and her husband and our two cousins. There was Jackson and me. And that seemed to be it. Who else would be in that house? I thought back to the church. A handful – at most – of Mum's friends to account for fifty-five-odd years of life. A friend from school, long turned into a penpal. A distant friend from somewhere she used to work. A sort-of friend from the school gates, when she used to wait for Jackson and I to file out with our satchels and rolled-up socks. Then there were the neighbours – friends only in a superficial sense, really. Friends she would peer at from over the fence, chat to about the weather, maybe the occasional TV show. Rarely, very rarely, one would go over to the other's house. The grand occasion of it! Shutting your front door and stepping less than a metre to the side, just to knock on the other. No, no, no: Mum's house was small, but it would look big with a guest list like that. There would still be so much *space*.

This bit about space – I got to that part when I was back in my house. I broke down. I only understood that phrase then: breaking down. I felt bones break off, cells misfire, organs unravel and explode. My hair was dragged away from the skull. Nails ripped off the fingers. Kneecaps collapsed to the floor. I lay on the sofa, a heap. I thought I'd never stop crying. I staggered to the toilet: my eyes were red raw, my skin was blotchy, I coughed up phlegm. My throat was all itchy from how much I wailed.

I scrubbed at my skin with a pumice stone. That didn't hurt enough, so I found some scissors and started to poke at my arms, then I yanked at them, hard, so the blood criss-crossed the skin. I managed to stop crying. I gaped at my arms and cast a finger over the lines. It was a better pain than the other pain. Thank God. I said that bit out loud. *Thank God.*

Except there wasn't a God, I could see that now. There had never been a God. It had all been fallacy. Supreme self-deception. Fantasy, and nothing more on my part. I pictured the space above me, the colossal wilderness. The (observable) universe: 78 million light years in radius at *least*. And most of everything, dark matter and dark energy: light-lacking unseens that we do not understand but which trickle through everything. Everything godless and vast and detached and precise.

I had betted on the future, hedged the risk with an understanding that I would find salvation in an afterlife, that I would be endlessly redeemed. I thought anything could be traded: even a soul. But I had been dealing with something that did not exist. My hands touched more imaginary grain than there could be actual grain in the world. A bird in the hand was worth two in the hedge, but my hands were empty. I was waking up to an unbearable present.

I wished for Nancy to die – and she died. But my father had died, and I never wished for that. And now my mother was dead and I never wanted that either. Despite all the anger and betrayal, the years of her eyes all dimmed, I had never wanted *that*.

When you get an illness or something fatal or incurable happens to you or a loved one – what is worse than the loss is the realisation, after several attempts, that wishes are unanswered and prayers unheard. No matter how hard you scream them. No matter how chafed the palms. I still rubbed my palms out of instinct, a defective flare gun to God.

The next day, I called in sick. I never called in sick. They knew it had to be because of the funeral. They didn't say anything. I hung up. I threw up in the toilet. I really did feel sick, but in a peculiar way.

My flat was oppressively big. All that space, all the *space*. My eyes welled up again. I wanted to cram myself into something small – a crack on the wall, a gap under the door. I climbed behind the sofa and lay down on my side, pressed up to the wall, so I took up less room.

As I've said before, it can take me a while to understand an emotion: to pinpoint it, name it, declare it officially as *this*. So I felt this feeling as only a vague gathering inside me. It took some time for it to scramble together before I could see what was there.

How did I become this person? How did I get here? When was the moment I decided to take those ill-fated turns – or had I made that sort of decision at all? I hated myself. I could feel it. A burn in the heart, a stab of bile in the belly. Self-hatred is like being stabbed from the inside. You can't even wrestle the knife out of somebody's hand.

Of course, there was never a God. There was only ever my mother and father. They were my creators, they were worthy of worship. They had constructed me from nothing, the ultimate magic trick. They had raised me, for God's sake: all-seeing, all-knowing, knowing they must never intervene. Oh, the guilt. The guilt.

Now I didn't have that, either. To be parentless is a terrible, intolerable thing. You feel that the world has no time for you anymore. It has nothing to give you. I was desperate for meaning. I needed to search for a meaning. I just couldn't bear it. The sheer agoraphobia. The swarm of total nothing. My roots pulled up from the ground.

I made myself go into work the next day. And the next. And

the next. But work deteriorated, like I knew it would. I had lost something – an innermost, sacrosanct thing. I walked about with my back bowed and my eyes blank on the pavement. I thought that everyone could notice it, was staring at it. This sinking, concaving, squishy jelly around my middle. I had gone *soft*. Something had sunk in and diluted me, made me mushy inside.

Finnegan called me in his office. 'Is everything all right?' Fuck me, he'd noticed.

'Yes,' I replied. The sun was hitting me straight in the eye. I squinted.

'I understand you've had a bereavement,' he said. 'One of the boys told me.'

'Yes.'

'I do wish you'd told me.'

'Well, it didn't seem pertinent—'

His eyebrows shot up. 'It's highly pertinent. It's affecting your work.'

I couldn't make out his face. Just the sun in my eyes. This dancing mesh of lights. 'But it's not affecting my work.' I put my hand up to my eyes to find some shade.

'And yet we've had a complaint.'

'A complaint?'

'Yes. From a client.'

'A client? Complained – about me?'

'Yes.'

'Why?'

'They say you provided some misleading statements. They say you downplayed some risks...'

'Right. Well, that simply isn't true. I can't even think which client that can apply to. Was it an official complaint?'

'It wasn't a formal complaint, no.'

'I mean, my clients haven't made any losses. At all. At least, nothing significant...'

'Any loss is significant if a client complains about it.'

'Right. I mean – of course.'

'We are a very small firm, Marcus. We are up against banks, multinationals... We specialise in the smallest of details. Quality of service. Perfectionism. Finesse. *That* is why our clients choose us. A client complaining – even informally – is *always* significant. Even if they're wrong. It's significant.'

'Yes. I understand. Of course. It's most unfortunate. I'm very sorry to hear it.'

'It's not a question of sorry, Marcus. It's a question of it not happening at all. We can't afford to make mistakes. That's it.' He held his hands up. 'That's all there is to it.'

'As I said–'

'If a client complains, it's a mistake.'

'Yes, of course.'

I could see that the meeting was over. I walked out very upright, trying to look blasé and urbane.

From then on, I knew I was being watched ever more closely. Finnegan was right: a small firm cannot afford to upset its clients. Our client list wasn't large, but it was lucrative. They expected a lot. Our reputation punched us above our weight.

A year earlier, I would have been distraught. I was an ant. All my day-to-dayness was for work; for the company; for the organisation of work. For work led to money, and money made you impervious. That was all the purpose I needed, that was my only pursuit. To stand on my own two feet, right at the top of the ladder.

Yet it's odd – I didn't know how much I loved my mother. I didn't think I loved her at all. Obviously there was an ancestral bond that yoked us, but I thought that was something superficial and perfunctory, like saying 'bless you' after sneezing. I certainly didn't think I liked her: mousey and apathetic, her eyebrows scruffed up in tufts, everything unkempt and coarse and traumatic.

I mean, it had been fun to be the favourite in childhood. It was so easy to orchestrate, so tirelessly amusing. But I didn't think I wanted her affection, not as I grew older. I was embarrassed. I would dawdle out of school in the hope that she'd move away from the gates and back into the banger. Her eyes wide and worried; Cliff Richard on the radio... No: in a million years, I could not have predicted that Mum's loss would hit hardest. Don't get me wrong: Nancy and Dad's knocked me sideways, dragged me down into pits. But Mum's...

Perhaps it was because I was once curled up in her womb; and she pushed me out slowly, gently, like a flower from a bulb. She changed my nappies; she clothed me, fed me, bathed me. She waited at the gates, she waited in the car. In her final days, in the last few years, she had no doubt been waiting still.

I couldn't put my finger on it. All I knew is that her death pulled something out of me and nothing could put me back together. It might have been her ultimate revenge. For now I was drab. I stared morosely into some middle distance. I didn't wash myself. I spent all the time squinting, my hands held up to my face, trying to find some shadow, trying to hide back in the dark. Our lives felt intertwined then, her genetic hold less weak.

I told my 'closer' colleagues about my mother's death. One of them must have told Finnegan. I don't even think it was worth the risk I took. The confession felt uncharacteristic and awkward. We didn't tend to trade in emotions.

True, bits of people had fallen off through the years. Some armour had rusted. Harry and Claire were divorcing. There were custody battles over kids and alimony. One day, he went to the toilet for a very long time, came back with eyes all slopped with blood and water. He coughed up about the divorce, with shaking hands; tried to dismiss it, but his voice wouldn't let go of the words. He never mentioned it again – but it was there now, around him, like a miasma of smoke.

And then there was the time that Philip got absolutely trashed. As in – the most drunk we had ever seen him. Right before the flood of vomit down his shirt, he blurted out that he was gay. Nobody knew, he told us, not even his parents. Some of the guys were a bit wary of him afterwards, but we mostly treated him just the same. Yet that night in the bar, in that night of wind and rain and revelation, some of us even encouraged him to come out and live the life that he wanted to lead. *This is the 21st century*, we said. *Nobody even cares anymore. You only get one life.* But come Monday, the masks were back. Our noses were hard: we'd been trained to seek out patterns, sniff up lines of order, you see.

I went out with the lads at the end of my first week back. Ben was picking up women like a party trick. Shots lined up on the table. Harry got hold of some pills. He shook them over his head, like maracas. The music thumped. All of our ties were crumpled and stained and the top buttons of our shirts tugged undone. I left very early. I didn't even understand why.

At home, I cried. Thinking of Mum. Her whole life a pregnancy that never got to the labour. I cried those big, sploshing tears that feel like you're expunging your insides. I was crying at everything, lately. It felt like I was getting a lifetime of tears in just under a fortnight. Everything was delicate, like being caught in a web.

I was slipping down the slope. If you are brittle, you are not standing upright. All the qualities necessary for my job were slowly ebbing away. How can you be confident about the future price of a commodity, when you don't even have confidence in your own future self?

I got paranoid. I assumed that Finnegan was waiting for an opportunity to bump me off: the merest slip-up, I'd be out on my backside. In a pre-empting act, I approached a large international, who had headhunted me previously. There was talk of a bigger role. There was talk of transferring to the US.

I went along to the interview. I put on that mask and I acted. The words tumbled off the tongue. It was well rehearsed. My greatest strength, my greatest weakness. A little bit of background. La di da, la di da. Then the obsequious zest for the company: the awe of its success. A flatter of the ego. The kickass presentation. The killer last slide, with the punchy closer. They seemed interested, leant forwards, doing that twiddly thumb dance and the gentle nod. They said they'd call me over the coming week. I saw the approval in their eyes and I wanted it.

But when I got home from the interview, I did something atypical. I sat in my favourite armchair, stared at the artwork some firm had picked out for me. Then I dialled my brother's number and I waited, hunchbacked and pale in my creased navy suit. It rang out like a trombone, or the forlorn bellows of a hunted whale. It rang into emptiness, it rang into space. It rang and it rang until it clicked into voicemail. There was the tone and I inhaled, audibly – but I didn't know what to say, so I ended the call.

Over the next few days, I did this several times. I called, he didn't pick up, I hung up. I told myself lies, like he'd probably switched phones. Then I tried dialling from different numbers – even stray telephone booths. He didn't pick up, but somehow this didn't assure me at all. Somehow he knew it was me, every time. Every time, he resisted, he rejected a reunion. I finally left a voicemail – broken, scattered, scratchy. I mumbled something about needing to talk. We were still brothers, after all. Just a lot of platitudes, really. I could hear the words coming out in my living room. I was talking to myself.

Of course, it wasn't ever just one incident that built the rift between us. Like all these things, it drip, drip, drips. I think, when we were young, really young, we might even have been friends: football in the park, the tug of wrestling moves, branches as lightsabres and the weekly sweets at the newsagents. But he was always falling back or acting out, and my parents always telling him off, and it made me suck up even more, feel a real thrill of divides. I don't know when that happened. When it fell beyond repair.

Jackson's profile was still on Twitter – nine followers (all but me were spam); a few tweets (all at me). I tried to contact him on there, too, but again there was silence. He had all but disappeared. I couldn't trace him on social media. I scrawled through search results, desperate for a forum post or video comment. He was now as difficult to find as I had once been.

I shrunk into myself and waited for the inevitable contact of a solicitor: the discussion of wills and property. Surely this would bring us together? Surely we'd have to meet up? But these were just words to try and stop the fever.

I knew I would never see him again.

On Friday, I heard back from the company. They were delighted to say that they wanted me. I asked for the weekend to think about it. They sounded surprised – but civil.

So I carried on like normal, gave Finnegan nothing to suspect. I turned down Friday drinks – no, not even the one – but that was probably acceptable, given my ma's recent death. I slapped Phil on the back and told him to have a great night. As they swaggered into the distance, they looked robotic and strange. On the way home, I picked up a bottle of whiskey. I don't even like whiskey – but it felt sort of apposite. I knocked it back the very minute I was back in that armchair.

I wanted to watch a film, but it seemed too intentful. I ended up skipping the channels. I liked the hypnosis of poking the remote. My brain couldn't concentrate, and I wanted monotony.

Red Nose Day was on – and the snivelling chatter was sort

of numbing and distracting, like smearing novocaine across your eyeballs. The celebrities were queuing up to do their duty and ease any nags of conscience. Oh fuck me, not Ant and Dec. Jesus.

I mean, once this was over, they could all return to their lofty apartments and vast Edwardian houses, full of incalculable stuff. It was the modern indulgence for the middle classes. Thank God, other images soon washed over me: potbellied children and flies, scorched earth and firewood.

The whiskey thrashed me. Soon everything was static and the room was rotating. I turned off the TV and lay down, trying to keep the ceiling in one place. But I was strapped to a circle, tumbling over time like a zorb. There was always another side, there was always another vista. If I didn't believe in my job anymore, perhaps all my beliefs were wrong. Maybe there was no right and wrong. Maybe there was only right and wrong. I had never thought like that before. Maybe there was a God, maybe not. I had no conviction. I just didn't know.

I somehow logged on to my laptop in this wiped-out state. It came back to me – my mother's favourite poem. I remembered the title, the poet. I found it quickly. I read it several times, but it didn't make any sense. The world was mysterious: both sublime and grotesque. I tried to picture my mother as a little girl, where she first found this poem. I tried to picture my mother reading it. I tried to imagine what it meant to her; what she read into those lines. There was nothing. The colours jumbled. I must have passed out. I greeted the morning with a banging head and the stink of acid.

Oh, Walt Whitman. What made you write these lines? What made my mother love them? What should I learn from them, or was I never the target?

'On the beach at night alone, / As the old mother sways her to and fro, singing her husky song, / As I watch the bright stars shining, I think a thought of the clef of the universes, and of the future. / / A vast similitude interlocks all, / All spheres, grown, ungrown, small, large, suns, moons, planets, / All distances of place however wide, / All distances of time, all inanimate forms, / / All souls, all living bodies, though they be ever so different, or in different worlds, / All gaseous, watery, vegetable, mineral processes, the fishes, the brutes, / All nations, colors, barbarisms, civilizations, languages, / All identities that have existed or may exist, on this globe, or any globe, / All lives and deaths, all of the past, present, future, / This vast similitude spans them, and always has spann'd, / And shall forever span them and compactly hold and enclose them.'

On Monday morning, I handed in my notice. On Monday evening, I booked the trip to Africa. Ever since, there have been weeks and weeks of banks, contracts, solicitors and embassies. Vaccination shots and getting the flat rented out for the year. But I'm finally ready. The admin is done. Tomorrow, I leave the UK and I will figure this out.

Part Two
White

Chapter Six

He scrubbed to get clean but couldn't get off the dust. The air was a haze: fine particles of powder, dead matter and silt. It mixed with sweat to form a sticky paste. Most people stopped scrubbing after a day or two. He reached in the bag for another wet wipe. He carried on scrubbing.

An 'official' person – he couldn't remember the name – passed something back to the driver, and saluted the passengers. The engine fired up and they bumped up the main road. A couple of people mumbled polite turns of phrase, but there was mostly just silence: except for the wind and the whistles of the driver. People had their faces pressed up to the windows; looking into the expanse as the light toppled out of it.

'We need to hurry up.'

'I know, I know.' The driver jabbed his finger in the air. The van veered a little too far to the right, and there was an audible gasp from the back. 'Think I don't know?'

'Sorry.' A woman at the front turned around to the group. 'There aren't any lights on the road. As you might have noticed.'

'Dark come quick.'

'Night-time comes quickly,' she said. 'You don't really get twilight.'

The man to Marcus's right: 'And we don't have headlights?'

'Yes, this vehicle does – but most others don't. And you have to be careful of the animals. Some come down from the hills and stray on to the roads.'

'Should we be worried? I mean, how long until we get there?'

'Oh, we'll get there in time. We'll get there before it gets dark. There's nothing to worry about.'

The driver swivelled around to laugh. It was polite captivity that made them smile back. 'No worries, no worries.' The car veered to the side again. Another loud gasp. He turned back to the steering wheel and gave a full-throaty crow.

'Oh they're used to it, here,' she explained. 'We'll just drive a bit quicker. We're nearly there.'

Everyone went quiet. The sky was sinking into the ground. The landscape throbbed with shadow. Occasionally they would pass a village and see woodsmoke swirl up from the sides of the road like fugitive spirits.

'We're here.'

The van skidded to a halt and threw open its doors.

'Come on.' Stephanie – that was her name – peered into the back. 'We're here.'

They had been travelling for almost twenty-four hours, but now they didn't want to arrive. Arrival was formal and final, and they didn't know what to expect. They were barely prepared.

The first to depart was a man to his right. The other three got out in tandem. Then it was him, in the cocoon of the car, hearing the clicking of insects. The last.

'We're here,' said Stephanie. She opened the door, and he felt obliged to step out of it. 'Come in, I'll introduce you to the rest of the group.'

He stomped through the dust, towards a single-storey house with a small crowd outside. There was a mix of black and white, young and old. A few children skipped at the front and waggled their hands. Two women ululated. Everyone seemed happy to see them.

'New recruits!' cheered a man, who handed Marcus a beer. 'Hi, pleased to meet you – I'm Aldo. You must be beat.'

'Just a little.'

'Well, drink the beer. It'll do you good.'

'Is it local?'

'God, no way. That stuff is vile. No, this stuff is Carlsberg. It's brewed here, in Blantyre – but it's not really "local" stuff. They rip the labels off, for some reason. Don't ask me why. But yep, it's all we have, I'm afraid. It does the trick, though!'

Stephanie appeared, with a face full of lines, eyelids drooped over the eyes.

'You all right, Steph?'

'Oh yes. Definitely.'

'Was it an OK drive from the airport?'

'Yes, it was fine.' She glanced from Aldo to Marcus. 'It was all right, wasn't it... I'm so sorry, you'll have to tell me your name again. I'm feeling a bit tired.'

'Marcus.'

'Marcus. It was all right, wasn't it?'

'Very much so. It was interesting.'

'Where do you come from, Marcus?'

'I'm from London.'

'This your first time in Malawi?'

'It is, yes. First time in Africa, actually.'

Stephanie and Aldo swapped meaningful looks. 'You'll get used to it, here. It gets under your skin.'

'How long have you been here, then?'

They both spoke at once.

'You first.' Aldo gestured.

'I've been here a year. I'm now Deputy Director. With Philippa. She's the Director. She founded the charity. You probably know that, from the website.'

'I've been here six months,' said Aldo. 'It's my time to go back, now. But I don't want to.'

'Right.'

'I might extend it further. It's just awesome out here. It's a great little charity, it's good that it's small, you get to know everyone. And you really see the difference you're making.'

'I bet.'

The chatter petered out. Marcus stared into some distance.

'Well, come meet the rest of the group. Did you chat to anyone on the way here?'

'No.' He added, by way of explanation: 'I was feeling a bit... overwhelmed. At the time.'

'Oh, sure. We all had that. Well, now's the time to do it. Let's go.'

'How many people are we?'

Stephanie walked beside them, her arms stiff and crossed. 'Well, we have some administrative help in the UK, but in terms of active volunteers... out here, right now... With you guys today, let me think – fifteen, yes, there are fifteen of us in total. We tend to change volunteers on a six-monthly basis. Aldo is staying, but most people don't.'

'Right.'

'They do this as part of a gap year, or they have a sabbatical from work. Anything less than a year isn't really long enough. But it's hard to get volunteers to commit to a year. Well – you must know how it is. Anyway, let's get you introduced...'

'When did all these other volunteers arrive?'

Aldo cut in. 'Some of them arrived with me, in another van. Others arrived last week.'

Marcus swigged his beer, gently herded around a pit fire. The village was being drained of its colour. He could just make out a ladder of lights behind a woman's shoulder.

She turned around, following his gaze. 'They're the fishermen,' she smiled. 'Out on the lake.'

'That's the lake?'

'Yes. You can't really see it now, can you?'

'No.'

'They often go out at this time. When it's just gone dark.'

He felt a vibration thud through him.

'They're the drums,' she said. 'I got here last week, so I'm a bit more used to them. Not completely, though. They're kind of loud. My name's Annabelle, by the way.'

'Annabelle. Right. I'm Marcus.'

'Nice to meet you, Marcus.'

'So, you arrived last week?'

'Yes.'

'Why are they drumming?'

'They're signalling to each other. Communicating something, I think. It's probably quicker than texting.' She grinned and crinkled her nose, but stared back into bewildered eyes that kept settling and unsettling. 'Well, I'm going to get another beer. Back in a moment.' Meanwhile, Marcus watched those pricks of light, drifting over the darkness.

Later, there were other introductions, other handshakes, other names to remember, other beers. There was a feeling of gaiety, like this was 'a moment'; like they'd stepped into a festival or a full-moon party, like life was being beckoned out of them, like pollen from a flower, this sweet taste on their tongues, with the scum and the dirt tightly gripping their skins like entry wristbands. Every scene was a photograph, every second was a memory, every conversation was something they would relay to their grandchildren. The drums thrummed ever louder and the beer beat their brains into muddles.

But that first night was a shambles. Stephanie addressed the group at a later point. A glass was struck and a shush rippled the crowd. Philippa came out of nowhere: a middle-aged lady, wearing a bright-coloured skirt, her curls pulled back into a big, dark bun that looked like a doughnut deep-fried in hair. She welcomed them all, gave further context, issued boundless thanks for helping out with the charity. Her voice dropped an octave and she gave some important instructions: tips about snakes and water and other things that people failed to take in. The stars were so deep, you could cut out the layers. He knew he should be listening but he kept looking up and feeling dizzy and bulldozed.

Soon, everyone was dispersing into bedrooms and shutting their doors. He was incredibly drunk by this point, couldn't see dream from fact. When recollecting the next morning, he thought it was Annabelle, the tall brunette, who half-carried him to the bedroom. He had a vision of her tucking him in with the mosquito net. He also had a picture of something else, in the corner. And when he opened his eyes, he wasn't too surprised to see another bed there, with another crumpled body inside.

Marcus closed his eyes again and floated back into light sleep. It was probably only for five or ten minutes, but when he opened his eyes, the figure was standing.

'Fucking hell!'

'Sorry, mate. Didn't mean to frighten you.'

He took a moment to compose himself. Then he propped himself up on one arm and tried to look casual, sociable. 'You must be my, um... neighbour.'

'Roomshare. Yeah. I'm Toby.'

'Marcus.'

'Good to meet you, Marc.'

'It's Marcus.'

'Marcus. Yeah, OK.' He sat down to squeeze on some shoes.

'It's just family who call me Marc. Only sometimes.'

'No worries. You coming to breakfast?'

'What time is it?'

'Seven.'

'Seven?'

'They only serve it until nine. Then we start helping out.'

'You've been here the week, then?'

'Yes, indeed. I mean, we get weekends off and all that. But Philippa told us last night–'

'I was a bit drunk.'

'Ha ha. I get it, I get it. No need to explain. It's play hard, work hard, I reckon. You did seem a bit worse for wear when you staggered in last night.'

'Sorry about that.'

'Nah, don't be sorry. Anyway, I'm going to go get some grub. You sure you don't want to come?'

'Maybe in a bit.'

'Right you are. See you laters.'

A sigh of relief once the body was gone. It was just him and his pounding head, the sweaty palms, constant retch of nausea. It was worse than any other hangover or comedown he had ever felt. He tried to get the world to keep still, but it was dancing in front of him, shaking the daylight from the sun.

What Toby didn't say was that the induction was compulsory in that first week. And at twenty to ten, there was a knock on the door, and when he didn't answer, the door pushed open and Stephanie was there, her knuckles clicking together.

He tried to close his eyes quickly, to pretend to be asleep. She cleared her throat.

'Marcus.'

He lay very still and tried to simulate rapid eye movement. He discovered this was a hard thing to do conscious. Then he felt himself prodded. He faked waking up: an unconvincing yawn and shocked widening of the eyes.

'It's the induction.'

'What?'

'It's time for induction. Everyone has to take part in induction week or you can't stay on the programme.'

'But I paid the fees.'

She regained her full posture and sighed. 'You didn't pay your fees just to lie in bed. You should have found somewhere out of a Thomas Cook brochure if you wanted that.'

'Touché.' He sat up. 'I feel...'

'Yes, I can see how you feel. It doesn't matter. We only do two induction weeks. You have to attend all five days. Other people drank last night too, and they're up. They're out there. Everyone else is up.' She gave her best icy headmistress stare. 'I'll see you outside in ten minutes.'

She clicked away into absence, and he followed the orders. It would be too embarrassing to be sent back to London, his tail loose in his legs. To fail at commodity broking was one thing, but to fail at 'finding yourself'; to be kicked out of volunteering by a charity that was desperate for volunteers! Word would get back to his old boss and work mates. They would laugh at him; trade witty one-liners. The thought of all that ridicule drew up the blood to his face. He had nowhere left to go but outside. Nowhere left to be but this continent: this epicentre of epiphany and deliverance. So they say.

He swallowed sick as he struggled into his clothes: outdoorsy bits and pieces that were hastily assembled from Kensington High Street. Everything looked too expensive, although he had deliberately ripped a few holes.

Sucked into the corner of the ceiling, a gecko hung upside

down: its shiny eyes were still and staring, the tongue flicking over the slits. Out of its mouth hung eight thick legs. It was waiting for Marcus to leave before it consumed its meal. It waited some time.

To Stephanie's relief, Marcus was not outside in ten minutes, as suspected, but he was there before her watch said 10am. His eyes were unfocused and his skin was pale. He looked unprepared. She handed him a bottle of sunscreen and left him to it; sitting at the back of the group, never uttering a word. He drank a lot of water.

At lunchtime, he stayed in his corner and scoffed the fresh fish and potatoes. People were still at stage one of their chats: finding out where people came from, what jobs they had fled from, what masks they had put on or pulled off. Instead, he chose to sit on the sand and gawp at Lake Malawi, with its invisible edges and its tidal dance. He had never seen a lake like it. He was used to the enormity of numbers, but not of physical things that he could not expunge. He felt very light, like he weighed nothing at all.

The induction week was a blur of instructions and precautions. The group familiarised themselves with the village: its small thatched buildings and its half-constructed school. The children would often throng about, grabbing their hands, tugging their clothes. The villagers seemed used to the charity, and they were friendly and welcoming. However, in solitary moments, they would stand and watch them – before sweeping the powdered-up ground into piles that would only rescatter.

The charity was 'multi-pronged' in its approach (a phrase they muttered like mantra) and assigned volunteers to the duties that fitted them best. Some people were obvious teachers, and would go to a nearby village, where there was already a school in place. They could start to build up their confidence there, with the expectation that another school nearby would be built within two to three months.

A few years earlier, the government had made primary school education free for all children. It was an aspirational statement: there was generally not the infrastructure nor quantity of teachers to allow this to happen. Plus many families still relied on their children for help, particularly at harvest, and did not see the point of keeping them inside to think when they could be doing.

A few charities, like Project Step Up, had surfaced in Malawi to manage the momentum of this goal. If a community built teacher housing, the government would usually provide a teacher from one of its training centres, although teachers were still thin on the ground. Volunteers from the charity were there to 'step up' and fill in the gaps: get the schools built in the first place, help with the teaching and try to lower the class size, while the government caught up.

Volunteers of the big and bulky kind, with too much energy, were best deployed with physical activity, such as making bricks in the kilns or building the houses. Generally, the charity endorsed using local labour, and keeping projects in the community (they were keen to stress this on their website, too). But sometimes there was muscle and punch that just needed exhausting.

Volunteers who were neither outgoing nor nurturing enough to teach, nor bouncy and brawny enough to build, were sent into the fine arts of decoration. They were given brushes and encouraged to 'express themselves'. They sourced resources and constructed furniture. They helped around the village with domestic tasks. They immersed themselves in village life.

Marcus saw straightaway that this was by far the easiest occupation of the three, requiring neither sweat nor thought. It was all a bit ridiculous, really – like the system was designed to reward the sensitive and weak. He resolved to hide himself in corners and keep his mouth shut. He anti-socially sat longer on the sand, watching the fishermen drag in their boats.

The final exercise of induction week was his downfall. Stephanie and Philippa introduced some interactive group exercises: mainly of the troubleshooting, lateral-thinking variety. Marcus intended to hold back, but he couldn't. He fell into a role of leadership and spoke up for his group, communicating the ideas back to everyone, unravelling their logic in careful, mannered tones. He felt the sweet swell of ego as Stephanie's eyes widened in respect, and she nodded hard at him, with thin, jutting-out lips. His people-pleaser pulsed. A smile fluttered from his face. She caught it, and spun one back.

The next day, the volunteers gathered around a board. They were divided into three small groups. Staring him in the face were the words 'Marcus' and 'teaching'. Most people were too pleased with their choices to see a snarl lift up his lip.

In Marcus's group was a posh guy called Reuben, who wore his hair long and thick (the one who sat next to him in the van); a short, lank chef called Ben, who seemed polite and thoughtful; plus the two girls from the previous induction. These included Annabelle, the tall girl who had carried him back to his bed that first night (or, so he remembered it). There was also Dora, the youngest in the group, who had just graduated in medicine, but acted as if she had lived a thousand lives already. Dora and Annabelle, although a few years apart in age, already clung to each other. They liked to sit and whisper conspiratorially; letting tectonic plates of gossip quake molehill mountains.

The next day, they were driven to the neighbouring village, where there was already a school. The journey was bumpier than before. Nobody spoke, apart from irregular giggles between Dora and Annabelle. There was a mood of trepidation. The sun was bright, and sweat glistened their foreheads.

They saw him before they passed him. A skeleton boy, painted white, with stick-thin arms and legs. His eyes did not track the passing car, but focused on some distant thing, beyond the road. He scrunched his hands into fists, sucking hard on a sugar cane.

'What the hell was that?' Dora's head swung wildly. 'Why was he covered in paint?'

The driver looked back at them. They had gotten to know him, his name was Kondwani, and he was a friend of Stephanie's.

'He paint white.'

'Why?'

'Why.' He allowed a couple of seconds to think. 'When boys twelve, thirteen, we send them from village. We make them white. White is spirits. Boys live alone, find food to eat. Talk to family ghosts, our... What word?' He clicked his fingers.

'Ancestors?'

'What ancestors?'

'Family from many, many years ago,' said Reuben. He was sitting next to Kondwani, at the front. 'Family now dead.'

'Yes, "ancestors". They talk to ancestors. They talk to spirits. That why they look like spirits. So they find each other.'

'But how do they survive?' Annabelle was pale. She leaned forwards on the driver's seat, as if to prop herself up.

'Village leave food. But not home. Must leave home village. Kill animals. Find food and not die. They go home and now they man.'

'So it's a rite of passage?' asked Reuben. 'A ritual to mark a time of change, or something like that. Like, from adolescence to adulthood.'

'Possible.' But Kondwani sounded doubtful. He wasn't sure how this was any different from what he had just said, but he knew the British often liked to say the same thing in a different way, as if they were the first to think or declare it. So much tautology and synonym!

Silence returned to the car. There were a few murmurings between Dora and Annabelle: indecipherable, on the whole.

Marcus managed to make out: 'Seems a bit harsh, doesn't it? He looked so young.' Then a grunt of agreement from Annabelle.

He felt a prod in his arm. Ben smiling, apologetically. 'That was a bit odd back there, wasn't it?'

'What do you mean?'

'A bit voodoo, if you know what I mean. Gave me a bit of a chill.'

Marcus shrugged. 'It was just a boy.' He'd seen worse in the City clubs on a Friday night.

Ben nodded and attempted a subject change. 'Gosh, I'm starving. And we've just had breakfast! This doesn't bode well!'

'Hmmn.'

'What do you think the children are going to be like? Not painted white, I presume!'

'Look...' Marcus closed his eyes. 'I'm really sorry, Ben; but I'm not feeling particularly great.'

'Oh. I'm sorry to hear that.'

'It's fine; I just can't talk at the moment.'

'Oh no. Is there anything I can do?'

'No. It's fine.'

'I could ask Kondwani if he's got any painkillers...'

'No, it's not a headache. Seriously, it's fine.'

'OK.' Ben turned his body away from Marcus, towards the window. The terrain was a patchwork of grey and green.

They arrived to a gaggle of children, singing and clapping their hands. Marcus stepped out of the car and his hand was snatched. 'Will you be my friend? You're my best friend.' He felt himself carried towards the school, like a leaf on an ant army.

Kondwani translated for them while the shy village herdman introduced them to the school and class. They also met their translator: a cheerful woman called Abikanile.

The building had only just been completed. This was the children's first day, and they were excited. They darted in and out of legs. Their faces were shiny and full of teeth.

Annabelle spotted Marcus, towards the back, leaning against a wall, his face down to the ground. 'Are you all right?' she whispered. The herdman was still talking.

He nodded. There was an exaggerated swallow.

She went to walk back to the front, but his words cut her short.

'I feel nauseous. I think I'm going to be sick.'

'Really?'

'Yes, really.' His face was full of sickness and loathing.

'When did it start?'

'In the car.'

'Maybe it's travel sickness?'

He shrugged. 'Maybe.' Then he shook his head and gestured vaguely to his lips. *I can't talk,* he seemed to say. She walked away.

As they drifted into the school, she dropped back again. 'How are you feeling now?'

'I think it's subsiding.'

'That's good. So it must have been the car.'

'Yes.'

'Good. That's an easy fix, then.'

'Yes.'

There didn't seem to be anything left to say. They followed the children into their new bright, clean classroom. They split the group into two, to try to keep sizes smaller, although there were children crowding in from everywhere. Either way, it was an easy class to teach, and the hours slid by. The first lessons were mainly introductions. A village lady – Bertha – had arrived, to take over translating and study their teaching. Her English was broken, but she told Annabelle that she was eager to learn. Annabelle didn't have the heart to say that none of them were teachers back in the UK. Although she wasn't sure this would matter: being white seemed to carry some prestige, as if you had the money and influence to solve problems, no matter how disparate or desperate. Her shoulders felt the responsibility of kings and messiahs. And yet this was a human who didn't know how to cook or grow guavas or measure distance with the stars.

They were all exhausted when they returned to the village. The tiredness was deep in their bones, like extra weight to lug. There was chatter around their evening meal, but it was polite and contained. People commented on the day's activities, informed the other two groups of their tasks. Nobody drank beer. Nobody tried to dominate. They leant back into their chairs and blinked up at the sky, almost willing the night-time.

Then the nausea came back: a writhing jam of acid in his belly. It kept erupting through his system and up into his throat, the burn of a digestive lava flow. He got up at one point and was sick on the sand, out of view. He went to his room to get a towel and then scooped up the sick with it. He made sure nobody could see him dump the acrid evidence into one of the waste bins. When he returned, the group were already bustling about, tidying up plates and unsetting the table. He joined in, warily, wondering if the stink was stuck to him. He worried his breath might flare out, like dragon fire.

Toby was in the room when he got there, pulling the bed sheets taut. 'You can't be too careful,' he said.

'Of what?'

'Spiders, snakes, centipedes – all that.'

'You're kidding, right? They wouldn't be able to get in here. We don't open the windows.'

'Oh, they could get in here, all right,' Toby replied, breezily. 'They've done it plenty of times, I reckon.'

'But you would notice a snake. And Aldo told me they don't have poisonous spiders here.'

'Not officially, mate. But Stephanie was telling me how

they've been know to get violin spiders, you know.'

'Right – and they're poisonous, are they?'

'Yep,' laughed Toby, as if the prospect delighted him. 'Their venom could kill you, all right. We've got nothing to worry about, but it's better to be safe than sorry, you know. So I like to pull the sheets really tight and touch the top of them with, like, the back of my hand, just to check there's nothing inside. And then I sort of propel myself into bed. Then I tuck the mosquito net into the sides of the bed.'

He proceeded to do this in front of Marcus, springing into the covers with a gleam of satisfied benignness. Marcus felt compelled to do the same. Toby then stretched an arm out from under the net, and switched off the bedside light. There was the low sound of an arm swooshing in again.

The darkness wallowed in front of them. It pulsed and eddied, like waves of nullity. Marcus held on to the sides of his pillow, so he wouldn't fall off this gyrating planet, suspended in space. He felt like he would never fall asleep. He kept thinking of his flat in London, its comforts and luxury. He could taste steak on his lips: the salty wetness of flesh oozing out on his tongue. A pang of homesickness so fierce that he had to blink back the tears.

But he must have fallen asleep, after all, to account for his waking up so suddenly. Sitting bolt upright, the sweat on his back, his breath puffy and rasping. He'd had a terrible dream. The horrors, even now, were flashing up in his vision, like he'd looked too long at something too bright. It had all been so vivid that he found himself shivering, shaking; at any moment, he might be sucked back in. He tried to think of anything else – anything at all. His first date with Nancy (Pizza Express). His favourite fruit (strawberries). Where he might live after London (New York). Annabelle in her underwear (she had an excellent cleavage). But it kept getting intercepted by his mother sitting in the bath, her zombie face twisted up at him, her eyes black and iris-less, the water muddy and low.

'Toby,' he called out. There wasn't an answer. He didn't know if he was pleased or disappointed. A mixture of both: one tied up with pride, the other, with fear.

He needed the toilet. 'Oh fuck, no,' he yelped. He couldn't see anything. He heard a patter on the floorboards – a spider?

He lay there for a few minutes more. He felt the pressure in his groin. An insufferable ache. Maybe he could just piss the bed. He would have to hand wash the sheets, but that would be fine. He was sure he could do it in secret. Somehow. There must be a way. How easy, how much easier, to just slacken his muscles, his pelvis, let it all flood away...

But the shame. The shame of being found out – Annabelle! Particularly by her, perhaps it was the cleavage. But by anybody, really... To discover that he had wet the bed and then slept on it all night, mummified in ammonia.

He whipped off the sheets and lifted up the mosquito net. He tucked the bedding back in, quickly, so he didn't return to any nasty surprises. He cursed himself for this situation as he felt his way along the wall to the door, hoping not to spring upon any latent bugs. Soon, he would be halfway to the toilets.

The whole world was conspiring against him. There must be a God, after all, and that God was showing off its dominion. Or perhaps it was the Devil. Either way, there was a vicious witchcraft in nature. All creatures, all wildlife, were the militia of some supernatural evil, some wickedness that lay deep in the soil, through pebbles, on sand, on the foothills around them, within the very veins of a leaf. Every living thing on the planet sought revenge. He was caught in the middle of a food chain: poked at and scratched at by tendrils, tentacles, umbels, follicles.

He went to the toilet at speed and was soon back in his room without incident. He thought about turning on the light and screaming, waking up the whole camp, the whole village. Something stopped him: some bottomless code.

He felt along his bed for the lump and bump of a malignant creature. While he did this, he heard the distant whine of a hungry mosquito. In a manoeuvre that would have impressed even Toby, he flipped himself into his bed, tucked up and secure, the netting tugged taut.

He listened to the whine of that mosquito for what must have been hours. He felt incredibly tired, but he could not sleep. His eyelids would get heavy, he would close his eyes, drift into unconsciousness (he could see it so near, right there in front of him, like reality had a horizon)... But then the feeling would leave him. He was back with his eyes open, the mosquito still whining. He saw the light creep into the room and the day force upon him. He had contracted insomnia. The World Health Organization had never warned him of this.

Oh, and the next few days were such a struggle. A passing blur of over-eager child-faces with chalk in their hands – like no schoolchildren he had ever seen before. And he had never seen so many black faces, even blacker bodies. He had no black friends. He had few black colleagues. He was used to being in the majority. So at first, he had stared at it: the contrast of their palms, soles, the white teeth and pink gums. Now it was normal and it was his face that looked odd: its freckles and sunspots, bloated pores and flat, wispy hair.

There was a party on Friday, once all the new recruits had survived. The trees were strewn with solar lights. The pizza oven was fired up to hungry roars. Aldo took the helm and could spin pizza dough like a pancake: this flamboyant flourish caused several whoops of approval. Other people stood by the sound system: a HiFi relic from the 90s with a temperamental CD player. The Spice Girls blasted out from nowhere and there was an even split between groan and cheer.

It is unclear what time the band arrived: an impromptu gala of locals who made musical instruments out of nothing, drumming with a scrap box and plucking an empty oil container with a single string. One of the older village men held his brown guitar quite high, with apparent pride. The A string was missing, but he worked his way round this with consummate skill.

It didn't take long before everyone was dancing. The beer was potent, the heat speeding up the effects. Marcus was the last to join in. His head was pounding with exhaustion, there was bitterness in his mouth. But the alcohol soon took hold, as it always does; and it seemed a better prospect than just standing there, talking earnest small talk with Philippa.

He excused himself to get another drink, and was willingly sucked into the vortex, arms swinging above his head, moonlight dappling his torso. Even Philippa joined in then, her feet keeping time to the drums, to the rhythm, to the soulful warble of the frontman.

A girl called Katie. He and she backed up against a wall. She seemed to smell the money off him. Shouting him questions, queries about his job, whatever. A rapidly raised eyebrow when he told her that he owned his property.

'In London?'

'Yes.'

'Zone 1?'

'Yes.'

'You must be loaded.'

'Not loaded, no. But I'm doing all right.'

'What on earth are you doing somewhere like this, if you don't mind me asking?' She blew on a canary yellow fringe: over-bleached and sun-dried.

He did mind her asking. When faced with this question, he felt his heart rate quicken, like he'd been found out for something; like he was on the run from the police, like he was under witness protection. Every part of him felt a peculiar sensation, a mix of adrenalin and nausea.

'I could ask you the same thing,' he said, trying to chuckle it out. In fact, he was employing a tactic, trying to cause conversational diversion. Everybody loves to answer questions about themselves; everyone is deep down gagging to be pressed on their life story.

'Oh you know,' began Katie. She wrinkled her sunburnt nose and snorted. 'I know where you're coming from. I have a bit of money, myself. Family money. But I hate it. I hate it.'

'Really? How so?'

'It's a fucking chain round my neck. I'm renting at the moment. I've refused to touch their money. It's given me nothing but grief. Don't get me wrong, it's not like I think all money is bad. My money, or my future husband's money – that's different. But my parents are academics and I was educated at about ten different schools. Expensive schools. Ridiculous. Really ridiculous.'

'Ten of them?'

'Oh, maybe not that many. But, you know – a lot. They kept moving around the country. I never saw them that much. It was ridiculous. Then they decided to send me to this hideous prep...'

So it goes. At an opportune moment, he slipped away to the toilet. He made his way there by keeping very close to the wall. He pricked up his ears for any rustle, scamper, patter. He could only get through the toilet business by whistling to himself and going as fast as possible. He touched the back of his head several times to make sure that nothing had dropped on it from the ceiling.

On the way out, he staggered into Annabelle. Her breasts were covered up in a loose tunic – but he still found it hard to remain on her face.

'Marcus!' She roared. The eyes darting around the sockets.

'Good to see you. How's your first week been?'

'It's been... interesting.' He thought that was a good reply.

'Interesting?'

'Yes.'

'That sounds... uncertain.'

'Well, it's been a tough adjustment, I suppose.' He loosened a button from his polo shirt. He was cornered, with his shackles down.

'I'm sorry to hear that.'

The first part was slurred. He saw an obvious change of subject. 'You enjoying the beer?'

'I'm not drunk, if that's what you're saying.'

'I didn't say "drunk". Did I ever say "drunk"?'

She stared at him, indignant, with iceberg eyes, and her lips jutting out. Then she fell about laughing. The mood swings of an inebriant.

'I am drunk,' she laughed. 'I'm incredibly drunk.' She flung her arms out. 'Isn't it brilliant?' She looked around herself. 'Have you seen Dora?'

'I think she's dancing on the sand. Everybody's dancing on the sand.'

'There's so much sand.' She nodded, sagely, and then collapsed into laughter. 'Oh dear. I'm sorry. I must be really annoying. You seem so sober. Why are you so sober? Here, let me get you a drink.'

He lifted up his beer bottle.

'Then why are you so sober? You mustn't be so sober.'

'I've drunk a lot of beer in my time.' And shots. And pills. And coke.

'I can handle my beer,' she insisted. 'And it's not like you weren't wasted that first night. I mean...' She belched. 'Oh dear, I'm so sorry.' Her hands flew up to her mouth. 'I can't handle beer. I don't usually drink beer. I'm really drunk.'

'That's all right. Most people drink to get drunk. Although you could stop there, if you like. Everybody's just dancing now, anyway.'

'It's so strange being here, isn't it?' she said, with an odd change of tack, as if answering a voice in her head. 'It's so different. Last week, or the week before – we were all in our different places. We knew – none of this. Crazy, huh?'

'It is indeed.' He nodded. *Christ*, he thought. Such *inanity*.

'It's such a mad thing to do. Being here. Isn't it?'

'I guess so.'

'But leaving behind friends, family...'

'I guess.'

'Do you miss them?'

He shrugged, a faraway look to him. 'It's hard to say...'

'I don't miss mine,' she said. 'I miss the scenery. If you wake up every day to the same thing, it sort of becomes part of you, doesn't it? Your identity.'

'Yes.'

'Where is home to you?'

'London.'

'Oh, OK. I'm from Manchester. Well, the outskirts – Cheshire, really.'

'You don't sound Mancunian.'

'It's just the odd thing, really. "Laugh". "Bath"'.

'Oh. Yes. Spotted it there.'

'It's probably more obvious when I'm drunk.'

'Not at all.'

'Well, I was born in Croydon. Lived there until I was six.'

'I was born in Croydon, too, actually.'

'No way! It's an honour, isn't it?'

'Yep. Very proud to be the holder of a "Born in Addiscombe" badge.'

'Oh my god, I was born in Addiscombe, too! I didn't mention

it as no-one's ever heard of it. Plus, it's a shithole. Sorry! Don't know if I'm allowed to say that... You might be very proud of your Addiscombe.'

'Of course I am. It's the bit of Croydon that made Kate Moss. And where would we be without Kate Moss?'

'I know, right? And I love the fact that I was born in the same ward as her.'

'Not Mayday?'

'Oh my god! Yes – "May-die", they call it. What a small world. I can't believe I'm in Malawi, of all places, and standing next to someone who was born in the same hospital as me.' She stumbled. 'Oh dear, I'm so drunk. I'm sorry. I just wanted to let my hair down, I think.'

'You've got very pretty hair to let down.'

This seemed to sober her up. She gaze him a quizzical look, tumbled her fingers through her hair. 'Yeah, well...'

He sparred with the awkwardness. 'Yes, well, I think it's time we went and danced with the others, don't you? Let your hair down properly.'

She bit her lip. 'OK, sure.'

He led her down to the sand, where the drums were still beating and the hips were still thrusting. The light was now a pale sliver, and the moon was a mouth, threatening to eat it all up.

A few songs later, a few glugs of beer, and he was running to the shoreline. He flung off his shorts, his top, kicked off the sandals... Dipping his toes in, then wading in further – the water, still warm.

'Marcus!' He ignored it. 'Marcus!'

Dora ran up to the water with a stick and prodded him. Now a small group was trotting down. The music stopped.

'Marcus, you're walking through reeds. Marcus, you've got to stop. Right now. That water isn't clear.'

He froze and span round. 'What?'

'Bilharzia. Remember?'

'Bull-what-now?'

'Oh, man. Just get out of the water. Now. Please, you idiot.'

He darted out. He didn't know what the peril was, but his skin was burning. He was itching all over.

Stephanie handed him a towel. 'Do you remember my instructions? On induction?'

'Yes.'

'So, it's "bilharzia", Marcus. We discussed it about five times over.'

'OK. I admit. I've forgotten. All right?'

'You weren't listening, you mean.' Dora was frowning with that baby face of hers. The medical martyr. It disgusted him. He wanted to strike her face.

'Well, I'm listening now. You've got my attention.'

'Marcus, I can't have any of you coming down with something like that. We've got some insurance, but it's really not much... Philippa can't afford to get sued.'

'You wouldn't get sued.'

'It's from the freshwater snails. They carry a parasite. The larvae enter your skin. Or through an orifice. Your *arsehole*, do you understand? It can give you diarrhoea, fever, fatigue. All the good stuff. If you don't treat it, it shuts down your internal organs. Do. You. Get. It. Now?'

'If you're swimming in the lake, *always* avoid standing water. So, anything swampy, anything with reeds, like here. That's a big risk area.'

The party disbanded after that. Literally and figuratively. He wanted to bid Annabelle good night, but she was gone. He was left with the animals and tailwind. The village candle blown out.

Later. In the whirl of darkness around his bed, he saw a slug thicken out of a puddle. It grew and grew, in a tornado of mucus, until it was seven or eight feet tall. It stood over his bed with its eyestalks twitching: for a few minutes, dripping, just staring at Marcus and Marcus looking back. Then a rasping tongue burnt through the bed netting like acid. Marcus went to scream but sound was impossible. Only the squelch of moisture as the slug sagged down and leaked juice on his face. Crumbles of skin sloughed off into his hand. Then an eyeball plopped out and there was nothing at all. He could only sense burning, this ebbing away. And when he lifted his hand to his head, he could feel only skull...

The screams woke the hallway. The light switched on and Toby was there, mumbling, ineptly: 'It's all right, mate.' Embarrassed grin. And that woman called Paula was undoing the mosquito nets and peering into his face. 'Are you OK?'

'Yes.' The sweat dripped into his eyes.

'You were having a nightmare.'

'Yes. OK.' But he didn't believe it.

'He had his eyes open, it was proper weird,' said Toby, to no-one in particular.

Marcus sat up and saw a small crowd around the doorway. Stephanie was there. She said: 'I really thought someone had been bitten.'

Paula turned. 'My first thought was snakes.'

The sound drifted into speculation: the murmurings and mumblings of hearsay. Marcus took these few moments to recollect. He hadn't been dreaming. He had been awake, he had been in his bed, he had been aware of the room. He saw that slug growing and thickening, he had watched it slide closer...

'Right, everyone back to bed.' Stephanie came forward to prod him. 'No cheese at dinner tomorrow, you hear?' Everybody laughed at this, everyone felt the matter reduced and resolved. But Marcus didn't laugh. His eyeballs were all red and stiff as they filed away.

'You OK for me to turn the light out, pal?'

'Yes.'

'Right you are.' Blackness. 'Night, mate.'

'Good night, Toby.' And he stayed like that all night: sat up, barely blinking, chest puffed up and shoulders thrown back, primed for a fight that would have no end. When morning finally came, he felt such relief that he cried into his pillow.

On Monday, they made their way back to the second village. He felt like there was nothing inside him, he was just a puppet wound up. The others chatted in the car, but he sat at the front and was silent. He didn't know how he was going to be able to teach a class. The sickness was returning, he felt it hatching in his stomach. He was resigning himself to going back to the UK and writing the whole thing off.

The class, however, went surprisingly well. He was always best with an audience, and this was the keenest audience you could possibly get. He enjoyed the happy babble that his questions prompted. He liked the chalk between his fingers, the spells he could cast with it. Their eyes widened at his stories of Britain and of London, of red buses and the Queen. Although they already knew a surprising amount about British history, especially the Commonwealth. Often they were the ones teaching him. Abikanile's eyes would twinkle when a child corrected him on some minor detail.

Outside, the group shuffled around the van, waiting for Reuben, who was chatting to Abikanile. Marcus's stillness had tainted them, and nobody else spoke, even Dora and Annabelle. The children bounced between them, while hands mechanically fluttered open and shut.

'What's that?'

'What?'

Dora beckoned. 'That.'

Everyone turned but nobody had an answer.

'Kondwani... Kondwani!' Dora tapped on the window.

'What?'

'What's that?'

'What, now?'

'That.'

'Ahh.'

'What's she doing?'

'Witch.'

'Witch?'

'Keep voice low.'

Annabelle's eyes stretched apart. She hissed: 'What kind of witch?'

'Spell witch, magic witch. Witch fly at night.'

'People don't fly at night, Kondwani.'

'Yes! Her!'

'So she's not a good witch?'

'Good?'

'Does nice spells? To get people better?'

'She spells to get people better; she spells to get people sick. You teach, she spells.'

'Why do we have to keep our voices down?'

'Everyone know she a witch, but you cannot say witch. In law, there is no witch. That is law. But sometimes a witch go to prison. Witch not always safe.'

'I don't understand,' said Annabelle. 'Why–'

Dora interrupted: 'How come that man's dancing around her?'

'He knows she is witch. Everyone know. He try to warn her.'

'Of what?'

'Sometimes people die by witch. Sometimes people want witch to die. Witch doctor knows. He look after village, like herdman.'

The witch doctor's dance grew frantic. He wore a belt of

shells that rattled together. There were bangles up his arms. He blew on a whistle. The children ran towards him, clapping.

The old lady tottered away, using a large stick to propel her. Her face was dark and scrunched, like her life had had several revisions. Even Reuben and Abikanile stopped talking. They were all facing the old lady as she headed their way; their backs pressed to the van.

She stopped and squinted into the sun. A bony finger unfurled and pointed. Her voice was as crackly and weak as a gramophone. She seemed to say the same thing again, but louder. Some children stopped dancing to look at her. Their faces were unreadable. The witch doctor danced on.

'What did she say?' asked Ben. His skin was paler than ever. The old lady hissed and walked away.

'Kondwani, what did she say?' Dora fidgeted with her dress.

'She said, "Fear the white man."' Abikanile paused. 'She said, "Children, listen: fear the white man, fear the white man."'

Abikanile's adoptive parents were American but her Malawian was flawless from frequent visits. She liked to let the words trip off her tongue to naive ears. So she continued: 'We say "bogeyman": "if you misbehave, the bogeyman will come and get you". We've all heard that, right? Their equivalent is "white man". Fear the white man. He will come and get you.'

'But why would they say that?' asked Marcus, piping up. 'We're the good guys; we're the ones who have actually come here to help you.'

She replied, 'Oh, you understand nothing', and swiped him away.

After that first day at school, the weeks rolled by on the train tracks of habit. Marcus was living on autopilot, just trying to get by, seeking to duck those nightmares and sudden feelings of panic. He mostly kept to himself.

There was a daytrip at some point – some river, some waterfall.

He wasn't really listening. Most people went. He opted out and slinked around the village, finding corners in the shade. Here, he lovingly dug out his Kindle and read motivational books about success and prestige. The dust crept over him and he felt very old, like he had already lived too long. Then he lay on his back and watched the clouds travel the sky. Always searching, always seeking; they never stopped. He tried to find patterns out of them, like he had as a child, like he had as a man, but now he saw only different shapes of the same thing. He saw only cloud. And just a short while later, Marcus disappeared into the landscape.

Chapter Seven

The strangest thing was the silence. It blew in your ears and it bloated your eardrums.

The second strangest thing was the darkness. Blinking and blinking, but never night vision. Just strips of lightlessness, all swaddled together; so tightly, compactly, that creation was snuffed.

The third strangest thing was Marcus: his very presence here, in the landscape. The way he dropped to his knees and lugged across the ground like an animal. The way he no longer thought about spiders or snakes or snails. The way his fingers grazed against the bark of a tree. He shot up a bough with surprising dexterity; stretching his legs out and falling asleep.

The sun was turning its spotlight. You could just about make out his skin marbled with white ash, or was it clay? Naked down to the boxers; a blanket swaddling his shoulders. Two rows of chattering teeth. He was unevenly balanced and looked ready to fall. A gecko sat on his kneecap.

The sun twisted the stage lights: the whole world lit up. His hands relaxed around the blanket. The gecko walked away. His forehead grew shiny with balls of sweat. His eyes opened up and they looked only pupil.

Marcus slid down the tree and walked further into the foothills. He wolfed down a breakfast of cricket clicks and chirping birds, sun streaks and sky. He tried to ignore the grumbles in his belly, which vibrated all the way through to the tissue.

Soon, the walking turned to gentle climbing. He walked like this for measurements of time that he no longer measured. The sun scorched his skin and he now used the blanket for protection, not warmth. He found another cluster of trees and yanked off giant lobes of leaves that he tied together with vine to make an impromptu hat. He found a long white feather, which he tucked into the vine, behind his ear. He did all these things with consummate care and attention, and these small tasks took up considerable mind power. He was so distracted with the now and what that he did not look into the past or future or ask himself *why* he was doing any of it at all.

At one intersection of time, there was a sound like shushing water. He changed direction and ran through yellow grassland, through a passing of trees, where a boulder was sheltering a dancing stream. He skulked about the edges, the thirst overtaking him; an intolerable urge to slurp up the water. Some latent and rational self was clawing him back, making him question the purity – was it safe to drink? He cursed his parents for not sending him to Boy Scouts: those hardy brats who always had a compass and penknife and the smug cotton blur of beige and khaki. Well, he could be just as prepared. He could be just as physically strong, as mentally awake and morally straight as those bastards. Those motherfucking Scouts.

He bashed a stone on the head of a lulling fish. It tossed about, pathetic. He did this several times until the water turned red. He didn't know a fish could bleed. Why had nobody told him that fish could bleed? Would a Boy Scout have known?

He picked up the fish and held it on the flat of his palm. There was still the odd flinch, the odd tussle with life. But these were lessening. So he gazed in wonder at the gaping mouth and darting eyes, things he had seen before, in some distant life, he remembered that now. He lay that fish out on his palm for many measurements of time, until there was only stillness, and the water babbling, and the sun following its inevitable trajectory across the sky.

He sat for some time like that, swallowing and swallowing, trying to produce extra saliva to slake his thirst. His eyes wafted over the horizon, automatic, without apparent thought. He stuffed the fish into his underpants. This didn't feel odd. While he stood there, his eyes kept wafting, until he saw a sheet of greyness ascend from the earth. It had to be woodsmoke.

There was running, and more running, until it caused his chest to explode. He broke down to a trot, then back to the beat of the walk. His skin peeled into dark pink strips. He licked his lips to stop them cracking. It cracked them even more so.

What Marcus found was a village that looked like the other one. Peroxide grass. Mud huts. Chickens. There were some gasps when he staggered into the centre and roared. Some women wailed. The men came out and stepped around him, in circles, jabbering words he did not recognise. One ran a finger down Marcus's side. He turned the finger over and gazed at the clay. He held up that finger and showed it to the growing crowd of people. There were no more human words or sounds. Just the chickens clucking, oblivious, locked inside private conflicts.

People moved away, then, as if Marcus had gone invisible. They moved behind him, in front of him, around him – almost right through him. He stayed there upright, his energy sapped, his mind in tailspin. He felt the gentle tug of his fish, but was unable to stop it. Then he slumped to the ground and covered his face in his hands.

The smell of food lifted him up again. Someone set down a couple of bowls: sweetly cooked chambo, a mound of mashed nshima. A jug of drinking water, which he turned to first. Then he scooped out the maize, loading it into his mouth so his cheeks puffed out. He went back to the water to wash it down. Then he picked delicately at the fish, like a chef or a gourmand; thinking thanks for its existence, for its role in his life.

He went over to the women. 'Thank you.' He was surprised by his voice; surprised it belonged to him.

Their eyes swivelled upwards. They didn't say anything in return and he could not read their faces. They went back to working. He assumed a lack of English held them back. But they stared at him, hard, as he staggered back into the thicket.

When the distance had gobbled him up whole, the people looked at each other in a deep and enduring silence. A man held up a hand to his throat, but the laugh ran away from him. Others were now laughing. Soon the women and children were clapping their hands and shrieking. They gestured at their underpants and told dirty jokes. A couple of jesters dragged out some fish from the nets and popped them into their trousers. The man who got the biggest laugh of all was the one with a fish head sticking out of his waistband. He moved the head up and down, made it speak in white-man language. 'Please, please,' he said, like the Queen. 'Thank you very much, please. Marks & Spencer, lovely jubbly.' A woman laughed so hard that she cried. 'Oh don't, don't,' she protested, and the children gibbered and grinned and touched her face. 'He tried to white himself when he is already white! A white man, but whiter!' She snorted. 'And he is a grown man, too!' This set them off again, and the fish got re-stuffed into underpants and paraded around. Any fear of white men and bogeymen was well and truly dissipated by recalling this spectacle: a strange and unusual sight and so completely hilarious.

'Where has he gone?' someone asked, at last.

'Into the trees.'

'Do we help him? Do we give him food?'

They turned to the headman for consultation. He frowned and peered up at the sky.

'I think so,' he said. 'It is all rather strange, but there must be a reason why he is here. We should protect him just in case.'

'But he's not even a boy...'

'I have never known a white man take part in this ceremony. But if he wants to call himself an initiate, let's hear him out.'

'But we don't have enough food...'

'We have enough. We can give him some scraps.'

'Give the rich white man scraps? This is madness! Appearances can deceive...'

'We only have appearances, so we will judge only appearances.'

They gave up protesting. The headman always had the last word. But somebody did snarl: 'We had the appearance of an idiot with a fish down his pants.' It was an interesting addition to a familiar proverb.

The headman continued, getting caught up in his gusto: 'We must respond to this moment, I know that good will come from this.' He raised his eyes like he was thinking of God, but he was thinking of money: white-man remuneration; rapper-dollar bills; gargantuan tips.

Chigayo had a brother in the city, who had gone to Lilongwe to open a restaurant and find some fortune. There was talk of rich ex-pats who worked at embassies. There was speculation of other people coming, soon coming, still coming, coming soon –

to blow all their bills on safaris and game. A 'holiday' they called it, a chance to find something different. Chigayo had never even seen an aeroplane, he could not imagine getting inside one and going to see something new. There was newness, every day. Each day was new, each second was new. Even though Edson, his brother, was the one with the steam in his eyes and an unfilled restaurant. Now Edson was changing his tune, he was babbling, 'They say we'll get richer, more people will eat out, we have to spend the money somewhere.' Oh no, Edson – here there is only poor, very poor and very rich. And the very rich do not eat out in Lilongwe, they'd sooner travel to South Africa and stuff themselves there! But none of this meant he pitied his brother more than he pitied that man. There was already a holiday in the next life, that was already a given. That lot seemed so unhappy – even the ones without fish down their pants. What did it all mean? What sense should he make from it?

While Chigayo was pondering, Marcus sought natural protection in the trees. He would stay in the lowlands, at a reasonable distance from the village. He found this comforting, as he was far enough away that he didn't see them as a threat. They had all seemed fairly normal, but he was in Africa now. He might be fast asleep tonight and one of them would come out to find him, wearing only a headdress and his goolies hanging loose; clutching a spear in one hand and something voodoo in the other. This was a primitive land, cursed by both humans and God. It was strewn with poison, disaster and death traps. Even McDonalds had no branch here.

Now – with time to think – Marcus mused on exactly how he had come to be here: in this continent, this wilderness, wearing only his boxer shorts. He could be, right now, in his perfect home, eating perfect food, picking up perfect women.

When these thoughts got too much to bear, he passed some other time by talking to the trees and hearing what it was like to be a tree. It turned out that trees were very remarkable and kept all kinds of secrets.

Then he passed other time by composing lists in his head: his top ten favourite films; his top ten favourite books; his top ten favourite lays. He said goodbye to the day while compiling his ten best sandwich fillings. This was more tricky to rank than he had ever expected.

That night, the cold whispered its way into his bones and lay flat like sediment. He seemed to sit in a husk, and he could hear himself rattle. Everything recoiling; everything turned inwards. He tried to stay still so he didn't waste any energy, but his limbs echoed out into dark empty space.

Noises were heard, like heavy paw prints on leaves, like the head of a lion, pushing its fur through the bracken, like the pant of a beast with stomach juice dripping over jeering fangs. Then something like the whisper of humans, the sharpening of spears. His head became stuck in a whirl storm of thoughts. The blanket over his face now. His body still shaking, ready for foreseeable death.

He must have fallen asleep, since he woke with the lights back on and the world reformed. All the dangers had disappeared and there was now a renewed optimism for an indefinable something. His smile grew wider when he saw a bowl of food by the trunk – protected with cloth and a stone in the middle to stop it blowing over in the wind. He said some blessings and tucked into the fried potatoes.

Marcus had long finished eating, and was now digging a hole to squat, when he saw a shape just beyond. He stopped what he was doing. His eyes fixed ahead. His father was standing there. He was holding a horse.

Marcus blinked a few times but his dad did not go away. He wore his hair slicked back and that pastel blue suit, for the special occasions. A hand hovered to shoulder height and waved, a bit shyly. Marcus waved back. They didn't know what to do next, so they both dropped their arms and their eyes settled over the forms of each other. It was all a bit awkward.

His dad stroked the horse's face. It was a rare white thoroughbred. There was some grey dirt over its chest and haunch, but its face was clean, and the hair pristine white. Even the eyelashes were white: fluttering over large slits of liquid black.

His dad was the first to speak. There had been some build-up. He started to shake and a supernova of blood vessels appeared in his eyeballs. He said: 'I can't spend my money. They won't take my money.' He let go of the horse and they both watched it lope into a distant place that they could not see.

His dad started to pace. In and out, in and out, weaving in and out of trees.

'Dad,' Marcus said, but the pacing didn't stop. He tried to catch his dad's eye, but he was wringing his hands, his eyes wide with panic. He stopped, looked Marcus dead-on and screamed: walking backwards, running backwards, his mouth a great hole in the middle of his face. The hole stretched wider and wider until the face disappeared.

'Dad!' Marcus ran after him, but could not see him. He had gone. The scream had gone, too.

'Marcus.'

He whipped around but saw nothing. Then a stone skimmed his shoulder.

'Over here, Marcus.'

His mother was sitting on a swing above the ground. She was kicking higher into the air, like she might take flight.

'Mum. Oh fuck, Mum. I just saw Dad.'

'I know you did. Don't swear, dear.'

'Mum; he didn't look happy.' Marcus paused; refocused. 'Mum – you look happy. What's going on?'

'Oh yes, I'm good, Marcus, I'm good. It's so much better

here. It's so much better not to be real, anymore.'

He swallowed. His insides churned. 'But of course you're real. I can see you.'

'Everything you see is you. You make it what it is. Your brain makes it. I am you. This is you.' She gestured around her. 'Everything is you. You're talking to yourself!' She laughed. 'How does it feel?'

'Wonderful,' he said. 'I never knew I was so interesting.'

'I agree,' she said. 'I always thought it was a shame we couldn't clone ourselves and then we'd have our best friend sorted forever. After all, we only talk to other people so we can validate our own opinions.'

'That's very cynical,' he said.

'That means *you're* very cynical,' she said.

'Yes,' he said. 'You're probably right.'

'I'm always right. I'm your mother.'

'But I thought you were me.'

She drew a circle in the air. 'And everything is complete.'

'You're being very cryptic,' he said. 'You're talking like Yoda or Mr. Miyagi. Like somebody in a film.'

'I don't know who those people are.'

'You must do if you're me.'

'Yes, but there has to be some realism involved, doesn't there? The playwright writes the play, but he still tries to write this panoply of characters – not just versions of himself. Anyway, I can guess what your point is. And I've got a riposte.'

'I'm not sure I ever heard you use the word "panoply" when you were alive. But anyway – what's the riposte?'

'Well, how would you like it if I started talking to you about the weather? Or asked you for the latest on Eastenders?'

'I suppose it would be disappointing.'

'Yes. Yes, it would be.'

They both mused on that for a moment, and then he

ventured: 'Mum. I'm not going to tell you I'm sorry.'

'I know.'

'I don't know if I am. I mean – I really hated you. Since Dad died, but also, maybe, before that. I hated you for falling apart. I hated you for not being like Dad. You were so wishy washy, you had no energy or ambition. You just seemed happy to die like you'd lived. I felt like you'd be happy with that lot for me, too. I felt like you suffocated me, like you could stop all my potential. I resented your genes. I didn't want to be like you.'

She stopped swinging. She folded her arms and sighed. 'Marcus, I know all of this. Why are you telling me again? I get it. I do.'

'I don't know. I guess it's freaking me out. That there's something else.'

'What something else?'

'That...' He didn't know why, but he was crying. 'I don't know.'

'You know this is what initiates do, honey? They're meant to commune with their ancestors. This is what's meant to happen.'

'I remember now.'

'You've always remembered. People pick and choose what they remember, but it's always there.'

'I thought I read somewhere that people never remember a memory the same way. There are only false memories. Memories change.'

'Oh, that's certainly true. The very act of remembering distorts it. But the thing itself, the core of it, is always there, like a photo: just waiting for retrieval.'

'You never talked like this in real life.'

'Of course, I didn't! That was real life. Oh you are funny, dear.'

'I don't like it here, Mum. I miss everything about home. I miss all the little things. I miss going to the cinema, broadband, my Friday night wine, a bit of steak béarnaise...'

'But you couldn't talk to me like this if you were back home, could you, honey? We couldn't *commune*.'

'So this is...communing?'

'Yes! How do you like it?' She resumed her swinging. 'Oh please stop crying, Marcus. I've not seen you cry since you broke your arm on that god-awful caravan trip in Wales.'

He tried to sniff away the tears. 'Yes. I think that was the last time.'

'You know that it wasn't. Stop pretending. You've cried a lot in the last few weeks. And of course you *did* cry when your father died; you just didn't show anyone. You cried in secret. To yourself. To the walls.'

'How do you know that?' His tone was defensive, embarrassed.

'Oh Marcus, do we really have to have this conversation again?'

His head dropped. 'No. No, I guess not.' He'd stopped crying. He put his palm up to his forehead, to feel his temperature.

'Are you feeling better now, honey?'

'Yes, Mum. I guess I got a bit overwhelmed.'

'How come?'

'Seeing Dad. Then seeing you.'

'A bit of a shock?'

'Yes.'

'How did it make you feel?'

'Shocked.'

'But what else? Anything else?'

'Oh Mum, stop it.'

'Honey, this is why people commune with ancestors. To get to the bottom of things! To set them up for the next leg of the journey. To become a man.'

'I guess I was just really pleased to see you. I guess I realised how much I've missed you. I miss you so much.' The tears turned back on, and they felt cool and remarkable.

'There you go, that's what we were waiting for. Why did you run away here? Was it to stop yourself crying?'

'I haven't been crying that much. You're exaggerating.'

'You know that anger is a kind of love, too? The opposite of love isn't hate, it's indifference.'

'Oh, that's such a cliché.'

'Such a cliché? Well, I suppose you're right. Someone should sack the scriptwriter.' They both laughed quietly at that.

'Well, OK, I've got something I want to know: why didn't Dad commune with me? Why did he look so sad?'

His mum stopped swinging again. She jumped down from the swing and sat cross-legged on the floor. 'You were the one that did it to him. Why did you make him so sad?'

'I'm not sure. I thought he was a happy man. That's how I remember him.'

'Ahh, remembering again. Are you sure that's how you remember him? As happy?'

'Yes.'

'Nothing contrary to that, which you may wish to retrieve?'

'No.'

'Okey doke, then.'

'Oh Mum.' He dropped to his knees. 'Mum, I don't feel so good.'

'Oh my little boy.'

He stumbled towards her, his arms outstretched. All he wanted was her arms, her big, grown-up arms.

'No, Marcus.' She held up her hand. 'If you come closer, I'll disappear.'

'No, you won't.'

'I will. Trust me. Trust *you*.'

'OK, then.' He stopped and stayed very still, his head

dropped on to his thighs.

'Mum, am I a bad person?'

'If you're asking the question, then you probably are.'

'Really?'

'Well,' she said. 'You're not a bad person, but you've got bad inside you. That's like everyone, really. You're probably no better or worse than anyone else.'

'Have I done bad things?'

'Of course. Terrible things.'

'Did I kill Nancy?'

'In a way.'

'Why am I out here?'

'What difference does it make? Here, there. There's always you.'

'Is there a God?'

'That's not an important question.'

'What do you mean? It's the most important question of all.'

'No. It's not. The answer's important, but not the question.'

'But surely I won't get the answer unless I've asked the question?'

'Oh,' she laughed. 'You haven't understood anything.'

He felt the heat whirl up within him. He looked up and she had gone. There was no swing. There was no mother. He did not know what had or had not happened. He felt consciousness drift in and out. He didn't feel so good.

The Tombe villagers found him collapsed with his limbs buckled up and his head all skew-whiffed. His eyes were open but he could not see. He stared at and through and into something. His face was all sweat and colour. The lips were moving but no words dripped out.

At first, they panicked. They worried that something had gone wrong with the fried potatoes. There was a bit of a debate. 'But nobody has ever been sick from fried potatoes' was the general consensus. Potatoes were solid and mild, all waxy starchiness. Somebody pointed out the toxicity of green potatoes and potato leaves, but the majority scoffed at this. They had not served the man green potatoes! They were not idiots. Beatrice, wife of the village headman, was brought forward, and confirmed she had not fried any green potatoes. Anyway, she had also given these fried potatoes to her family – and were they not upright and well and joining in with the discussion?

The debate died down quickly after that. Marcus's bones were dragged like firewood. He was shifted to one of the mud brick houses and his body lain out on the floor, in the dust, so that his hair streaked with grey and the beetles scuttled over him.

A village meeting was called, although not everybody could come: people were in the field; some had gone out to beg. But there was a relatively good attendance and decisions were made. A rich white man could not survive alone for long in Malawi, wearing only his underpants and waving whole fishes about, without even a pocketknife. They estimated that he had been wandering the land for no more than two to three days. They guessed that he had not gone far. They surmised that even yesterday some sickness had hollowed him out and sucked out his soul: hadn't he worn his eyes all wild? Hadn't his face been all puffed and paled, like the weight of the sky was pressed on it? No, this wasn't the work of the fried potatoes: or even the fish or the maize or the sunburn or thirst. This was the work of the insides. The eternal internal thing that winds us up like a spring but can suddenly snap or turn rusty. Whether a mechanism in the head or the heart, it was impossible to know. But something had failed him. What these wealthy westerners didn't realise is that somebody can be dead but not physically dead; just like someone can be physically dead but forever alive. This man was dead. The sing'anga, the village herbalist, wholeheartedly agreed. He beckoned a few people to help him roll Marcus onto a straw mat in the corner, as a sign of respect. Duly respected, the crowd wandered out.

Tombe fell between two other villages. They summoned a man called Dixon, to run to the one to their east. They knew a charity was based there, full of white smiling folk, always burnt and bitten. It was the obvious place to try first.

This village lay at a distance of 15 miles. Dixon had made the trip before. He was the village messenger and he was as lithe as a leopard and as fierce as a hippo. He had calves as wide as fire pits.

He went back to the house, to look in on Marcus. He made a mental photograph of his features, his height, his hair and eye colour. He stored this information and banged the soles of his feet to the earth, felt the earth shudder through him.

This was when Dixon was happiest: with the wind sailing through his hair and the feel of his body in motion. The only thing that saddened him was that he would eventually grow tired and would eventually stop. It was sad to think that he could not run forever. It was sad to think that he could not run over borders and continents and oceans. He wanted to explore every corner of the world. He wanted to know where rich white men came from. He was twenty-four and had never left his district. He just ran to and fro and back and forth and in and out of the square metre. If this district were the entire world, he would be the world's most travelled traveller. He might even be famous.

Stephanie was the first to notice Dixon; an ever-growing speck on the horizon. She called to Philippa and they spoke in raised, dramatic voices. Then they sat on the wooden bench on the compound's porch: hypnotised by Dixon's thrashing legs, their thoughts excitable and keen. When he was within hollering distance, they gazed at their hands and the ground, at the scurrying of insects. It seemed wrong to maintain eye contact at such a close distance. It seemed to break something human and sacrosanct. They waited out his running in their own discomfited ways. The silence thronged between them.

In the final few seconds, Stephanie looked up and rose to her feet. A hand was held to her forehead, eyes wincing from the glare of the afternoon sun. She recognised Dixon, and waved.

'Dixon,' she croaked. Philippa stayed seated.

'I have message,' he said, as he slowed to a halt. His English was rough, but he knew a few basic phrases. He had been practising these in his head for most of the journey. He coughed into the mounting tension, then spat on top of it.

'Man,' he continued. 'White man. We have white man.'

'Marcus?' Philippa stood up too now; she was smoothing down her skirt and trying to look composed. Inside, she was a maelstrom of insurance claims and solicitor bills and bad PR for the charity. They had never lost a volunteer before. It was unheard of.

Dixon shook his head, but this was because he did not understand. Stephanie, recognising the difficulties, turned to Philippa: 'I'm going to get Kondwani.' Soon, Kondwani was standing among them, the smile tugging at his cheek, his usual sanguine self in the face of adversity. As he chattered to Dixon, the smile only grew wider.

'He talk of man. I think it Marcus. He sick. He cannot speak or see. They think...' He trailed off and tapped his head.

'What does that mean?' urged Stephanie, the hysteria swelling up.

'Something wrong in head.'

'What?'

Philippa shrugged. 'He may have a medical history. Something we didn't know about. We can't be responsible for this.'

'But we definitely got clearance from his doctor, didn't we? In the application...?'

'Oh, that doesn't mean anything. You know what GPs are

like. They'll sign anything just to get you out of the door.'

'Well, what are we going to do?'

Dixon continued to stand there, patient and statue-like. He had gone from post van to post-box.

'We'll have to drive him to the hospital in the sugar estate. His insurance will cover it.'

'It's still quite basic, though.'

'If he needs anything more, we'll have to get him out somewhere else. There are better hospitals in Zambia.'

'Do you think we can do that?'

'I don't know. Worse-case scenario, perhaps we can fly him home? Or at least fly him into Europe. Sometimes the insurance covers that.'

'I don't think so. They usually do anything they can in the clause to wriggle out of that one. It costs them tens of thousands. No, I think we're jumping ahead of ourselves. We haven't even seen him yet. We can't possibly know how he is. Let's pick him up and take him to the hospital.'

'One of us should do that, but one of us should stay here.'

'You stay here and I'll go pick him up.'

'Are you sure?' Philippa grimaced with relief. She didn't like hospitals; especially not Malawian hospitals.

'Yes, it's fine – and I'll have Kondwani with me.'

Kondwani nodded. He spoke all of this back to Dixon. 'He say, plan good. He run back now.'

'What? But that's ridiculous. We can give him a lift in the car.'

Kondwani relayed this back to Dixon.

'He run.'

Stephanie shrugged. 'OK, then. That's fine. Goodbye, Dixon. Thank you.'

Dixon understood these words, so he bowed his head and started to run again: both his legs and thoughts.

Kondwani and Stephanie bumbled into the car. As they drove off, they saw Aldo and a man called Chris; they strode towards Philippa, gesturing to the car, a keyed-up wonder about them, a closet delight in the drama. Kondwani's habitual grin gave nothing away; Stephanie wore her best poker face. She didn't like the idea of anyone feeding off someone's bad fortune. She thought about this for a few minutes as Kondwani sped off down the dirt track, the car bumping up and down, grit spraying off into corners. She supposed she had this ridiculous righteousness about her. Everything was crystal clear. She found the world so frustrating. If only she could be prime minister, head of the UN, or *something*. She dreamed such impossible dreams. She taunted herself with–

'Woah!'

'What was that?'

'You not look?' Kondwani motioned in front of the car, perplexed but eyes twinkling. 'We almost die, my Stephanie! We could die, and you think about... What you think about?'

'Oh, I was a million miles away.' She started to explain the expression...

'Yes, I know, I know. You tell me that one.'

The car trundled on, past the gawping family that clutched the goat Kondwani had almost killed...

'They come out of nowhere,' he said, repeating another English express he liked. 'Dead goat – dead family. You see? That goat is life. Goat feed them.'

'Yes, I see.'

'These bloody roads!' Kondwani had learned a lot of English swear words from the group. He enjoyed them immensely. 'They are not roads!'

Stephanie had to agree with that one. Even the highways were just tracks of dirt. She had never been to a country with such poor infrastructure. It made her spin into hopelessness.

There was so much to do.

Her thoughts drifted to her time in the charity: would she ever go home? Even Philippa returned to the UK every so often, to visit her grown-up children and take lunch with friends. Everybody went home eventually: either permanently or just to visit, to reconnect with a way of life that they all desperately missed. She was the only one who did not do that. She was the only one who had nobody in the UK that she really wanted to turn to; or whom she felt she could.

Stephanie glanced at Kondwani's hands on the steering wheel. How the pulse of the car thudded right through those hands. How his legs twitched at the pedals. How his eyelashes fluttered over the eyes that stared right ahead of him. His chest breathing so regular. These roads were some of the most unsafe she'd known, but in a car with him, she only ever felt safe. She felt miraculously safe.

He looked over. She blushed.

'I have food on my face?' he asked. They both laughed.

'No,' she smiled, embarrassed. 'I'm sorry. I wasn't staring at you, I was staring into the distance. But it must have looked a bit odd. I'm sorry.'

'Even my wife not stare like that!' he roared. And at the mention of his wife, Stephanie's hands folded up into her lap and she crossed her legs very tight and peered out of the window beside her. She looked very still, but there was a trembling.

When they arrived into Tombe, the women yelped once more, and a crowd of wriggling children opened and closed their hands over the hot metal fizz of the car.

Kondwani spoke to the headman. Stephanie caught a few phrases, which Kondwani had taught her, but she couldn't hold her own. The language was so painfully dialectical. She kept trying and trying to learn it.

Kondwani took her hand and led her into a house a few

minutes' walk away. The headman nodded, said something, and left them.

'Shit.' Kondwani dropped her hand and shook his head. 'He look bad. They say he... What is word?' Kondwani did an impression of somebody shaking, their eyes rolled back, the tongue sticking out.

'Fitted? He had a fit?'

'I don't know if that is right word. I don't know word.'

'Does he have a fever?'

'Don't know.'

'Do you think it's an illness? Something contagious?'

'We hope not.' He was now moving forwards. 'I carry him. You stay. I am strong. I get no sickness.' He made a spectacle of bending his arms, moving a small mound of muscle. 'I carry him.'

The village stayed their distance but mumbled sympathetically as Marcus was lowered on to the back seat of the car. They offered food, which was refused. Instead, they gave thanks, and also offers of food in return: the villagers also refused. All grateful tokens of food refused, and everyone appeased, Stephanie and Kondwani slotted back into the car. They waved at the villagers as the engines revved up. The villagers waved back. There was no laughter about fish and underpants today. There was something too pathetic about this man, now. He had surpassed even laughter.

The hospital was a slow and matted mess of insurance claims and misunderstandings. Stephanie spent a long time on the phone, wrangling and scrambling. She located the nitty-gritty detail of his policy: no, it did not cover medical evacuation; yes, it would cover medicine. She then set work on her best negotiation skills, via Kondwani, to guarantee Marcus a private bed. This mostly involved bribing. However, she did not have any notes on her, and her pleas about Marcus's credit card –

which he would access when better – did not work. There was not enough space. Besides, Marcus's condition was assessed as non-urgent, so he was wheeled into a long corridor with a line of other trollied beds. She sheltered herself around him.

His eyes were now open. He was blinking at the windows. He went to speak, but felt a surge of embarrassment. He was going to pretend to fall back asleep, but Kondwani prodded him. 'Alive?'

'Yes.' His voice rested strange on his lips. His lips were dry.

'You take drugs?'

'What?'

'They want to know if you've taken medication in Malawi,' said Stephanie. 'Or drugs.'

'You know,' grinned Kondwani. 'Malawi gold? Smoke some?'

'No!' Marcus tried to sit up, but failed.

'Do you know why you're here? You've been sick. You ran away from the camp. Do you remember that? What do you remember?'

'Nothing,' said Marcus. But then – 'I saw my parents.' A bit more came back to him... 'I think I slept in a tree.' His eyes were wide and lunatic. 'Oh god. Oh god!'

'It's all right. It's all right, Marcus. Something has happened and we're just trying to figure out what that is.'

He swallowed. 'Aspirin. Something else for headaches – something stronger, I forget what it is called. But I only took it a couple of times. Oh, and my anti-malaria medication.'

'Yes, they were particularly asking about that one.' She beckoned to a passing nurse. 'You wanted to know about his anti-malarial medication?'

'It's Mosaquine.'

She said something to Kondwani. He translated. 'She ask, is it one? A week, I mean?'

'Yes. It's a weekly medication.'

'That's strange,' said Stephanie. 'I thought they were always daily.'

'I didn't want to take daily. I always forget to take things daily. I got this one – Mosaquine – because it's a weekly one. I wanted weekly.'

Kondwani spoke some of this back to the nurse. She nodded. She wrote something down and walked away.

'What did she say?' asked Stephanie, anxiously.

'She talk to doctor.'

They lived out the time as best as they could, in their different ways. Stephanie's foresight meant she had a book in her rucksack. She read this very slowly, as her mind drifted on to different things. Kondwani entertained himself by talking to all the patients, hearing their life stories, offering sympathetic noises, touching pregnant bellies. Marcus just stared up at the ceiling and saw his past life spin into substance out of spider webs and blocks of shadow. Why had he run from it? Hadn't he been happy? Hadn't he been a success?

The doctor finally entered in a parade of handclaps. He shouted something jubilant at Kondwani, who dashed over from the dialysis room. 'He says he read on internet... Mosaquine no good!'

'On the internet?' spluttered Stephanie. 'But that's... He's a doctor, right?'

'Yes, doctor. Nurse read at internet café. Drug side effect. Head side effect...' He searched for the word: tripped it off his tongue, syllable by syllable. 'P-sy-cho-sis?'

'You pronounce it "ko". Psy-ko-sis. And you don't need to say the p. It's a silent p. So, that's what they think it is? Psychosis?'

'I'm not psychotic.' Marcus rolled his eyes. 'We're listening to a doctor in a third-world country who sent his nurse off to the internet café to look something up. I don't think we have to automatically believe this diagnosis.'

The doctor said something more to Kondwani. Kondwani translated: 'One in ten people dream strange. No sleep. Yes?'

Marcus paused. Then nodded.

'Oh god, that nightmare you had... When you shouted out.' Stephanie glanced around herself, frantic. 'Could that have been a side effect?'

Kondwani continued: 'More symptom. Sadness. Worry. Headache. Dizzy. Vomit. Memory all bad. Want to die.'

'Suicidal?'

'Probably. And see things. Pictures. Not real things.'

'Hallucinations?'

'Yes! Those. Like with Malawi gold.'

'Yes, like Malawi gold.'

'Oh god,' groaned Marcus. 'I think it was the tablets. I think they're right. Oh fucking hell – those fucking tablets.'

'All right, Marcus, it's OK – calm down.'

'But... Why didn't they tell me any of this?' His eyes swivelled up. He felt pathetically small just lying there, cramped into the corridor corner. He felt outraged by the impudence. He felt so embarrassed.

'Oh!' said Kondwani. The nurse had handed him something. 'This...' It was the nurse's printout of the information.

Marcus snatched it and started to read. His vision blurred over. He couldn't believe it. They didn't even prescribe this junk in EU countries anymore: the UK had for some reason continued to hand it out to tossers like him, who didn't have the mental aptitude to handle a daily pill... What an idiot he was! What an idiot! He shook in the bed and struck out at himself.

'That's not going to help. Why are you so angry? It's all right. We'll get you some other drug. There are lots of other ones. We can pay for a stash of it with your money and then claim it back with the medical cover. It's fine. Really.'

'This is all I need! Some poxy fucking psychosis! I'm getting out of here.' He swung his legs over the bed.

'No, no, no. Just stay here a bit longer. They need to do blood tests. We need to check that it's all out of your system.'

'I haven't taken it for...' He paused: poised on the bed, with his hands gripping the metal. 'How long have I been gone?'

'You left the camp two days ago.'

'Is that long enough for it to have left my system?'

'I don't know. I mean – if it's a weekly pill...'

'Oh right. Yes. You're right. Oh fuck. So today is...'

'Wednesday.'

I always take it on a Sunday. It's still going to be in my system, isn't it? Oh fuck.' He started to shake. It was like some bizarre horror movie, with the monster inside you, its claws in your blood.

Stephanie and Kondwani persuaded the hospital staff that Marcus was safe to leave. They both had a hunch that the environment was whisking him up into another mental episode.

The hospital staff, however, were disappointed to see them go. They'd all been getting along so well. Stephanie slipped the doctor some notes from her bag, to soothe over any ill feelings. The doctor took them with relish and held them close to his chest, as if cradling a newborn.

The atmosphere in the car was tense and terrible. Stephanie found her mind drifting again. She did not feel weighted in her body. She looked down at her hands and could not see the connection.

Kondwani was smiling his usual smile, but his hands shook on the steering wheel. He could feel the strain of Stephanie's body, and he did not know how to help her. He had grown to like this strange and skinny white woman. But he had never known anyone so fragile and coiled. And now, if that wasn't bad enough – as if he didn't sense that she was burrowing herself into one of her moods – he had this psychotic in the back of the car. A man who, at any point, could leap up and bite his neck. Or crush his skull with a rock. Kondwani kept glancing into the rear-view mirror.

Meanwhile, Marcus was struggling. He couldn't decide upon the least psychotic-looking pose. He sat with his arms crossed, but this seemed a tad surly and aggressive. With his legs flopped forward, he felt like a sexual predator. Even worse was the face: did he smile, like a manic, or risk looking blank like a sociopath? And woe betide if the corners of his lips drooped downwards, or his eyes accidentally watered from the winds.

Kondwani was first to break the silence: 'There is no doctor in these villages.'

Stephanie roused from her head travels. 'Sorry?'

'If Marcus die. What if Marcus dead before Dixon run?'

'Well,' considered Stephanie, blinking. 'That's just how things are, Kondwani. There aren't enough hospitals. There aren't enough doctors.'

Marcus leaned forwards. 'And the hospitals you've got aren't much cop, if I'm honest.'

'What?'

'For god's sake, watch the road, Kondwani – or we're going to end up back at one. It's an expression – "not much cop". It means it's not very good.'

'We poor. Who cares?' He sniffed, hurt. 'But I change it. For our village.'

'How?'

'Get Madonna to build a hospital on top of it?' quipped Marcus.

Kondwani swiped his hand through the air. 'No, no, no. Serious, now. Government train people to care in village. Like doctors. Give drugs. Eleven weeks. Train and you get money, yes? More money than charity give.'

'Oh yes, I've heard of this.' Stephanie nodded, slipping back into her body. 'They're called Health Surveillance Assistants, I think...'

'Yes!' Kondwani clicked his fingers. 'Yes. I want to be that.'

'But Kondwani, I think you need to be a secondary school leaver.'

'What now?'

'You need to have finished school. Big school.'

'No, no, no. Two years.'

'Oh. I thought... Well, even so: did you do two years of school?'

He shrugged. 'Yes.'

'Kondwani...?'

'They want two years of big school. I have two years of big school.'

'I'm not sure that's how it works.'

'Yes.'

'All right. But why?'

'Money. More money for family.'

Stephanie winced. 'Yes. I can see that.'

He glanced at her. 'You not happy.'

'If you get through... If you complete it... Of course I am happy for you.'

'I am most clever man in village. I not miss school.'

'Yes, but secondary school. Big school.'

'My father pay. He find money.'

'Yes, but how long were you there...?'

He smacked the roof of the car and unease pervaded everything. 'It no matter. Stop now.'

'Kondwani, I'm sorry.' She smiled, although her eyes stayed static. 'I'll just miss you, that's all.'

An involuntary smile twitched at his mouth. 'Really? Is that why you not happy?' He leant over and kissed her cheek. 'Princess Stephanie.' A rumble of laughter. 'Ahh, we have fun, yes?'

'Yes.'

Marcus leant in again. 'In all seriousness, I think it's a great idea. The village needs a clinic. It's living in the Stone Age... It's backward.'

'Marcus.' Stephanie whistled through her teeth. 'You're not helping.' She turned around to face him. 'You're volunteering in a developing country, one of the poorest in Africa. What did you expect?'

'What you expect?' repeated Kondwani. It was one of his favourites. He liked the tone of it.

Marcus flopped back again. 'Just something more... You know, a drive to improve. A drive to get better.'

'With what money?'

'Look, they still believe in witchcraft, for god's sake. It's weird.'

'They don't all believe in witchcraft.'

'Most of them do.'

'Well, anything can be witchcraft. Science is like witchcraft to me. Religion, philosophy.' She tried to move the conversation on. 'Kondwani, you know these Health Surveillance Assistants... A lot of them don't even get bicycles. There's not enough. You'd have to do what Dixon does. You'd have to run around the villages by foot.'

'I am muscle enough! No?' He flexed his muscles and they laughed. He added: 'I am not old.'

'I know you're not,' she said, softly.

'My children will laugh.'

'Why?'

'They see dad run to villages, red and hot and this belly.' He grabbed it and gave it a shake. There wasn't much to shake but he liked to see Stephanie laugh, her pale lips giving way into teeth. 'I sweat now. This weather! Bad.'

'Now it's my turn: what do you expect?'

'Marcus...'

'Isn't this just Africa? It's hot. It's fucking hot.'

'Why angry?' bellowed Kondwani. 'You big psychopath.'

'I am not a psychopath.'

'You are! Doctor say so. You big, crazy psychopath.'

'I am not a psychopath!'

'Please.' Stephanie's voice was tired and world-weary. 'We're almost back now. Can we just calm things down? And by the way, Marcus, we're in Malawi. You shouldn't just say "Africa"'.

'I not drive you. I leave you in hospital with cockroach and rat. I tell you, this is rainy season. This is rainy season but no rain. We need rain. We have rainy season with no rain.'

'OK, I get it. Rain.'

'It rain in "Africa country" too, you know. Psychopath.' He was really enjoying the sound. He liked to practise new words. Bonus points if it was something that could antagonise stupid white people.

'I remember it was the opposite problem last year,' recalled Stephanie. 'I remember the rain just suddenly coming and pouring down and never seeming to stop. For so long, there was nothing, and then there was this... torrent.'

'It sounds like you're never satisfied, basically.'

'The rains aren't meant to be so unpredictable, Marcus. The rainy season is meant to be this steady, continuous rainfall. Not absolutely nothing and then a downpour that floods everything. All the crops died. It was terrible.'

'Never like this when I boy,' growled Kondwani. 'Never like this.'

'Oh, we're here.' The turning was coming up. Thank goodness. The medication had turned Marcus hostile and bellicose. Sharp words could pierce Stephanie like wasp stings. She couldn't wait to get out of the car. Kondwani was sitting too close. She didn't know what it was; she was getting worse...

Just this horrible fixation, such disreputable daydreams. She was better off steering clear of him.

Darkness crept towards the village as the car pulled in. People were gathered in the porch. Some stood up and pointed at the car lights. A couple called out his name. 'Marcus!' 'Good to see you again, Marcus.' A few kept back in the shadows, wearily casting their eyes over him, now seeing him as the man who crossed lines. There was no greater societal sin.

Marcus tugged at Stephanie. 'I just want to get into bed.'

'Don't you want to say hello?'

'I can't deal with this right now. I'm not even wearing trousers. Please just take me to bed.'

Philippa walked towards them, while the others stayed back. 'Marcus,' she smiled, but her body held back. She twitched briefly at the pants. 'We're so glad you're back safely.'

He nodded, embarrassed. He twisted his body to the side so there was less of him to see.

'He wants to go to bed. He's really tired.'

'Of course.' Philippa waved her hands towards the sleeping quarters. 'We can talk everything through in the morning. Good night, Marcus.' He didn't reply. He was trying to ignore the Christmas fairy lights, which had been strung up in his absence. He passed a shiny plastic tree on the way to the bedrooms.

Stephanie went to go with him, but he resisted. 'I'm fine, honestly. I just need to get some sleep.'

'You'll remember to tie up the mosquito net and everything?' Her eyes screwed up, worried and uncertain.

'Yes, of course. I'm not feverish or anything right now... Honestly.'

'All right, then. Well. Good night.' Within seconds she was just a pair of shoes, clip clopping into night-time. He listened to the sound of her peter away. Then he faced a delicious near-silence: far better than the shock of true silence or the shriek of cacophony. Wordless voices swelled out on the veranda. He let it babble all over him.

In a short while (impossible to know how long), he heard voices in the corridor: more distinct, this time. He could just about make out what they were saying.

'I'm not sleeping with a psycho.'

'We think he's all right now, Toby.'

'I mean it; I'm not sleeping in there with him. He's fucked.'

'All right. We'll see what we can do. All right? Anyway, let's move along from here, or we'll wake him up.'

Somehow he fell back asleep and then it was morning. Another day to live out. He thought about breakfast but the shame nailed him to the bed.

There was a knock on the door. The door creaked open. Annabelle.

'Stephanie wants to know if you want any breakfast.'

He cleared his throat, uncomfortable. 'I think I need some more rest. I mean – I feel too tired to get up.'

'I could bring in your breakfast if you like.'

He thought about it. 'Yes. Yes.'

She waited for a please, but it didn't come. Biting her tongue, she went off to get his breakfast. Stephanie wasn't in the habit of allowing people to have breakfast in bed, but at the same time, she couldn't face having him there today. She was still so tired and wound up. 'Yes, all right,' she said to Annabelle. 'If you're OK bringing it to him...'

Annabelle went into the room with the breakfast tray and perched next to him on the bed. 'How are you feeling?'

'All right.'

'You've given us some brilliant drama,' she grinned. 'But don't feel embarrassed. If you are. Because other things have been happening, too. Want the gossip?'

He didn't. He hated gossip. But he wanted the drudgery to

earth him, to cut out the live wire inside him that kept frothing and sparking.

She chatted to him, idly. He liked the way her face moved when she talked. It relaxed him. He felt his eyelids flutter. There was a gentle drift into a low sensory state.

When he awoke, it was dark, and Annabelle was gone. He thought he might have slept through the day. He couldn't remember the last time he had slept through the day. He panicked. Then he heard some sounds outside, the clatter of plates. Dinner?

He rose out of bed and dressed himself, then pattered out on to the veranda, where people were laying down plates and getting themselves seated for food. The chatter stopped, and people didn't know what to say. They nodded at him, but wary. Stephanie said: 'Oh Marcus, you feeling better?'

He said: 'Yes, I am – thank you. Listen, I want to go to the school tomorrow, if that's all right. I need to say goodbye to the children. I want to go home.'

But before she could answer, they heard the sound of screaming.

Chapter Eight

For two months, people dropped dead like flies. Death smells like stewed fruit, sour milk, wet wood. There was a strange feeling to everything, like resolution unpixelating. Life holds you up to the light elements of the universe and exposes you as monumentally small and susceptible, in a constant wait for your fate.

The scream had been Ben's. His was a hollering scream, a wailing scream, a something-from-the-pit-of-your-guts scream. The sort that shudders through tunnels and bubbles up mud. It felt like insect wings and cobwebs. It had the brute strength of elephants. It was a hard sound to forget.

A villager dead from meningitis (so it turned out to be). And what happened was this: Ben came across a body that was cold but not too cold, lips pale as candyfloss but not yet blue. Nobody knew why she had crawled out of bed, why she had dragged herself by the hands and knees into their yard. People debated it over breakfast, coffee breaks, the ever-churning pizza oven.

It worked out strangely well for Marcus. Everybody seemed to forget his psychotic wanderings; his peculiar puberty ritual, his symbolic rite of passage (at the tender age of twenty-nine). There was a new conversation on their lips. People recited facts that they had read online: the average life expectancy, the HIV crisis, the changing seasons. It tainted them all, and a foreboding hung about them, like the very air itself was made up of malevolence and trickery.

One day, he saw Stephanie sitting on the veranda, quietly watching – what? What was it? She was staring at something intently. Occasionally she would sigh and gather her shawl around her. She'd probably call it a 'pashmina'. But Stephanie was definitely the kind of woman who wore shawls.

Everybody had gone to schools, to their projects on the periphery of the villages or elsewhere. The camp was silent, except for non-human noise.

Marcus had escaped teaching that day by playing his 'recovery' card. He felt a little odd, he might stay back – it wasn't fair to the children, etc., etc. They were all so terrified of mental illness, of the unpredictability of emotions, that they gawped and nodded, not knowing which words to speak, what they could possibly say. This worked in his favour.

Now he had Stephanie to himself. He approached her, quietly, he didn't know why. He wanted perhaps to startle her at the last possible moment, to gain her utmost attention in a concentrated second.

She jumped.

'Marcus! Oh my word.'

'Sorry.'

'I forgot you were here.'

'I stayed behind, remember? I wasn't feeling too great.'

'You've got to be careful. Don't push it.'

'Exactly. That's exactly what I'm doing.'

'Relapse and all that.'

'Exactly. May I sit down?'

Her eyebrows shot up, she blinked several times in succession. 'Sure.'

He dragged out a chair and planted himself down.

'Beautiful day,' she said, panicking at the prospect of sustained conversation.

'Well,' he considered. 'It's a bit like any other day.'

'Well. I suppose so. But... Warmth, sun. It's a rare thing in England sometimes.'

Pause. 'I've always wondered why people associate sunshine with happiness. What makes this a "good" day and not a bad one? What makes it beautiful? Is it a rush of vitamin D? A serotonin boost? Is it social conditioning? Isn't there something beautiful about mist, as well? Snow, rain, fog? What is "beauty", anyway?'

'Well,' she said, flustered. 'I hadn't quite thought of it like that.'

'What is this meaning we give to a blue sky? What is this human element that we project on to it? Because it's just a sky without any cloud in it. It's just a colour. It's still just the carapace of a void. And why are clouds bad? Clouds signal rain. Rain helps our crops grow...'

'We could certainly do with some rain here.'

'It's too simplistic to say that these constructs of beauty–'

'I was just making conversation,' she snapped. 'My god.' she instantly regretted the outburst. She bit her lip and turned to him, anxious, scouring his face for any hurt or outrage. On the contrary, he looked quite chipper.

'I'm sorry,' she said, anyway. 'I'm a bit tired.'

'Thinking about the villager? The one who died?'

'Yes.' She continued, despite herself. 'She's the first person I've known to die here.' Then she trailed back off. He counted to ten. She still didn't speak.

'Stephanie?'

'Yes?'

'I've been meaning to say. I still want to go back soon.'

'Back?' Her eyes widened. 'Oh yes. Yes. Right. You said. That's right...'

'I don't think this is quite what I expected,' he said, gesturing around, at the ether itself.

'Oh right.' What *did* you expect, she thought (to borrow Kondwani's favourite phrase); but she let the thoughts circle around in her mind, her lips lowered like a lid on a boiling saucepan.

'And the whole... malaria thing. Apparently you can get flare ups. It takes a while for those drugs to leave your system. I'd really feel much happier at home, surrounded by – you know, mod cons, technology, normal 21st century stuff.'

That isn't normal for most of the planet, she thought – but, again, she said nothing. She held herself tight.

'And it makes sense to go back now – just before Christmas. It's really weird to be out here, with all this tinsel and fake snowflakes sprayed on the windows. Honestly, I think I'd rather go back.'

After a few seconds of processing, Stephanie said: 'We can help you book your flight. But it's going to cost a lot to fly back at this time of year. And you will have to pay Kondwani a flat fee to take you to the airport.'

The thought of the camp disintegrating, of the camaraderie ebbing. Everyone was a bit spooked, already; people acting as if meningitis was something you could catch, like measles. What if they all packed up now, what if she never saw Kondwani again?

'Can I persuade you to stay, though?'

'Persuade? God, no. Sorry. I'm made up.'

'Well, I respect that. I do. But it's just... We have so much to do. So much to accomplish. We promised the village–'

'I appreciate that, but–'

'What if we paid you? I mean, it wouldn't be much. But it would be something. As a token for your time. You couldn't tell the others. It would have to be a secret. I'd clear it with Philippa. I'd find a way to...'

He hadn't thought about money for a while. Money. That golden ticket. The piece of paper that justified everything, which could fool you into thinking that you were living your life well, that you were achieving your goals.

'Couldn't you just stay for a month? With us paying you, a bit. And then see how you feel? We can achieve so much, I know that we can. But if we all disperse...'

'Can't you just get some more volunteers?'

'It doesn't work like that. We have to get people visas, sort out their flights, make sure they get their jobs. We have to fill out forms, do checks on insurance. We have to train them. We're only a small group. We are such a small charity. Every day is a battle, a battle to survive. To achieve what we set out to achieve. Please.'

'Money would help,' he admitted. 'I could be earning big bucks at home. This would be... a kind of compensation.'

She blinked a few times. 'Well, like I said, it wouldn't be much.'

'But something. That's good.'

'And the children have gotten to know you. Have you gotten to know them?'

He shrugged. 'They're just children. They seem nice enough.'

This time she didn't blink. She stared at him for several moments, her eyes wide and her pupils constricted. 'Can I say something?'

He waved his hand to signal consent.

'You don't fit the profile of our usual volunteer.'

'Oh? What's that, then?'

'Well,' she floundered. 'Liberal, humanitarian, compassionate...'

'Compassionate?'

'Sorry, I suppose that's too strong. But you know the type. *I'm* the type. Feeling guilty at the state of this world, this terrible burden on your shoulders.'

'Guilt?'

'Yes.'

'Guilt.' He pushed the seat back away, stood up from the thighs, so his torso and shoulders stayed rigid. 'I don't feel any guilt. Why should I?'

'Well, that's kind of what I meant.' She hesitated.

He mumbled something inaudible, his eyebrows hunched down to the bone. 'I'll stay for a month,' he said, and walked back to his room. But today he found the peace too disturbing, and he popped in his headphones and shut out everything but songs: singing along to the lyrics so there was no room for the words in his head.

#

It was a good month. It's true that the skies stayed dry and the crops stayed shrivelling. An unspoken panic true enough to cause some villagers to creep around the pizza oven, clumsy hands held out for charity, knowing what it was like to starve hollow and desperate because nothing would grow. And it's true that everyone thought about that young woman and her early demise, although improbable that anyone missed her. They'd already forgotten her name.

But Marcus had a good month. He found their Christmas to be surprisingly fun. He didn't usually like Christmas because his father had died just before it, on the way to buy presents. Marcus had badgered him all year for a PlayStation, he just had to have one, he'd gone on and on about it for weeks. So after that, he never really liked tinsel or crackers or mincemeat. Yet he decided to treat this one like it was just an extra-colourful party, of the ilk he'd had in student days. Cheap bottles of wine and silly, flirtatious games. It all ebbed away in an indulgent blur.

He also enjoyed the teaching, in a way, now that it was 'work' and earning a wage. Even the children were growing on him, you could say – there was something of him in them, an eagerness to learn, to try and be something, do something. Of course, in other ways, they were different – they seemed to have everything figured out much better than he did. They seemed to know a secret in life that they would not share. They stared at him sometimes, and did not look awkward when he returned their gaze. They just kept on staring.

Best of all, Marcus was now sleeping again: deep, restful sleeps with normal, colourful dreams. He ate a lot of pizza from the pizza oven. He'd always loved pizza. And he made an almost friend, a buddy: Chris. They bonded over a competitive tournament of charades on Boxing Day – both on the winning team, no less. It was funny because Marcus hadn't spoken to Chris before that moment, but he discovered that Chris was in finance, too; that he was doing this trip as part of some elaborate favour to his boss. Playing the long game on the court of promotion. Marcus understood and related to those reasons. Although even Chris could be a touch too pious sometimes, and a bit of a pussy (a teetotaller, non-smoker, strictly faithful to his girlfriend back home), he was perfect for a touch of kick ball or a chat about women (which he grudgingly gave in to, after a little persuasion... And turned out to be as lascivious and perverted as the best of them). His biggest asset was his willingness to talk. Pretty much everyone ignored Marcus completely – whether for his mental hiccup or for something else, he didn't quite know. But he didn't give a rat's ass. Which he told Chris repeatedly, as they lay in the sun. Chris would just murmur or nod or offer reassurances to the contrary. Marcus didn't care for this half of the conversation: it was the talking he savoured. Luckily, Chris was weak and genial. It was a good month for Marcus.

One small annoyance was the day he drew short straws with Annabelle to stay behind and man the camp, while the others went off on a boat trip excursion along the Shire River, the day before New Year. He had been desperate to leave these confines, to try to capture some kind of holiday feel. People came here on holiday. There must be fun, 'holiday' things to do, besides swatting mosquitoes and sweeping up dust.

'It's full of hippos, anyway,' said Annabelle, as she stretched out her legs and opened up a book. 'They'll probably all be killed. Then we'll be pleased we drew the short straws, won't we?'

'Oh god,' he drawled. 'Do you have to turn everything into a silver fucking lining?'

'Yup.' She said this with a proud tone, but nonetheless drew her legs up to her chest, and sucked in her lips so she looked sort of hurt.

'Are you fucked off with me?'

'Nope.'

'If you are, can you just say so, instead of moping around all day?'

She lowered her sunglasses. 'Would you be sorry if I was?'

'I wouldn't be sorry, but I'd be relieved to know where I stood.'

'Oh great. I'm so desperate to relieve you of this burden and not even get an apology for it.'

'Yep. You're fucked.'

'Oh—' she began, and flung down the book.

'Yes?'

'Nothing.'

'You were about to say "fuck off" to me, weren't you?'

'No, I wouldn't sink to that.'

'You were, too!'

'I wasn't.'

'You really were.'

'I don't think I was, actually.'

'You know what?' she said, now shoving the book across the table... 'I've been so nice to you. Why do you have to say such mean things all the time?'

'I wasn't trying to be mean. You're just always so... Upbeat.'

'I'm not upbeat!'

'You are. You're always upbeat and smiley and optimistic and super nice.'

'Why are you spitting out those words like they're bad things?'

'I just don't get how somebody can be that way for twenty-four hours a day. You must be acting or something.'

'Me? Acting?' Her eyebrows trapezed across her forehead. 'You're the one who is acting. Trying to be sane when you're clearly mentally ill!'

He put his book down. 'That's better. Some truth at last.'

She looked away, embarrassed. 'I'm sorry. That was super harsh.'

'It's OK. I don't care what people think of me.'

'Well, I wish I could be like that.' Her eyes went dreamy. 'I always anticipate judgment.'

He could see the plan to read was suspended. He lay down and closed his eyes. 'Hence the super-niceness, then. You're trying to get everyone to like you.'

'No, I don't think I'm doing that, Dr Freud! Maybe I'm trying to like... Oh, this is getting too personal. And I can tell that you're bored.'

'I'm not bored.'

'You've got your eyes closed.'

'I'm just blocking everything out. Focusing on your words.'

'Really?' Her voice was incredulous but soft, pert...

'Yeah. Whatever.' She was so easy to win over. Nancy at least had more dignity. She'd have kicked him in the balls by now.

'Well. Anyway. It was strange at school yesterday. Wasn't it?'

'What do you mean? No, not particularly.'

'An odd atmosphere, I mean. When Blessings asked us about Britain.'

'Why was that weird?'

'I didn't know what to say.'

'Right... Well, it didn't matter. I jumped in.'

'Yes, but then you just started talking about Nando's and high streets and binge drinking and iPhones...'

'So?'

'So, it was strange. I could tell the children were baffled. Just completely astounded. Trying to imagine this land where everyone can ride into these giant supermarkets and you have all these motorways and cars and central heating and office blocks. All those things we take for granted.' She gestured towards the generator. 'Electricity, I mean. Turning on the light like it comes out of nowhere. Like it's not even special.'

'They have their cities. I mean, this lot don't live there – but many do.'

'But their idea of a city is nothing like ours. Compare Lilongwe to London! Come on! Think of the station, with those big piles of plastic. And that smell. That smell, like sweet and sour–'

'Well, they've heard it all before. They know our country's really rich and theirs isn't. They know we have different lives.'

'But didn't you feel embarrassed when you were telling them that? Making the distinction out loud? I was curling up inside. I couldn't even look at them. I felt really ashamed, Marcus.'

'Why were you ashamed?' He half opened his eyelids.

'Because they know we're all going to go back to that. That lifestyle. We're just going to leave them floundering in this one.'

'So what?'

'I felt like a hypocrite. That's all. None of them have anything to eat right now. The soil's rubbish, they're out of fertiliser. It's not even raining, is it? I'm a hypocrite to even be here.'

'A hypocrite?'

'Yes, a fraud.'

'You're mad. They'd go back to Britain if they could. They'll probably try to sneak under the back of our aeroplane, tie themselves to a wing. They don't blame us for it. Why should we? What are you going to do, stay out here indefinitely, out of some twisted sense of guilt? Just count yourself lucky.'

'But that's all that divides us, then. "Us" and "them". Luck?'

'Well...' He considered a fuller reply, but trailed off. 'Then you get into politics and shit. It depends on your ideologies, doesn't it?'

'I'm not sure it does.' Her voice was sad and broken. 'I don't think it has anything to do with that. I think you were right the first time. It's luck. Historical luck. And we've just exploited that, ever since. We had a good first hand and we've just exploited it.'

'Come on. You're beating yourself up for nothing.'

'Well, I saw their faces when you were speaking. When I finally got the courage to look at them. And they just looked confused. I guess maybe some looked enchanted, like you were telling a fairy story. A children's book or something. But a couple of them – including Blessings... They just looked sad. Defeated, I guess. Defeated and resigned and all given up inside. I could see it hit them. This awful sad anger. Thinking about how the rest of the world lives. All these things they'll never have. All these things we take for granted.'

'Of course they can have it! They just need to grow their economy. Sort out their shit. Stop lazing around and believing in witchcraft.'

She swivelled her eyes, tough as two pricks of frost. 'You don't seriously believe that?'

'I do.'

'These countries can't get rich as long as we keep feeding our greed.'

'Wow. Everyone has an agenda, don't they? Yours is communism and self-flagellation.'

'Most of the world can't live like we do. We live in our little bubble and we talk about the new millennium and the 21st century. We say, "Ooh, are we all going to ride hover cars in fifty years time?" "Ooh, are we going to invent some injection which means we'll all live forever?" "Ooh, isn't the internet great?" "Isn't progress great?" We think that everyone lives like we do. But they don't. The majority of the world does not. We're the elect. We're the elite. And that's just how this shitty world runs. They're condemned from birth.' Her voice rose higher. 'What are we educating them to be, Marcus? Tell me.'

'What are you on about?'

'We're going into these schools, we're teaching them stuff. What are we educating them to be? When the best most of them can hope for is to maybe work as a cleaner or in a shop. Maybe get married in a year or two, if you're a girl. Or maybe just fall under the radar and belong to nowhere at all.'

'They've got hospitals, nurses. They need nurses.'

'Most of those kids won't even get to go to secondary school. They know this. You know this. And even if they do, come on, their prospects aren't great.'

'That's the problem with you lot. You cry about all these injustices and you don't realise that you're the one that's being bloody patronising. Maybe they're happy how they are. Maybe they're doing all right.'

'But they don't know any better.'

'But you're basically admitting that our economic system is the best one. That it's good to live in a major capitalist country. And, by the way, there's plenty of poverty in our own country if you wanted to look for it...'

'This has nothing to do with being anti-capitalist, Marcus. This is to do with how capitalism works in a rich country and how capitalism works in a poor one. There's not enough to go around. Don't you get that? We sit there and educate them and it's the wrong kind of education. What they need is a wake-up call.'

'Yes, let's get them to revolt! Just what the world needs – another loony country that hates us.' He was getting carried away on the wave of his rhetoric. 'I'll tell you what we need. What would be good. More war. Let's have more war! More revolution. There's not enough war in the world.' But he looked over at Annabelle and she wasn't even really listening to him anymore. She was slumped down with her lips stuck out. Her eyes dancing with indignation and tears.

He didn't know whether to continue the argument, or if she needed a fuck, or if he should just walk away. At last, he broke the silence: 'At least you're not Miss Pollyanna for once. That's worth missing hippos for. I mean it. It literally is.'

He caught her face. It slid between outrage and humour. She gave in to the latter and chuckled to herself and stared up at the clouds, while he picked up his book again. As he scuffed at the pages, she saw herself as a dot on an atlas, pinned to this sliver of a country; shaped like an intestinal worm, a throwaway thought, like it was tossed on the map, just the scraps of a meal.

A little later, on New Year's Day, the second death showed up.

John, seven, was walking along the side of the road, taking his time, returning from bend-down market errands. These mobile markets slam-bang across different sections of the main road; wares spread so low on the ground that you have to creak your back to get a good look. When you finally lower yourself low enough, you have to sift through stacks of tat, rejected by every charity shop in the West. But one man's tat is another one's treasure, so the saying goes – and John had scored some superlative tat, as authorised by his father just an hour or two earlier.

Now the lights flickered out and John saw the start of his village. He was thinking about woodsmoke : and food : and stars : and the garlic gust of neem trees.

The truck skidded to the side and ripped John's body in two. It flipped over and skated on its back for several metres, metal crunched up in a ball and glass smashed up into grit. Nobody got out because the passenger was dead and the driver was dying. He lived only five minutes more. There was not enough air in his lungs left to scream.

The news didn't reach the village until the early hours of the morning. It came after countless pacing and retracing John's steps. Torchlight stomped into barren corners. Tears were shed. Somebody told the father about the accident. The body had been taken to the hospital, they said. The father got into his car and drove to that hospital, where he identified some body parts as his son. He clutched the upper half of the body and he wailed like a baby, trying to squeeze whatever life really is back into that child-size skull. He didn't leave the hospital until he was certain that the tears had dried up. He had to be strong for his family. He had to wear his face like a mask.

When Kondwani returned to the village, he sat for a few minutes in the car with the engine left running. There can be comfort in mechanical sounds like cars or aeroplanes or radio static. It's the sound of automata; white-noise balm for the ceaseless babble of brain fizz. He lit a cigarette.

When Dziko saw the cigarette, she sank to her knees and

screamed. Kondwani didn't smoke. Nobody really smokes cigarettes in Malawi, although most of the population depends on tobacco farming to survive. But a previous charity worker – long since returned to home comforts – had given him this particular pack as a gift.

At the time, he told his wife: 'I will save these for a rainy day.' He had caught the English expression, and he liked to say it often. 'Is today a rainy day? No, not today.' Or: 'Yes, the sky is raining, but it isn't a rainy day, is it, my love?' And: 'Let's hope that rainy day never comes, love. Thanks to God, thanks to God.'

The smoke wound around his body and rolled through the car like a ghost snake.

He stayed like this – his hand poised in the air, the vapour biting and stinging and pricking his face – as he watched his wife screaming and beating the ground, his other children swirling about her, upset and uncertain. When some villagers came to hold her and move her away, she looked up into his eyes and he took a deep drag and slowly shook his head and held his breath without coughing.

The mourning lasted for days. The family gathered on the side of the road, outside the house. Dziko wailed. Branches were spread on either side of the road, so people could spot the residuum of death. Friends of the family sometimes sat with the family, sometimes slept among them. At different points, the charity workers themselves – friends of Kondwani – sat beside him and stammered out platitudes. He nodded and grunted but never replied. He wanted to sit very still, in silence, as robust as a statue; not a frail straw body, all stuffed out with pain.

Stephanie was one of the first to sit with him. She was terrified of Kondwani's face. She was used to seeing it laugh and smile and joke and dance. To see a face like that turn as stock-still as stone was as shocking as seeing snow in the summer.

She whispered words of consolation and prayers of solace. She gave these mostly to Dziko. She hugged their children and held the baby. She leant towards Kondwani and gave him money for the funeral. 'From the charity,' she said. 'On behalf of us all.'

He did speak then. He told her, thank you.

Dziko wailed and Kondwani looked up at the sky. When Dziko and the children went to a neighbour's house for some food, Kondwani said he wasn't hungry.

'Can I stay with you a bit longer?'

Stephanie watched the family trail off; Dziko staggering into the shadows.

'Yes. But no talk.'

'We don't have to talk.'

'I remember fact in your book,' he said.

'Book?'

'About Malawi.'

'What, the charity leaflet?'

He shrugged. 'I remember. One in thirteen children die before birthday number one. One in seven not go to five. This is Malawi. This is my country. This, my dead child. How many more?'

'I'm so sorry.'

'No more talk,' he said, irritably, as if Stephanie had started it. 'No more talk.' Then he said: 'Is everyone gone?'

'Your family's eating dinner. There's nobody here.'

'Hold me.'

She blinked.

'Hold me. Please.'

Her arms were stiff and awkward as she enveloped his thick, broad chest. She rested her chin on his shoulder. He writhed around in her clinch and barked. It felt like an exorcism. The back of her top was soaked. It was a terrible thing and yet she was happy. She wanted someone to press the pause button. But nobody pressed it, and life went on; those minutes, those hours, those days. Of course, the embrace had to end. That day had to end. All lives have to end. There is always an end.

But Marcus wasn't at the end, just yet. He tailspinned into a new chronic state. Anxiety feels like you have metal in your lungs. Something cold and hard swells up from the gut and lodges in your centre. Your breath cannot flow through it. It has to stagger around. It jumps up for air in these stop-start spurts.

He remembered that god-awful DJ on the radio. The middle-of-the-road voice, geographically unidentifiable, all smooth and neutral and the consistency of milk. He remembered her eyes blinking in the rear-view mirror as she pulled out of the driveway, that thick blonde hair... A hand reaching up to scrub away surface tears. The buzz of the door. The police saying those words, the world ripping at the seams, nothing quite holding it up. Her body now somewhere along the West Coast. Was it even a body or was it just dirt? How long does a body take to decompose? How long does it take until the face rubs out?

John's death, the car accident... It brought it all back. This whole African episode had thrown him into a trance, into some wild distraction, and he had suddenly come to. He cried most nights for Nancy. Nancy – who died all those years ago. Who would get so very young as he got so old. Why the hell did he still care? He couldn't talk to Kondwani; the pain reminded him too much of his own. He recognised that hunched-over back, eyes of horrifying blankness. He left him alone, and he grew very quiet, less cocksure, licking away at his wounds.

There was one particular night when a violent thought swung at him: he didn't want to go home, after all. There wasn't a home. At least here, in Malawi, there was diversion and routine and a sense that he mattered – that people depended on his efforts. He felt some dots joining up but they joined over his neck like a noose. He accepted this fate, pulled it tighter still.

He didn't go to John's funeral, but he heard from Dora and Annabelle and some others that it was surprisingly similar to western funerals. The village headman had notified surrounding villages, and the turnout was good. With help from the charity, John was able to lie in a coffin. People gave speeches, and sang, and read extracts from the Bible. It went on for hours, and Philippa said they were not expected to stay for it all.

'I didn't know they were Christian,' he commented.

'Most Malawians are Christians,' said Dora. She curled her feet under her body, on the chair, the way children do. Her cheeks were flushed. She liked excitement and drama and the relaying of gossip; as if more people knowing something made it even more real. 'Didn't you know that? Didn't you read the leaflet?'

'What leaflet?'

'The one on Malawi. The one in our welcome pack.'

'I didn't read the welcome pack.'

'Oh Christ, Marcus, there was a whole profile in there. Well, most are Protestant but a few are Catholic. Can't remember the exact percentage.'

'So how can they believe in witchcraft? And things like that?'

'I guess they just fit alongside each other. Some people might say turning water into wine sounds a bit like witchcraft. Like a magic trick.'

He rolled his eyes. Dora, always trying to sound so clever and grown up, with that punchable face, with that unlined skin. 'Well, what about multiple wives? Like Useni? And some of the others?'

'Kondwani had one wife.'

'Yes, but some of them have more.'

'Like I said, I think they adapt it.'

'How convenient.'

'Back to the funeral, Dora.' Annabelle was in the corner,

filling in her diary.

'I don't think Marcus even cares,' she sighed, leaning back with folded arms.

'Does every female in this camp have to be hormonal and aggressive?' He thought of lovely pliable Lisa, growing thin and possessed.

'You sexist shit. I'm not being aggressive!'

'It was a nice send-off.' Annabelle's voice, low and flat. 'Some of the songs were beautiful. One of his children sang. His older girl. I can't remember her name. I don't know what she sang but it was beautiful.'

'A lot of the kids in the other village are Muslim. I saw the Koran in the classroom. A couple of the women wearing veils.'

'Yes, there are Muslims in Malawi.' Dora made an exaggerated sigh.

'How does that work, then?'

'I think it all works out fine, Marcus. Jesus! You get different faiths in the UK, for God's sake. And not everyone is as backward as the States when it comes to views on Islam.'

'I have no idea what you're talking about.'

'They just get on with it. I don't think there's tension. I think there is less division between religions. It's all just worshipping a god. As long as you do that, it's fine.'

'Kondwani is leaving.' Annabelle shut her diary and sat up straight. 'I heard Philippa telling Stephanie this morning.'

'What, leaving the village?'

'No, not the village. He won't leave the village. The charity, I mean. He's leaving the charity.'

'What's he going to do for a living?'

'I don't know. I just overheard.'

Dora's eyes wide and unblinking, trying to swallow the facts. 'Well, what did you hear?'

'I just heard he was leaving. Really, that's it.'

'But why?'

'I don't know, Dora. I said I don't know.'

'OK. Tetchy!'

'I'm sorry.' Annabelle's face went calm and affable. 'Ugh, it's been a really long day.'

'It's no longer than any other.'

'Relativity, Dora, relativity.' Marcus fired a disdainful glance. She screwed up her face and then got up and left. They both watched her go. Exchanging glances.

'I don't think she's too happy with you.'

'Why? Because of that? That was nothing. She's going to have to tell families that their loved ones are dead when she grows up to be a doctor. She's going to need thicker skin. She likes to get the last word. That's all. She's a baby who acts like she's a fucking guru.'

Annabelle snorted. Then laughed. 'You have an interesting way with words. It's kind of nice to see your spark back.'

'What?'

'You've been quiet, lately. Not your usual self. If you know what I mean.'

'I'm never the loudest. Dora is definitely louder. And don't get me started on Toby...'

'Quiet's the wrong word. I mean – I don't know... A bit more squishy.'

'Squishy?'

'Yeah, you seem a bit more delicate. In the last few days. Is it because of John and Kondwani?'

'I'm not more "delicate". Oh god, I need to find Chris...'

'What do you mean?'

'I need some male conversation. I'm suffocating here.'

She swallowed. She was trying to swallow the anger. 'Well, you're in luck. I think dinner's ready now, anyway.'

He followed her through to the veranda. By the time they

reached the table, all the conversation had stopped. There wasn't much to say these days. Some quiet buzz about the weather. The scraping of metal cutlery on ceramic plates. The hollow murmuring of approval for tasteless food.

Stephanie's eyes were cast down throughout. She didn't even look up when Philippa confirmed that Kondwani was leaving them. That he was taking a break. That they were flying over a new driver who wasn't native Malawian; he was a second-generation Brit, but he still spoke Chichewa. He knew the culture very well. He visited often. He was delighted to join the charity. His name was Daniel. Etc., etc.

The next day stretched out like every other day. The intense sun bore down on them, like extra weight on their flesh. Dogs stopped running and sniffing and pissing in doorways. They lazed in the heat with their tails tucked under. Their bodies panting, thick tongues oozing out. Flip-flops kept whipping up the rubble into clouds. People staggered into their duties and chores. Heads jerked up at the sky, wondering when it would rain. It had to rain soon. It just had to, didn't it?

'What are they eating?' asked Marcus. It was another day, at last. They were outside the village school, with the children running up to him and Annabelle: taking their hands and touching their clothes. They popped small white granules into their mouths like candy.

Abikanile shook her head. He didn't understand the gesture.

'They've got a lot of it,' he added. 'Considering the drought.'

'It's millet,' she muttered, but then her face went puce. 'It's birdseed, you idiot. It's fucking birdseed!'

It was the only time that anyone had heard Abikanile swear. The group hurried into the school, into the calm and orderly presence of Bertha, who never let feathers ruffle. She just sat there, stoic, as always. Annabelle had once caught her crying. She said it was just pellets of tears down an impassive face.

But there was more to come. The third death, a murder.

They knew something was wrong when the dogs stopped sitting and panting and basking in heat. They heard them howling, went over to look, and they were huddled in a pack, grinding up a corpse with their maws and their noses blood-wet.

People beat them with sticks, so they could drag the body to the side. They saw a stab wound in the stomach. The knife chucked away, just a few metres to the left.

The next morning, after a complicated tournament of 'paper, scissors, stone', Marcus set out to carry a gift to the grieving mother.

The village house was typical. No cement or brick, just basic mud. A thatched roof held up with sticks. Inside, some basic provisions. The colourful swirl of river clay adding extra decoration.

The mother sat with her hands clasped together and the stars in her eyes. He could not comprehend all the fire within her.

'Hello,' he said, uncertain.

'Hello,' she replied, before the translator could speak. 'Hello.' She knew that much. She split open her lips and her mouth was full of holes and charcoal gum. Her face stayed fixed and no more English fell out.

'I am very sorry to hear of your loss.' He waited for Abikanile to translate.

The woman stared at his face while Abikanile spoke – as if the words were still his voice. She closed her mouth and nodded.

'My name is Marcus.' He waited.

She mumbled something. 'She is saying her name. You know her name, don't you?'

'I've forgotten.'

'It's Sigele.'

'OK.' He continued.

'Sigele, we've brought you a gift from the charity,' translated

Abikanile. 'We are all very sad that this could happen in such a beautiful village, full of such kind and wonderful people.' He felt a little off-kilter for relaying such sentimental trifles, but the others had helped form these words, and he felt compelled to recite them.

The woman patted the wooden seat beside her. He offered the stool to Abikanile, but she refused. He sat down instead and surveyed the dust and dark before him.

The woman started to speak and Abikanile chirruped over her; towering above them, her hands on her hips.

'She says that it is not the first murder.'

'Really?' He shuddered at this land's barbarity; giving into a temporary amnesia of London and its back-alley stabbings and street-gang crime. 'Well...' He knew he was stepping outside of the boundaries, but it just seemed too tantalising. 'And do you know why your son was murdered?'

The fire dimmed a little. 'No, she does not know. She says she has her suspicions. There was a feud. But she cannot say any more.' Abikanile waited, patiently, while the woman bubbled out sounds. 'She says she wants the violence to end now. And also...' She frowned. 'She says it must have been God's will. Her crying is done now. No more tears for what cannot be changed.'

He sat back. He thought of Nancy and the ten commandments. That all seemed so far away. All very petty and childish. The fish and the piss and the married woman. The hairs flinched up around him.

Sigele leaned forwards. She tapped him on the arm as she spoke.

'She says that she has to trust in God. Death is everywhere. If he had not died of that, he might have starved. She is starving.'

'She used that word? She didn't say hungry?'

'She used really hungry. It translates like starving.'

'Well... That sounds like translator's licence.'

Abikanile bristled. Meanwhile, the woman's hard face twitched up and down. She murmured, inquisitive.

'She wants to know what we're saying.'

'Say that I didn't know that the village was as hungry as that.'

Abikanile translated. 'She says that you can only live so long on grasshoppers and crickets and caterpillars. These things are tiny. But she's excited that someone gave her a goat as a gift.' Added as an aside – 'For her grief.' Then: 'This is a great honour.'

Sigele's hands fluttered around her like they were held up by string. Her lips smacked together. Her face shone with vigour.

'She is telling the story of her son.'

'Can you give me the highlights?'

They waited while the voice droned on. To him, it just sounded like clicks and tuts. Like a tongue in spasm.

Finally, silence. Sigele's face darted up to Abikanile. There was a new loudness to it. He sensed she was irritated.

'OK, she's wondering why I haven't spoken yet. So I'll give you the "highlights", as you put it. Her son was a taxi driver. A bicycle taxi. He drove people from village to village. He had the strongest legs you had ever seen. But, anyway, you wanted the highlights. He was a good boy, such a polite boy, blah blah blah. He saw and heard things on those bike journeys he should never have seen or heard. He would drive to the city. He would carry the money on him. He would give her nearly all the money. He loved her very much. He hardly ever spoke; for years, they thought he was a mute, they thought he might have been born the wrong way up. But he could speak. He just preferred to listen. And then there was some other stuff too, but to be honest, I've forgotten it now. It's hard recapping this rather than speaking as she speaks. So there you have it. The story of her son. Voila.'

'Are you angry about something?' he asked, pulling the skin off around his fingernails.

'Why would I be angry?'

Sigele started up again.

'She said death stays with you always but you can learn to live with it. You must get rid of the blame, of the anger. You must live in the present.'

He didn't know where it came from but his eyes watered up at that. Even Abikanile saw this, and her eyes opened wide. 'So you're human, after all.'

'Shut up,' he grimaced. He snorted back phlegm. Sigele's face was twitching very close to him.

'She asks if you are also sad about a loss.'

He didn't want Abikanile there. He wanted her gone. For a moment, she was. He tried to block her out. 'I have to confess something,' he said.

'What? Do you want me to translate that?'

He whispered something in Sigele's ear. He started to cry.

'Oh Marcus, keep it together, will you? What are you saying to her? She can't understand you.'

Sigele's face cracked into a smile. She spoke.

'She's just saying it was their time. God has a purpose. She lost her husband a few years ago. You have to trust God.'

This dried up his tears. He sat himself up. The poorer the people, the more they needed that myth. There has to be a reward in the next life! Oh, there just has to be! Otherwise, this crushing sense of unfairness would simply be too brutal. He wasn't so fooled, anymore. Something had turned on the lights and she could not dim it. But he felt better for offloading his secret, so it wasn't time wasted. There are all kinds of weights in this world and they are not all physical.

When he got back to the compound, they told him that they'd arranged a gaming excursion for Saturday. Philippa had organised it with a tour company – no doubt to fix the broken mood.

And it worked. Saturday was a riot of laughter and chitchat.

The change of scene broke through, and the whole thing suddenly seemed like a break, a rest. Some tourists even tugged along in another truck: a jamboree of wealthy travellers and gap-year kids. They waved at each other and all whooped into unison.

The park spread before them seemed so much lusher than their village. So many shades of yellow and green. They didn't know there were so many shades. The sky was the palest blue with a few tufts of slow cloud. In the distance were leopards. There was a yell from the back. The truck trundled onwards and they stumbled on buffalo. Then the biggest cheer of all gathered up for giraffes: peering into the treetops with sashaying necks. At the end, came a lion tearing up a gazelle. Nobody spoke. They wanted to look away, but they couldn't. They all reached for binoculars and zoomed into the gristle.

It was a long day. Some were ready for an early bedtime; others lit up the fire and opened bottles of beer. They reminisced about the things they had seen. They swapped cameras to stare at photos; the confirmation that this had actually happened. They were united in an instant nostalgia.

In the distance were fishermen: lights twinkling on an endless lake. Male voices called across to each other. The sound of nets tossed into water. A kind of beauty in the pursuit of hunger, when it is framed like this. Marcus made his fingers into the square of a lens to catch it.

Perhaps it was the escapism of the day, or this sight, or the beer bubbling up in his stomach... But Annabelle had backache, and he murmured some suitably sympathetic words. He went to get her some beer. He even offered a massage. She politely declined, with a few blinks of surprise. Her whole body lifted, though, just for a moment, as she flashed him a smile. You can let someone up, as well as let someone down.

Chapter Nine

A week later, they awoke to a sound. The sky was the colour of bones. Rain fell in every direction. And when they looked outdoors, they gasped. It has to be said: the landscape was strange without that sun-smoked glint. Though the light was tamed, the colours were richer. The ground was orange and the air felt thick with a hot, sticky tang. The sound was like the thrashing of wheat. The sound was like a tyre let down. The sound was like a lot of things. It kind of swept you into it; into a sort of trance.

The villagers ran around excited, gesturing up to the sky, kneeling down, giving thanks. Abikanile said they had names for different kinds of rain and that this was planting rain. Everyone wanted to grow their crops.

But soon stretches of road were flooded. The drive to the nearby village was difficult, so the group did not risk it. Some people volunteered to help in the fields, but they just seemed to get in the way. So most of them sat around playing cards, reading books, chatting idleness. Philippa said this was all perfectly normal, and the rain wouldn't stay that way for long. She said that it usually switched to raining at night, so you still had the long, balmy days. But even normal can be terrible. There was talk of straw roofs swept away in nearby villages; entire families huddled in tiny cold stone rooms. Some people slept in termite mounds. Philippa did admit that every year the rain seemed to fall longer and harder. She tried not to dwell on it, tried to shift the talk on.

Marcus was in a buoyant mood, despite boredom and rain and the shuffling of bodies. The last few months – the last few years – lifted up and away from him. It was as suspected: he needed to treat death with more death. It was the vaccine approach: to find death in its purest form and inject it in you, so you are cured forever. It was all so prosaic and predictable. He was now immune to the effects of it. Thank you, Africa. Thank you, Malawi. He had chosen well.

He was even popular. Well, 'popular' was a stretch. But he was socially acceptable. He was back to his genial, charming, chameleon self. He was done with being honest and heart-worn. He cracked jokes when they were needed. He helped more with the chores. Stephanie even commented: said how much she appreciated it. He said, 'No problem,' very cheerfully, but was distracted by her face. She was growing grey around the temples. She was prematurely ageing. He didn't like ugliness or aesthetic slight, so he kept his distance thereafter.

However, he did enjoy Annabelle's company. She was always the nicest to him. She made an extra effort to draw him into conversations. She would leave him her leftovers when she'd grown too full. She force-fed him news. 'Stephanie's in love with Kondwani,' she'd say. 'Everyone knows it.'

'What – they had a thing?'

'No, I don't think so. I think it was unrequited. Or maybe requited, but it wasn't returned. Something like that.'

'Well, she's got no chance now. He doesn't even want his wife. I saw him the other day. He was just facing a wall. Talking to himself, I think.'

Annabelle frowned. 'Yes, it's so sad. He took his son's death so badly.'

'Or maybe this is precisely the time that Stephanie should just walk up to him and get her tits out. When he's not in his right mind.'

'Marcus.' She shot him a disapproving look, but he was bulletproof.

'What?'

'That's horrible. He's married and grieving. And, anyway, Stephanie's lovely.'

'I know, I was just trying to lighten the mood. And point out that she's not exactly a looker.'

'Oh, really? Well, who is a looker, here? Huh? Who meets your high standards?'

He slid into a comfortable groove. 'Well. Some are more easy on the eye than others. I like the cut of your jib. For instance.'

'The cut of my jib? Oh, you are hilarious. And thank you for the compliment. I feel so validated as a woman now.' She said all of this in a sarcastic tone, but her cheeks were pink and her eyes had sparkle.

Yes, he enjoyed flirting with Annabelle. Longer bursts of her could be intensely irritating. All that guilt and hand-wringing. A bit like Stephanie. But unlike Stephanie, she had a figure to die for and a loose, chatty tone. She wasn't his usual type, but maybe that was a good thing. She didn't look like Nancy and that made her an excellent distraction. A hobby for the rainy season. He toyed with her like a piece on a board game, knowing every move that he made was a winning one. But there was also this pleasant sense of pursuing something other than money or status, something with a human at the heart of it, with an attempt to like and be liked.

Except it wasn't long before he was heading over to breakfast and the rains had cleared up for a bit and he went to take his usual seat – and Annabelle wasn't anywhere to be seen.

He saw Katie loading up food on her plate. The others bustled around. Katie's hair was dyed again: the colour of sloe gin.

'Is Annabelle still sleeping?' He knew this was unlike her. A lie-in, to her, was a waste of time. A dress rehearsal for death.

'She's sick, I think.'

'Sick? With what?'

'I don't know.' Katie shrugged. Apart from that talk at that party, in the early days, she was still a bit distant. And usually hungover. 'Ask Stephanie.'

He looked over and saw Stephanie. She was still suffering with spots. A large whitehead gobbed out of her chin. He thought he'd ask Aldo instead.

Aldo kept a diary. He was recording another entry as he sipped his tea with a furrowed face. 'What can I do you for, Marcus?'

'Is Annabelle sick?'

'Who told you that?'

'Katie.'

'Excellent. Just the sort of privacy she'd hope for.'

'Is it something serious?'

'It's not serious, but it could have been. She's still at the medical clinic. They're assessing her. She may need to go back.'

'Go back?'

'Home, Marcus. England.'

'But you can't tell me what it is?'

'I can tell you that back ache was a symptom, and she was

right to listen to her body. She knew something was wrong, and it was.'

'But she'll be OK?'

'She'll be fine, Marcus. Fine. Frankly, I am delighted you care so much.' He laughed and slapped his back. It seemed a signal to leave him alone.

After that, the days lost their contour. Marcus felt a little out of odds, like he was losing his mojo. The listlessness came back: that familiar lull of non-feeling as you sink into the mattress and never want to spring up.

The only thing to shake him out of this state were the locusts. That day burned impressions in his mind; so even when he closed his eyes at night, all he could see were those long broad bodies, the long, flexed hind legs, the shiny armour of their spines.

The locusts didn't come to the village. The attack was further south, near Lake Chilwa. Grasshoppers were decimating huge tracts of land. But beyond flying a few planes to spray insecticide, there didn't seem much they could do to help. It was Ben, of course, who suggested sending some food baskets. Everyone agreed that it was a token effort but would be much appreciated.

Daniel, the new driver, could finally show off his mettle. He asked for someone to go with him and Marcus shot up an arm. He hadn't told anyone – but it was his birthday that day, the last one in his twenties, and he was desperate for a present; no matter how it was tied up and given, nor what it contained.

After a week of gathering soon-to-expire food items from the fridge, and rolling large tomatoes and avocados from the vegetable plot, the back of the van was filled with modest provisions. They set off the next morning.

Daniel was not a talkative sort. He was as smiley as Kondwani, but lacked the infectious passion. He preferred to tap on the steering wheel to the sound of clubby house music. Occasionally, he'd lift his hand and gesture a finger up to the car ceiling, in his own private rave.

Marcus did not mind. He stared out of the window and watched the landscape peter in and peter out. It grew greener and lusher, large birds soaring through the sky, their shivering wingspan, their fixed black eyes.

'Fuck,' he said at some point, despite himself.

Daniel turned. 'What?'

He reddened a little. 'It's crazy beautiful.' He didn't know why this was embarrassing. Maybe because he was a jumped-up city prick. City pricks shouldn't get this kind of awe in the fecund hills, in the endless ground. He was born for metal and glass and asphalt and brick. He was wired up to the grid.

Daniel cocked his head to one side, scratched out some ear wax. 'It's all right.'

'You don't like it?'

'I don't *not* like it. It's all right, man. You know – it's fine.'

'Fine. OK. You wouldn't write that on a postcard though, would you?'

'What?'

Marcus turned down the volume.

'Jesus, man! What you doing?'

'That bass line feels like it's cutting my skin open.'

He grunted. 'That's a sick beat, right there.'

'It wasn't a compliment.'

He shrugged. 'Whatever. Man, you're kind of uptight.'

'Uptight? I'm really not.'

'I thought everyone at this charity was meant to be, you know, slick and laidback and hippyish and whatever.'

'Well, you're here. Are you slick and laidback and whatever?'

'Kinda.' Daniel pursed his lips together, then opened them up for a smile. 'I mean, I needed the money, truth be known. This is good pay. Not a lot of people willing to come out here, speak the language, you know.'

'So I'm guessing you've been to Malawi before?'

'Oh yeah, once or twice. Family reasons. When we've really had to, you know? Like – a great auntie dying out here, or my dad needing to go pay his respects. Then we'd come out here. But it's expensive, you know? And my dad doesn't like to come out here. None of us do.'

'Why?'

He grunted again. 'You ask a lot of questions.'

'Well, usually things are pretty sociable, here – people interact with each other. I don't know if you were told.'

He shrugged. 'You're one to talk. Pardon the pun, like. But, anyway, I don't see the point. It's not like we're going to be pals or whatever.'

Marcus stiffened. 'Who said anything about pals? I was just making conversation. I don't want to be your friend. Trust me. I fucking don't.'

'All right, all right,' he laughed. 'Let's not get wound up now. Wow, I touched a nerve, eh? Anyhoo. To answer your question, since we're making conversation–'

'Forget it. I don't care.'

'Oh, he don't care. Look. It's a shithole. This country's a shithole. My dad couldn't wait to leave. He got lucky. Really lucky.'

Marcus had his arms crossed, his eyes lifted up to the sky again. There was a thin line for a mouth.

'Come on, you so curious before. Don't you want to know how he got lucky? Mate?'

'We're not mates, remember.'

'Oh come on. You wanna hear this story?'

'Yeah. You're just going to tell me anyway. So yeah.'

'A British woman. My mum. She came over to help with the church. She wasn't your typical churchgoer, you know? She didn't wear her hair in a bun, a prim little skirt, and whatever.

She was a pretty lady. Everybody said so. And she came from a good family. She had some money in the bank. And of course she'd been snapped up already, like you gonna expect. Married, proper, the lot. But my dad – he was badass, man. He was poor as shit, and a couple of years younger. But he was built like a fucking stallion. And she left her husband, everything – got a divorce right away. Managed to get him over to England on some temporary visa or whatever. They got married. They had me. Then they had my sister. Then another sister. They were fucking like rabbits, you know?'

'OK. That's kind of weird.'

'What?'

'To talk about your parents like that.'

He shrugged. 'Why? I like the fact that they were fucking like rabbits. They were in love, you know?'

'Were?' He saw the foreshadowing of death, disaster, departure. He should have known.

'No, mate. Just a figure of speech. They're still together. I reckon they're still fucking like rabbits!' He let out a guffaw and whacked the steering wheel. The van wobbled a little to the centre of the road. Marcus flinched. He saw Daniel take his eyes off the road to peek at him. 'Tell you what, though – my mum never went back to the church. She couldn't. She was Catholic. Divorced. I'm a child of sin. Love is a sin! Can you believe that? True love is a sin.' He leant over to turn up the volume. 'You don't really mind, do you, mate? It helps me concentrate. On the driving. These roads are fucked.'

Marcus couldn't quite belief that these musical thumps and klaxons could help a man drive. But he was done with conversation. It hadn't worked out well. And the land truly did look beautiful – although it pained him to think so, to sever geography from economics. It might not be the best place to live in the world, but by god it was beautiful. And even that... Some of the villagers looked so cheery, so contented, nonplussed, you could say – would they really swap their lives with him, given the chance? Well, OK. They would. Or would they? It was hard to know. So he gave up the thoughts to the ether, and his mind danced around objects.

When the car was near their destination, he saw a smear of orangey red. Involuntarily: 'Shit!'

The car skidded. 'Fuck me! You scared me. What is it, mate?'

Marcus pointed to the near horizon. 'That's not them, is it? They're not the locusts.'

Pause. 'I reckon it must be. They're red locusts, right? The air there looks *red*, man.'

'Shit. Fuck.'

'It's all right, they're just insects.'

'Can we wind up these windows?'

Daniel curled his lips, as if to titter. Then he reconsidered. 'Yeah, man. Sure.'

An electric wheeze as they whooshed towards red smoke. Now he could make out each locust in the air: darting and diving against the endless blue. Others stood out like scabs on the tall bleached grass beside them. There was humming and buzzing and clacking. One sucked itself to the windscreen. The antennae juddered. It disappeared into the swarm again.

'They look like lobsters. Like little lobsters.' Daniel laughed, but it died away quickly. There was something unsettling about nature when it was this unstoppable.

'I mean,' said Marcus, as if revving up mid-sentence. 'I've read about locusts and seen them on TV, but this is something else altogether.'

'Yep. That it is.'

'I saw this programme, once... David Attenborough or something. And there was this fact. About their brains. Hold on. Yes – swarming locusts have bigger brains than solitary locusts.

Something like that. Isn't that incredible?'

'What do you mean?'

'Well, locusts are usually solitary. They just hang out on their own. They're even a different colour.'

'Right. To what?'

'To how they are in this state – their swarm state. Something sets them off or something. Makes them turn from a solitary locust into a swarming locust. I think it's something about... getting food better. Surviving better. They work better as a pack. Anyway, it goes round in cycles.'

'Right. So what was that bit about the brains?'

'When they turn into swarming locusts, their colour changes. But also, their brains get bigger. I think they get about a third larger, or something. Something incredible like that. Their brains actually change. I think it's mainly to do with learning and processing and that kind of thing.'

'Right.'

'And I think it's even their brain chemistry that changes. I seem to remember that they have more *serotonin*. In a swarm.'

'What now?'

'Serotonin. It's a chemical in the brain. It affects things like your mood. I think it does a lot of other things, too, but I can't remember what. I'm not an expert. Like I said, this was just from the TV.'

'Right. So how does this work with locusts, mate? Ordinarily, they're sitting around, crying into their little leg thingeys? Talking to psychiatrists?' He went to laugh at his own joke, but the frown lines stopped him.

'I think they're just normally very shy. And the serotonin helps them deal with the swarm. It makes them more sociable. More aggressive. It's cut-throat out there, basically. They need to adapt to their circumstances.' His inner eyes drifted to the scrolling numbers, the briefcases, the two-faced handshakes. He clicked his tongue against his mouth.

By the time Annabelle returned, just three days later, he had grown quieter and quieter until he was barely anything at all. He was a husk in the hammock; a book held over his face like a tombstone. He wasn't really eating and he certainly wasn't drinking. Every time that Chris suggested football, he shook his head. He got up to go to the school, on autopilot, but felt like the children were not victims or humans or anything at all – just characters in a book. Something he could not attach to.

He saw the car skid down the dirt road. Daniel's hand thumping on the roof, the vibration of bass bolt through him. There was someone in the passenger seat, but the sun glared off the windows and cancelled them out. He saw a hand wipe away hair.

The car disappeared and then he heard the engine switch off. Two car doors slamming. A commotion of voices, the high-pitched squeal of women jumping up and down and hugging. Some clinking glasses. Some scraping of chairs.

Dora by the terrace, her face flushing with delight.

His head poked out of the book, an eyebrow raised.

'Annabelle's back!' she hollered, without looking back. A minute later, she was scurrying past him, waving a bottle opener.

He waited a few moments, listening to the sounds of the group. There is something both lovely and lonely in listening to the gentle hum of other people's merriment. Then he managed to freeze them out and battle with his head instead. Pros and cons, yeses and nos: back and forth, back and forth. Mental indecision is so tiring. In the end, he got up: brushed himself down, put on a 'social' face.

He stood on the outskirts of the welcoming committee, feeling awkward and shy. It was peculiar to feel these things. *This is what happens when you scrub yourself raw*, he thought – or words to that effect. He still had these damn sensitive insides, like some people have sensitive skin. Just about anything seemed to set off the itch, now.

Nobody spoke to him, and he did not know what to say. He tried to smile, to look unfazed and controlled. Dora dashed over with some wine. He physically forced himself forward, clinked glasses with Annabelle. But he chose a clumsy moment. She was locked in a vigorous conversation with Philippa, and it felt rude to intrude, and yet strange to step back. So he had to hover around them, aware of some invisible social ribbon that he had ripped right through. He knew it was weird, but he clinked glasses with her anyway, not saying a word; just turned his back on them both, resolving to go back to the hammock. Then he felt a hand on his shoulder, and her voice all around him: 'Marcus!'

He spun. Philippa was gone. The others were there somewhere, but somehow he couldn't see them. He just saw this pale, moon-like face beaming down at him, her eyelashes wet.

'I'm back,' she said, shyly, gesturing at herself.

'I heard. I heard the party from the hammock.' Somehow his voice sounded accusatory, so he tried to smile. 'Are you all right?' he added, trying to make his voice sound warmer.

She shrugged. 'I guess so. It was a bit scary though. The hospital wasn't the best.'

'I know. I remember being a bit shocked myself.'

She nodded. 'So... Has everything been all right, here?'

'Well. It's only been a couple of weeks. Not much has happened.'

'Sure. That's a really silly question. I guess it feels like I've been away forever.'

'Do you mind me asking what was wrong?'

She bit her lip, cast her eyes around her. 'Oh, it wasn't anything too terrible. Just really, really painful. The worst pain I've ever felt, actually...'

'Wow. I'm sorry.'

'That's OK. It was... Well, it started with that back pain. Do you remember? Anyway, I left it and left it. Turns out it was a kidney infection. I had a really high fever, I was vomiting. It was the middle of the night. It was pretty intense. Really horrible, actually. And I didn't respond to the antibiotics, straightaway... Ugh. They wanted to get me back to the UK, where there are stronger antibiotics. But I just...beat it myself in the end. Thank god.'

'You weren't tempted to go back home?'

'No.' She tipped her head to one side. 'I wasn't.'

Dora slipped in between them. 'Top-ups?' she railed. She was bouncing off the walls.

'I can't drink, remember?' Annabelle pushed her affectionately, laughing.

'Yeah, it's pretty awful to get a party going in your honour when you can't even drink. That's really bad of me, isn't it?'

'Oh it's not so bad. I like it. It's nice to be back here. That hospital – my god...'

'And Mr Mystery here has been pining for you *the entire time.*'

'What?' Annabelle looked up at him, blinking. 'Oh don't be daft, Dora.' She was glowing a little.

Marcus's face hardened until the veins in his temples stuck out. 'What the fuck are you about, Dora?'

'OK, OK. Calm down. It was a joke.'

'I just wanted some time to myself. Is that such a fucking crime in this place?'

'Look, it was just a joke. Christ. Come on.'

'No, you fucking come on. Just fuck off, you fucking bitch.' He threw the glass into the bushes and strode off to the hammock, his face pulsating. How dare she. How dare she? How fucking embarrassing. How fucking moronic. The fury grew so much that it was almost unbearable. He threw a fist into a wall and recoiled with an odd kind of pleasure. Then he sunk into the hammock and cried.

'Oh no. For God's sake, no.' He heard footsteps. He went to get up and go to his room, but she was already standing there.

'Marcus, what was that about?'

He placed the book over his face. 'Did I kill the party?'

'Just a little.'

'Well. I'm sorry about that. But she's a fucking cunt.'

'Marcus. Can you not talk like that? Please.'

Ordinarily, he would scoff at that, maybe laugh at her Pollyanna-ness, maybe jibe at her delicate ways. But he didn't have the energy and he was now deflating too rapidly. 'OK. I'm sorry.'

'She didn't really do anything.'

He sighed. 'I think she did.'

'What? She was just teasing us. That's what Dora does.'

'Well, it's embarrassing.'

'Oh. Right. So it's that terrible for somebody to suggest that you've got a thing for me. I'm such a hideous witch.'

'No, I don't mean it like that. Oh god...' Talking to women could be such a tactical game, he thought. So many traps to fall into.

'Can you at least take that book off your face?'

He waited a moment, heard her quick, shallow breath. 'All right.' He slid it down his body. Now she could see how on fire he was, how red and livid.

She perched beside him. 'You know what, Marcus? I'm just going to say it. I was thinking about saying it the entire time I was in hospital.'

He closed his eyes, expectantly.

'You're a twat.'

They popped open. 'What?'

'You're a total twat. You can be so rude. So inconsiderate. You pick fights with everyone. You can seem...heartless. At times. Callous. Cold and indifferent and detached. And then flying into these ridiculous rages. It's embarrassing. Seeing you act like a twat.'

Somehow this made him feel better. 'I'm not going to deny it. It's kind of nice to hear you say it. I'm a twat. It's true.'

'Except...' She leant forwards. 'Sometimes you're not one. Sometimes I feel like there's more to it than that. Anyway, I could be wrong. But, either way, here's the thing. I really like you. I mean, I really, really like you. And I don't know what it is: your smell, your eyes, I don't know. But I've liked you the entire time. And I know it's been obvious.'

'Mmmn.'

'That's all you've got to say?' She cast down her eyes. 'Well, it doesn't matter. I just thought I'd give you the chance. Let you know that it was OK... If you did like me. Because I like you, too. But I don't want a holiday fling. That's not my thing at all. So I want you to understand that. But I'm just... I really like you. Oh dear.' She covered her face and shuddered. 'This is coming out so bad.'

He shuffled up to one side and patted some room behind him. She hesitated a moment and then clambered in. The hammock swayed wildly. They giggled, nervously, like schoolchildren. Both of them stared up at the blanket of night, at the stars studded in it. He stretched out an arm around her head. She wiggled deeper.

'I like you,' he said, after some whittling away of time. He felt her tense.

'There's a "but" coming.'

'There's no "but". All right, maybe there is.'

'Well, just tell me then. Just give it to me.'

'Like I said, I like you.' He didn't even know why he liked

her. It was like liking a sheet of blank paper. Her skin was so thin – literally. You could see the veins right through it. 'That's why I've been acting like a total dick. Following you around like a dog.'

'I did wonder,' she said, wryly. 'I did think – maybe he does like me. But sometimes you would just act so cool and indifferent.'

'That's just my style.'

'Well, it's really annoying.'

'And sexy?' he teased.

'Hmmm.' She waited a few moments. 'Yeah, maybe. A bit. Annoyingly.'

'You don't want to admit it, but I know that girls love the bastards.'

'Well, maybe there's some who do. But I never thought I was one of those. And I really, really hope you're not a bastard.'

'I've never been put before a judge.'

'Well, what do you think?'

'I think that I probably–'

Suddenly there was an explosion of silence and the lights cut off. A collective groan from the dining terrace. The frantic searching for torches.

'The generator,' said Annabelle, stating the obvious.

'That generator's so old.'

'Yep. God, it's so dark here. I can't even see my hand in front of my face.'

'Are you frightened?'

'Of the dark? No! I'm not six years old.' But she was frightened. And so was he.

'All right, all right.'

'Do you think we should go help them out? With packing everything away?'

'No, let's just lie here a little bit. They'll come looking for us if they need us. Let our eyes acclimatise.'

'OK.' She breathed out extra long and hard. 'I guess it does make the stars seem even bigger and better.'

'Yes, it's sort of scary though, isn't it?'

'Ahh, so you're the one who's frightened!'

'Well... You've got to admit it's pretty primitive. Blackout – the curve of space – the sound of animals and insects all around us.'

'OK, now you're freaking me out. Shit, what if there's a spider on me right now? About to climb over my face! Marcus, this might not even be safe...'

He was wondering the same thing; fighting between instinctive fear and the enjoyment of an attractive woman snuggling up close to him. 'OK, let's give it five minutes more. I'm comfortable. This is nice. We've got privacy at last.'

'All right,' she said, unsure. 'Maybe you're right. Just five more minutes. So how long have you liked me?' She rolled her eyes, coquettish, like she'd earned the compliments.

'I kind of liked you from the beginning. And when you told me you were born in Addiscombe–'

'What? How did that help at all?'

'I like a coincidence. I always have. Somebody once told me to look out for them, to see them as a sign. Like somebody was writing your life and trying to show you where the story is leading...'

'I like that.'

'I even kept a book once. With every coincidence inside it. I used to scan it for signs. Didn't really make sense, though. And I didn't bring it to Malawi. Don't even know the last time I updated it...'

'But what kind of coincidences? Stuff like that Addiscombe thing?'

'Pretty much. I don't really remember too many of them,

they never seemed to make sense, just this trail of clues that didn't reveal any great mystery. Well, I do remember this one entry, for some reason. I've never liked fiction, but this girl I was sleeping with, she did read a lot. And she kept going on about this book she loved, *The Comforters* – I think it was Muriel Spark. And one time she read a lot of it aloud, and there were all these mentions of *Brompton Oratory*, it's this church in Knightsbridge. And I'm not even sure why that bit stuck in my mind. I remember thinking – Brompton Oratory. I've never been there, I wonder what it's like, I don't really know that bit of London. What's an Oratory? That kind of thing. And the very next day, on the radio, this song comes on and it sort of grabs my attention. And the DJ says, that's a song, Brompton Oratory, by the singer Nick Cave. And I don't really know Nick Cave, but I looked up the lyrics – and I find out that it's not even a new song – and I was looking for clues, and these lines just stuck out at me, and I thought – are they significant? Maybe they'll help me. And I wrote them all down in that little book, that Book of Coincidences. I wrote it all down. Stuff like that.'

'Wow. That sounds fun. Maybe you need to revisit the book.'

'I might do. But I know what you can tell me,' he said, self-conscious of his monologue. 'Why you're here.'

'What do you mean?'

'Why you came to Malawi. Why are you here?'

'Well, I don't know why you're here, either.'

'OK, but I asked first. How did you end up here?'

She sighed. He fluttered his hand up to her hair and started to stroke it. 'That's really nice.'

'Well, now that you're comfortable, how about you tell me your story.'

She stretched out her body and wrapped herself into his limbs. 'Where do you want me to start?'

'Well, that's the decision of every story. Does it start with your birth? Does it start with your parents? Their parents? Their parents' parents? Or does it start with an event: an event that changed your life forever?'

'Wow. This is intense.'

'We have the universe as our audience. The stars are in the front row. I think we need to talk about more than just our hobbies, don't you?'

'Well, I think I'd actually begin it with a hobby.'

'All right. That's your decision. You're the author of your life, after all.'

'Yes. I'm going to start it there.'

'Where?'

'With my tennis.'

'Tennis!' He laughed. 'I really didn't picture you as a sportswoman.'

She whacked him in the side. 'And why not?'

'You're not that athletic looking.'

'Tall and gangly, you mean?'

'No. Graceful. Like a ballerina.'

'Ballerinas aren't five foot eleven, you charmer. Anyway, I want to begin it there.'

'OK. Fire away.'

'I just sort of took to tennis very young. I had a natural gift for it. I was really, really good. And my parents, understandably, saw a talent there and thought I should at take advantage.'

'Well, the tennis player with the advantage wins the point.'

'Yes. Very good. I didn't even mean that as a pun.'

'Sorry. Carry on.'

'Well, I got coached. I got entered into all these tournaments. It became pretty serious. I was genuinely being pushed towards taking up tennis professionally. Entering professional tournaments. Trying to get a ranking. But all this time – and my parents didn't know this – I was going through inner turmoil.

That's not even an exaggeration. I hated it. I was just doing it to please my parents.'

'You hated tennis?'

'No, I loved the tennis. It was brilliant. But I hated the spectators.'

'What?'

'The minute you start taking tennis seriously, you start to get spectators. I'd be standing there, about to play my serve, and I'd suddenly become aware of all these grinning faces. All staring at me. Fixed on me.'

'They were probably checking out your legs. In those teeny skirts you wear.'

'I wore shorts to play tennis.'

'Really?'

'Yes.'

'Oh. OK.'

'Don't sound so disappointed. I was playing tennis, I wasn't out there to titillate perverts like you. I wasn't a stripper.'

'OK. I'm sorry. Although you still had your legs out. Lovely.'

'Well, anyway. Let's move on.'

'Sure. So you hated the spectators?'

'Yes. I mean; I properly hated them. I started to get these panic attacks. I suppose you'd call them that. I mean, I fainted a couple of times on court. Honestly. I even stopped eating. I was too nervous to eat.

'And it just seemed so unfair. Why did we have to have spectators? Why does sport have to be public? Biologists don't have to do their experiments in an arena. You don't buy tickets to watch a carpenter make a bench.'

'But sport is meant to be entertainment.'

'I didn't see it that way. I just wanted to play a game against my opponent, with just a ball girl or boy and an umpire – that's that. Play it in isolation, under lock and key, with nobody else watching. And then you could release the results afterwards, to the fans.'

'It doesn't sound like it would be much fun to be a fan, if I'm honest.'

'Well, OK, but that's what I wanted. I loved tennis, I was good at it. I was actually great at it. I just didn't want to be watched. Of all the things I had to be good at – it had to be that.'

'So what happened then?'

'I eventually told my mum and stepdad that I was going to quit. They were devastated. We didn't have a lot of money – still don't. I think they saw me as their ticket out of the sticks. I didn't want to let them down entirely, so I paid more attention to my studies, but it was a little too late. When you're seen as being good at sport, you're sort of taken out of academia. It's a given. Everyone sees the two as diametrically opposed.'

'Well, you learnt to use phrases like "diametrically opposed". So you can't be that thick.'

She whacked him again. 'I didn't say I was thick. But I didn't come out with the grades that I needed at the time. And I was disillusioned and unsure of myself, and I left school at sixteen.

'I don't know why I was so self-conscious about being watched like that. I think I've always been shy, always been aware of myself. Hyper aware of myself. I've always carried this guilt. I guess it must stem from something; I guess I can think of a couple of things. But who knows? Anyway, I sort of decided that you had to help others to be happy. I started volunteering for a charity and I just drifted into this: a lot of temping, some short-term contracts, some voluntary stuff. This is the first time I've done it outside the UK though. I really wanted to see it for myself, you know? I know that sounds terrible. Really patronising. But I wanted to see a developing country for myself. I wanted to escape suburbia and all those tennis clubs. My mum and stepdad always made me feel like we were so hard-up and hard-done-by. I guess I wanted to feel *lucky*. Oh god, that sounds sick. Doesn't it?'

'No. I don't think so. It's good to appreciate the fact that you're lucky.'

'Well, do you feel lucky?' she slurred, like Dirty Harry. 'Seriously, what's your story? I told you mine.'

'It didn't really feel like a story. More a vignette.'

'Well, it was some of it, at least. Now tell me some of yours.'

'If I told you my story, it would probably be full of lies. That's what I've done my entire life. Tell lies. Con people. Take advantage.'

'Seriously?'

'Seriously. It's always been so much easier to just embellish things. It kind of just happens without even thinking about it.'

'Give me examples.'

'Well, if I wanted a day off work, I'd ring and say the house had been sucked into a sink hole. Rather than just saying I had a cold. You know, it gave life a bit of colour, something for people to talk about. I mean, can't life be dreary and dull, without a bit of colour? So the lies would just tumble out of me. And sometimes I'd use those lies to mess with people's heads, give me what I wanted.'

'Well – that's horrible.' She pulled away from him. 'Why even tell me that?'

'Because I'm getting tired of it. When I got here, I thought I'd try out honesty for a while. Be brutally honest, for a change. Say out loud what I'm thinking and to hell with how people think of me. But then I had this idea that a few lies are OK, maybe it's just the intention that needs changing. But, anyway, I don't have that urge to lie to you. I don't know if it's this forced situation. But I like you in ways I don't ordinarily like women.'

'Right. Thanks, I guess. That sounds kind of clinical.'

'Maybe it is. But let me start with my job. I basically make more money for rich people. I see food like a banknote. But I don't want to be sentimental about poverty, either. Being poor really sucks. And it doesn't make you a nicer person, actually. It can make you angry and stressed out and resentful. You can't think of anything beyond what you're going to get on your plate. That kind of survival, day in, day out – it hardens you.'

'But being rich doesn't make you that nice, either.'

'Well, either extreme takes you out of reality and, I guess, only deeper into yourself.'

'OK. So you were out for yourself, looking after number one. But you quit that job. You came out here.'

'Yes. That surprised me. I didn't know I had it in me – to try and mellow out here, get used to being somewhere like this.'

'Was it guilt? Like – for me?'

'No, I didn't feel guilt. I felt chosen. I used to, I mean. But there were all these deaths in my life that knocked me back very hard. I used to have this incredible belief in my thoughts. I could hold up planes. I honestly believed that. When I flew on planes, I'd have to visualise the plane flying for the entire flight, to keep it up. It took a lot out of me. Long-haul flights knocked me out for days. No, seriously, they did. But then I felt like I'd been wrong all along. I wanted to try something else out, for a change. I wanted to feel very small and like nobody at all. I wanted to see what that would do to me.'

'Well, it's worked. Hasn't it?'

'In some ways, it has; in some ways, it hasn't. I wanted to feel smaller – but this has just made me feel bigger. I mean, we're like gods to these people.'

'Steady, now. I wouldn't put it like that, myself. But anyhow – this all started with losing somebody?'

'Yes.'

'Well, it can really change you. I know that. I saw a death

once. I mean. I saw someone die. I thought it was going to be spiritual, I guess? I guess I'd seen too many films. I thought it was going to be spiritual, but it was just – mechanical. Like a dial on a speaker being wound down to zero.'

'That's funny. I've had lots of people die on me but I've never seen anyone die.'

'That's lucky.'

'Maybe. And maybe that's why I feel there's just so much more than that.'

'Than what? What do you mean?' Her breaths getting deeper.

'Than a piece of machinery. I feel like I'm my feelings, my thoughts, my memories. That's got to make me more than just mechanical.'

'But that's just it. I thought seeing somebody die would sort of conquer my fear of dying. Because I'm really scared of it. I thought it might be like that therapy when they make you hold a spider – when you're scared of spiders? For ten seconds, twenty seconds – until you're holding a spider in your hand for an entire minute, then two minutes, ten minutes, even.'

'Desensitisation.'

'Yes, I thought it would do that. It would "desensitise" me. But it just made me more scared.'

'Of dying? How?'

'This feeling that one day I'm going to get switched off like that. All these emotions, all the memories – like you said. They're not going to exist anymore. They'll be nowhere on this planet, and life will just go on without me.'

'But even if you don't believe in God, that's no reason to be afraid,' he persisted. 'That's what I've been thinking. It will be just like before you were born. You didn't exist then. The world was there – without you in it.'

'You see. I don't buy that argument. You can't compare the two states.'

'Sure you can.'

'You can't! That was totally different. That was "pre" all these thoughts, all these feelings – all this *you*.'

'So? One is pre and one is post.'

'But that's so different. It's really, really different. I mean, without wanting to sound too sixth-formy about it. One is nullity, the other is annihilation. Don't you think? You've been snuffed out. You exist – and then one day you don't.'

'So you'll live on through the photos, through the people you meet, the people you love, the actions you take, even your Facebook statuses.'

'That's not the same. That's not living. That's not the same at all.'

'Fuck. And you said I was intense.'

'I'm sorry.' She laughed. 'Maybe you've met your match?'

'Yeah. Sure. But can you talk about football?'

'I can talk about football. I can ramble on about the weather if you'd like.'

'And I thought you were a Pollyanna.'

'I always seem like that. When you first meet me. I'm actually a total killjoy.'

'You can say that again.'

'Well, anyway, what about you? Who died for you?'

'Jesus.'

'Ha ha.'

'Oh, you know.' He coughed, uncomfortable. 'Just some people.'

'You don't want to talk about it? While we're getting all up close and personal?'

He really didn't want to talk about it, and yet she was so easy to talk to. She was one of those people who convinces you that you've always known them. It makes you want to believe in souls and past lives or the circularity of time; there must be some mysterious reason behind it.

'You don't want to know. Trust me.'

'No, trust *me*. Come on.'

'Well, I'm technically an orphan. For a start.'

'Woah.'

'Yep.'

'Since you were a kid?'

'No. My dad died when I was a teenager. My mum, not so long ago. But it's still pretty weird to be my age and not have parents. It's really weird.'

'I bet. I'm so sorry.' She squeezed his hand in the darkness.

He took a long deep sigh. 'And then I killed someone.' She let go of his hand. 'What? OK, you're messing with me, aren't you?'

There was a pause. 'Sure.'

'Come on, Marcus. You're messing with me.'

'Well, what I mean is that I wanted it to happen.'

'I'm confused.'

'It was my girlfriend. My first love. Actually – my only love. So far.'

'Were you together long?'

'A few years.'

'Hold on. You mean – this girl. Your first love. She's dead?'

'Yep. Car accident. She was twenty-two.'

'That's terrible.'

'It was. It is. It kind of...' He trailed off.

'But why did you want her... You know.'

'Dead?'

'Oh god. That sounds terrifying out loud. I'm feeling like maybe I should get out of this hammock with you.'

'Look, it was just in the moment. We had an argument. Things weren't going so well for us. And I wished for it.'

'Well, that doesn't make it your fault.'

Another pause. 'Manslaughter. Doesn't it sound arcane? Man. Slaughter. Like you're suddenly a Viking or something.'

'But it wasn't manslaughter. Everyone wishes bad things on people sometimes. That just makes you human. This is just like what you were saying about the planes. Like you're in control of a plane. But you're not. Anyway, to have so many loved ones die. I can't even imagine it. I'm so sorry. I feel bad we even got onto this subject.'

'No, it's all right. The concept of blame is an interesting one though – isn't it? I guess that's what it boils down to. Why I'm here, I mean. I'm just trying to figure out blame. Who's to blame? There's got to be somebody. Somebody's got to be held accountable.'

'It's just life, Marcus. Life is messy. There are losers and winners. Anyway, shall we change the subject? This is starting to ruin my mood.'

He wriggled up to her. 'So, what would improve it?'

'Oh, I don't know.'

'This?' She couldn't see the movement that preceded it; the wet brush of lips. Tongue, touching. A hand at the back of her head, tousling hair like violin strings.

'Yeah, that definitely helps' – and it felt like a brilliant line in a movie. Something Lauren Bacall would deadpan in sunset. The shades of the world hoisted up into Technicolor. Fade out. Film over.

But we need to fade in again. New scene. Cover of night. He dreams of Nancy. She is sitting in their old flat, on that shabby, mousey sofa. Her legs tucked in beneath her backside. She hugs a cushion to her chest.

He says: 'So you're not dead?'

She says: 'No. Why would I be dead? Don't be silly.'

And he believes her. Because that's her voice – so clearly. And surely nobody can mimic a voice that well? And these are her mannerisms – down to the smallest detail. The light streaming in through the windows. He knows something isn't right, but he cannot remember what. He just resets himself here: she is alive and he is in the flat and this is reality. He steps forward for a hug. He thinks: is that warmth? Is that the warmth of her arms? Can he feel it?

She laughs. And it is her laugh so exactly. It rings off into the trill intake of breath.

He couldn't remember all of the dream when he woke up in the dawn. He seemed to remember something weird about a garden. Radiation in a cabbage. Was that right? What had it been? He blinked into the daylight. The coos of the dove outside the window.

He looked down. He expected to see Nancy's face cuddled up to his chest. Instead, there was a splay of dark hair and a body tilted on its side. A leg twitched out. Of course. It was Annabelle. Nancy didn't exist anymore. He looked around him, at the sun that streamed through the windows. Sun that Nancy could not see. The sounds of birds – things that Nancy could not hear. And yet he had reconstructed her like Frankenstein; made her up out of the magic and matter of his head. Her voice... It had reeled off like a recording. How had he done that? How does the brain do it?

He wondered if he had constructed Annabelle, too. She felt pretty real in his arms, though. She felt pretty real last night – when he led her back, furtively, to the dark of his room, and they had coiled up together like they were snakes being charmed.

Now he started to wonder about the rest of his life. Last night, he had confessed a lot. The alcohol had gone straight to his head. But hearing it out loud made him feel he could actually shake off the past like skin. He could be a better man. Maybe he could try and do something incredible, out here in Africa. He didn't know what, exactly – but something. It's never too late, is it? Yes, he would sell his flat back in London and give the money to charity. He'd do whatever it took. He'd never forget the lessons these past months had taught him. He'd never forget how rock-bottom he had felt and how sky-high he was now. He wanted to help people and change the world. After all, you only get one life. You only get one world. You should only get one masturbating ghost in your bedroom.

Part Three
Either / Neither / Both

Chapter
Ten

This is how I proposed.

The pyramids of Giza were all stuck out like giant sandcastles. I could see the tip of the crumbling sphinx. Camels trailed at the edges, a chain of minivans. Crowds roaring towards the limestone mountains.

Annabelle could only see me – and the salad cart.

We were sitting in Pizza Hut. We had a table view. I was slurping my coke, looking at those triangles, thinking I had expected them bigger. But now was the moment. We'd just made our order for deep-pan pizzas – cheesy crust – and who knew how quickly the blasted things would arrive...?

When the waitress left us, the whole moment felt spiritual and exquisite, like we were on our own stairway to heaven, lifting us off from this sacred ground that still held dead pharaohs. There was an old-fashioned romance; an electric buzz to the air. I was Indiana Jones in human form.

I stumbled to the ground, and it was kind of awkward. I bruised my knee. I said 'Shit' beneath my breath – but I don't think she heard. Because by then I had whipped out the box and flicked the top open – and there sat the ring, shining brilliant in sunbeams.

'Oh my god,' she said, flipping back a bang. 'Oh my god.' She started to laugh. 'Oh my god!'

'Annabelle,' I said, clearing my throat. 'I was going to say this outside, but I was worried about the hawkers.'

'They'd probably nick it.'

'They probably would.' She obviously couldn't see it was cheap. 'And we've got a splendid view here.'

'Splendid.' She was still giggling. Giggling and blushing. In fact, it was getting annoying.

'This isn't a joke, Annabelle. I've thought about it long and hard. All the time during these few months of travelling. And I know it might seem kind of crazy. I know it might seem fast. But...' I waited a split second; I wanted the tension to tease up the hair on her neck. 'Will you marry me?'

'Oh my god,' she said, as if still in shock; and I know it is terrible, but I wanted to hit her.

'Annabelle, please give me the honour. I've fallen for you hard. I haven't been this happy for years. I mean – ever. I know that we're right together. I know we can make each other happy.' I was starting to lose balance. My knee was fucking killing.

'Oh my god, Marcus,' she said, but then the pizzas arrived.

The waitress spoke broken English, but it was clear that she had no precedent for this. She looked between us – at our moment – and gave a smile that said absolutely everything and nothing. 'Pizza,' she said at last, heaving the eleven-inch monsters on to round wooden mats. The cheese was still bubbling.

I tried to keep my eyes focused on Annabelle but it was difficult, with that smell drifting up to my nostrils. My attention wavered to these giant carbohydrate slabs: as impressive as ancient masonry if you haven't had breakfast.

It could be she was hungry, too – because she seemed to hurry up then. She spluttered 'Yes'. A smile danced over my face and I dragged her close and smelt her hair. I slid the ring on to her finger, and it was a little bit loose, but we didn't comment on that. We just stared into each other's faces with absolute wonder and delight. Then we fell back on our chairs and, without really realising, we were munching on lunch and back to chitchatting idly. A bit of crust got wedged in the (fake) diamond centrepiece. I tried to lick it out for her. It felt very erotic. I wanted this moment to last forever.

'We're going to get married,' I thought. I couldn't quite believe it. I still can't, really. That's how I proposed. Right by the pyramids. I mean: you could see them from the bloody window.

I'd bought the ring from some dodgy souk stall, but it looked kind of vintage and sweet. She was now twisting it in her hands and pointing out scratch marks. I told her (over ice cream) that it had been my mother's, and her mother's before her – I wanted to make the story better, a bit more romantic. Never mind the implausibility if you stopped to really think about it. No, of course she blushed all over her body and flung her hands up to her face and gasped. She said 'I love it' and 'Oh my god!'

But how did we get here? How did I turn so soppy? Do I need to rewind?

Let's go back to Malawi. I was lying in bed, listening to that cooing dove. I was holding this woman, this magnificent body that I had fucked just a few hours prior. I could still taste her in my mouth, all sour yoghurt and tamarind.

Well, it was kind of awkward at first. Now that we'd screwed, she was out of my system. The allure wasn't so great; the mystery had gone. But I had sworn not to be one of 'those' guys. So I tried to be nice to her: we kept hanging out, sneaking off for secret rendezvous. I didn't mind. I got laid. Other people probably noticed, but we liked to pretend that we were being all cool and hush-hush. Besides, people didn't really talk about me anymore. My sudden bursts of temper had me down as psychotic. People tended to keep their distance.

It was weird how it happened. When I wasn't around her, I would start to really miss her. We would creep into each other's rooms at night. We'd lie all night spooning and cupping. That sure wasn't easy on a single bed. And we didn't always fuck each other, either. Sometimes it wouldn't happen that way, if I'm honest. We would just lie there, soft and tender. We fell slowly into intimacy.

Not long after, we announced our coupledom to the group. People tried to look surprised, but their eyes were cold and reconciled.

'I hope this isn't going to be a problem,' said Annabelle.

'Why would it be a problem?' asked Philippa. 'It's not the first time it's happened. And it will happen again. We're all thrown so closely together.'

I wondered if Philippa had ever had a Malawian romance. It was hard to even know how old she was. She could be forty, fifty, sixty... Her hair was so tightly pinned back, the grey wisps all greasy and flat.

'I don't want it to affect that closeness,' said Annabelle. 'I've made such good friends here.'

I have to admit that I looked up wildly at that point. Friends? She'd made friends? I couldn't count a single one of them as a friend. Even Chris. He was a thing that played football with me, something mechanical and reflex.

At first, we carried on like we'd always done. We went along to school to teach the children. We watched the new building bloom before our eyes. It was painted in brilliant candy pop strokes.

At night, I would retire to my room to read books on business and economics and maths. My brain felt like it needed the stimulation. If I was too tired for that, I would retreat to the hammock and try to find constellations in the stars from some old astronomy textbook.

While I read or studied, I would hear Annabelle with the others, laughing and chatting and always seeking approval. Now she had admitted that part of herself, it was a little bit painful – even embarrassing – to hear her out there. Her voice would sound so desperate. She laughed at everyone's punch line.

Then she would creep back to me, the smile dropped from her face, looking worn and fatigued. She would reach out her arms and scramble beside me. I'd stroke her face or rub her nipples. I just liked the physical heft of her.

Soon that wasn't enough. We wanted to be together all the time: not necessarily saying anything, but being close, almost touching – like two plants twisted together at the roots.

I started to get really resentful, hearing her out on the veranda. And she became less tolerant of the charade. Increasingly, we would hide away together and carry on with separate tasks, but intertwined: me, reading my book; her, scribbling or sketching.

But we were always aware of other people: their footsteps, murmurs, snores. The pressure of them grew into a colossal intrusion. We felt their presence when we had sex. We were conscious of them as we kissed. We could feel their existence in every stretch of the village.

Our feelings grew deeper – fuck, what else do I need to say? Basically, we just had enough. We started to dream up these fantastical thoughts. Late-night conversations about the great continent we stood in; how there was still so much we had to see. We daydreamed endlessly about having some privacy, about living for ourselves.

When we announced we were leaving, we heard Stephanie

gasp and Dora cry out. Philippa beseeched us to stay – 'There is still so much to do. And we're almost there. Let's at least complete the project. Can you stay just a few months more, just so you've done the full year?' I felt Annabelle's hand stiffen in mine, so I shook my head firmly. I recounted the long tourist list of Africa. We were still very young; now was the time to do it. The truth is: the more we cared for each other, the less we cared about anyone else. Isn't that the same for everyone?

That night, tucked up in bed, Annabelle glanced at me with her long, pale face: 'Have we done the right thing? I feel like I'm letting them down.'

'You haven't let them down. We've been here ages. We've seriously done our bit.'

'But we're going to leave the children. Just as they've gotten used to us. They get so excited every time they see us.'

'We only ever signed up for the year. They'll get excited about the next people, too. It's not us they're excited about – it's just the attention they get.'

'But we said we'd try to do great things here. We said we'd try to make a difference.'

'We still can. We just need some time out. We can always come back.'

'That's true,' she said, crinkling up her nose. 'I hadn't thought of that.'

'We just need some time together, Annabelle. Some quality time. We need to have fun.'

'It's true,' she laughed. 'There's so much squalor. It feels so hard to fall in love here.' She flinched suddenly: realising what she had said. I was terrified of the word, but I didn't let her know it. I just smiled and reeled her in: my catch of the day.

\#

It was odd seeing them all grouped together like that: waving us off. All those faces in line: bodies I'd been cooped up besides for months and months. Now retreating into another part of my brain, being stored slapdash in some file that I knew I would seldom retrieve.

Annabelle hugged and kissed them all. She exchanged Facebook invites and email addresses. She cried so much that the mascara came out of her nose with the snot. 'I'll never forget them,' she sobbed. 'This has been the best time of my life. I'll never forget this country or its people. I'll never forget a single thing about this. It's life changing,' she said, her hand gripping my thigh for emphasis. 'You don't forget an experience like this. Not ever.' It was a long and tedious journey out of there. My shirt was forever ruined by her tears.

She cheered up once we were in the convertible. The South African vineyards before us. The sun melted on us. The mountains staggering up into air. And these long, neat lines of structured greenery, everywhere that you looked. We had the sharp burn of alcohol in our throats. She sang along to the radio. I tapped my hand on the roof.

We stayed in youth hostels for a while, and it was fun at first. It felt like a grand adventure. Annabelle liked to talk to the other guests in the common room. I'd usually distract myself cooking some pasta on the hob. But we'd end up in bunk beds and the breakfasts were terrible. It felt like we were still stuck in this fixed grin of communal poverty.

I checked my accounts in Cape Town. It was the first time I had done it for a very long time. I'd be lying to say I didn't feel a heartbeat stampede to see that big number shine back at me.

I shook myself together, threw a wad of cash in my wallet. Although standing by bulky building blocks and ornate bell towers, I had seen the scrap-metal slums that huddled around this city: their stink and rust and ruin. I knew that these people would be rabid with envy. They had probably picked up the scent of my wealth already.

I hurried back to Annabelle. She was sitting in a café, engrossed in a guidebook. That's all she ever seemed to do: delight in the endless possibilities. 'We could do this'; 'We could do that'. I don't think it even mattered what we did. The daily lists and plans were enough to build her a fortress of optimism.

'Hi,' I said.

She looked up, smiling: relaxed and pink. 'Hi.'

I slid into the booth, opposite her. 'I've got a plan.' I stretched out my hands. 'Let's stay in a really nice hotel tonight.'

Her eyes narrowed and darted around. Her lips jutted out. She looked like a cartoon version of confused. 'What do you mean? We've already called the hostel. I spoke–'

'We can call them back. Let's stay at a nice hotel.'

'Marcus,' she sighed. 'We haven't got enough money to–'

'I've got enough money. Just one night. I want to treat us. Please.'

It took another few minutes of persuasion before she finally acquiesced. Then it was time to stand outside and make some quick calls on the cheap mobile that I'd picked up at the market. The radiation burned against my temple. I didn't notice too much though: I was swooning inside at the hotel I'd booked. It was the most expensive place in Cape Town.

She blanched when we first walked in. She said: 'Marcus, how can we afford this?' The sweet, innocent thing – I don't think she really realised how loaded I was.

When she saw the suite, and the terrace Jacuzzi, and the champagne on the bed, she involuntarily squealed. But then the guilt set in, and we had an hour of that. 'Oh god, but those slums,' she moaned, small hands splayed across her face. 'To think of those people living in those boxes of tin, and we're sitting here...in this.'

And then it led back to Malawi. 'Those children we taught would not even be able to conceive of something like this.

Something as grand as this. Oh my god. It just feels wrong. I feel terrible. It feels a bit vulgar; don't you think so?'

'It's just for one night, sweetheart,' I said. I'd found out quite quickly that the word 'sweetheart' was like valium to her. It steadied her nerves: made her woozy and weak. 'I just think we deserve it,' I persevered. And I did – I was so sick of those bunk beds. I was so sick of the sticky air. I turned the air conditioning up high. I threw back the Egyptian cotton sheets with an ecstatic shiver at the thread count.

'Well, it's just one night,' she relented.

I grabbed her hand and pulled her near me. She felt so soft and pliable. I lifted her t-shirt and felt the turning cogs of passion: once started, it is hard to stop.

I gave in to her the next night, and we returned to the hostel. But I could see that she missed the mini-bar and room service and the room with a view. The 'off' smell smelt 'offer'; the bed sheets felt coarser.

In the morning, she banged my top bunk. I peered down. She said: 'I had a terrible sleep.'

'Really?' I had, too – but I wanted to hear the confession.

'Oh my God, don't tell me you didn't hear those people come in really late last night?' She was hissing the words, pointing to a group of travellers opposite, fallen asleep in their clothes. 'They were so bloody loud.'

'Yes, I think I did wake up a few times. Now that you mention it.'

'I don't think I got any sleep at all.'

The blood was rushing to the front of my head. But I held myself there.

'Marcus,' she began – falteringly. 'Marcus, the hotel yesterday was ridiculous. Brilliant – but ridiculous. But maybe... If you've got enough money... And of course I can try to help a bit, too... Well, maybe we can stay in hotels. For this trip. I mean – not overblown hotels like the one last night. Not five-star hotels. But nice, three-star hotels. Three-star equivalent. You know – normal, decent hotels. OK, so they're a bit more expensive. But, I think... If we're not able to sleep here?'

I tried not to look triumphant. 'OK, sweetheart. Let's go and get some breakfast and talk it over properly.'

And of course: over slimy eggs and anaemic toast, it was all agreed and settled.

I booked the hotels after that. While they weren't up to the calibre of that first luxury pad, I always paid a bit more than Annabelle knew. If we were going to travel, then let's do it in relative comfort. Just because we were in Africa, it didn't mean we had to live like Africans. After all, wasn't that just the tiniest bit patronising?

Now that we had giant beds to ourselves, and roll-top baths, it was easier to have long, languid sex and deep, cosy conversations. She mostly did the talking when it came to personal issues. I learned to nod my head in a very interested way. (It wasn't that I didn't like to hear her voice or her views, but my god, those conversations could go on.) I also became adept at sidestepping most of her questions. I would usually end all replies with an affirmation of my feelings for her: this would distract her and move the conversation on. I then took the topic on to academic, learned things. I felt quite turned on when I lectured to her about science, finance, history. She lay there naked in foamy water, screwing up her forehead in ponder-pose, and it all felt like an X-rated *Educating Rita*. Fuck me, it was sexy. And I envied her, really – there was still so much she didn't know.

By the time we were stood at Victoria Falls, we had fallen in love and were categorically submerged. She said it there. 'I love you,' she shouted, over the roaring of water. Her eyes blinked, expectantly. I was searching myself for cynicism, for obstacles –

but I felt strangely serene and wide open, like my body was the prairie or the Serengeti plains.

'I love you too,' I shouted.

'What?' she hollered.

'I love you too.'

Her face broke into pieces: a lopsided lip, a fierce blink, a darting eyebrow. Individually, it looked odd and horrific. Together, it was the most beautiful thing I had ever seen.

'Thank God,' she laughed. 'I'm so happy you said that.'

We huddled our bodies together: squelching anorak fabric and waterproof trousers. She pointed, yelping: an elephant tight-roping across the rocky precipice. He made it along, the trunk lifting up to a rainbow, and I watched the light dancing in her eyes. It was a gift from fate.

Well, the world just seemed to fall away there. The luscious, green land had been slashed down the middle. You could see the spray hanging in the air. It felt safe to cry. No-one could know. Our faces were already moist.

There I was, with the waterfall in my eyes and this woman in my arms. Ruminating on 'love' and what it could mean. All I knew was this: when she said it, it just felt natural and effortless to say it right back. 'I love you.' I tried mouthing it to the wind and heard it wailing back to me.

Time moved on, and so did we. My God: the things we saw in Tanzania. Peering up at 6,000 metres of Mount Kilimanjaro, jutting whiteness into picture-postcard blue. In front of us, giraffes, wandering free with bandying legs. An ever-changing terrain – a bit of life here, a bit of life there; then the ground seaweed-green and endlessly desolate.

I once read the human body is mostly just space. You see, the matter in an atom is just a tiny fraction of the whole. If we let out our space, we would sink down to near nothing, just a lump of limp balloon skin.

That frightened me at the time. But now this expanse made me heady with love. I felt like I had all this capacity to absorb her, to stuff myself full of her.

We descended into the Ngorongoro crater, one of the largest calderas in the world. We saw zebras, buffaloes, lions – and so many flamingos that the lake was dyed pink. We sat on the lodge balcony. This green and brown patchwork was just spread out before us. We sat in our robes and we drank ourselves silly; giggling about the big old world and all the creatures inside it. We watched these animals hunt and seek shelter and struggle to survive, through binoculars or phones or the lens of a camera.

The lodge had an internet café, which meant Annabelle could carry on posting her blogs to the world. I didn't know what she wrote, and I didn't really care much, as long as it kept her happy. But she would often drag me to these places (usually involving an hour-long search in a small and grimy town or village). Then soon she would be tapping away, her forehead furrowed, her lips involuntarily smiling. 'There,' she would say. 'I'm so glad I did that. It's good to keep the blogs regular or your audience loses interest.' I was going to ask her who this audience was – and how she had found one – but by then I'd lost heart.

In Tanzania, in the drunken splendour of surveying such ancient survival, she started to talk to me about this blog.

'It's called "A picture is worth a thousand words,"' she said. She would upload a photo or drawing she'd done in her travels, then write 1,000 words about it: her impressions of the place, or how it made her feel.

'So that's why you've been drawing so much?'

'I've always drawn,' she shrugged.

'And people are reading this? This blog?'

'Oh yes,' she said. 'I get over a hundred hits a day.'

'Right,' I said, slowly, thinking of the average circulation of the top newspapers and magazines. 'Well, that's great, sweetie.'

'I wish you would take a look at it sometime.' She stretched herself out and ruffled my hair.

'You know I don't read blogs. I don't even go online much.'

'I know. You're my little throwback, aren't you?' She often called me her 'little throwback'. In fact, she said it so much that it was now legitimately a pet name. I didn't even know at that point why she called me that.

'Why do you even call me that?'

'Because.' She giggled.

'Because what?' I tried to sound light, but I knew there was a brittle annoyance to my tone.

'Well,' she said, rolling her eyes. 'It's not meant to be insulting, Marcus. It's just a sweet little thing. I call you it because you are so sweet and old-fashioned and Luddite, and basically like nothing else in this century.'

'I'm not a Luddite. I used to work in finance, I was surrounded by screens. I have a fucking iPhone, for God's sake.'

'You're still out of time. And please don't get cross.'

'Well, thanks. I guess.'

'Cheer up!' She thwacked me. 'Look at this! Look at everything around us. Do you know how wonderful this is? Huh? How lucky we are?' She still said this over and over, like a mantra – but now she said it with less conviction. 'We can be anything!' She threw her arms up to the sky. Her speech was slurred. 'We're human beings, not human doings.' She must have read this in a book, she looked so pleased when she said it. 'We can live like this, like nomads. We can travel the world!'

I was obviously more sober, as I said: 'With what money, sweetheart?'

'We don't need much money. You don't need much money, Marcus.' Now she sounded irritable. 'You don't need much money just to travel the world, earning money where you can. I could work in a bar, you could work in a bar. Or I could waitress. You could get a temporary job somewhere, working on some business or something. I don't know! But we could do it, couldn't we? We could do anything we wanted. Be anything we wanted to be.'

'You're not even saying it in the present tense.'

'Marcus,' she yelped, her irritation brimming over. 'Are you not getting what I am saying?'

'I'm getting it,' I said – and I was. The world was a giant oyster and we were the pearls inside it.

She leant into my arm. I kissed the top of her head. 'And when we've finished travelling... If we decide to settle somewhere... You can do your drawing or blogging or whatever–'

'Oh yes!' she interrupted. 'I'm already thinking I could get a book deal or something. Maybe. I mean, it's possible, isn't it? I got this brilliant comment the other day–'

'And I could do something in policy. Some really great think tank. Somewhere that wants to make a difference. You know, fuck it, I could even go into politics. Shake the system up a bit, make some real waves. I mean, why don't we think big? You know, I've learned some lessons in Malawi, and from this whole trip, and I'm not about to throw that away. I want to start my life over. I want to quit finance. I want a fresh start.'

'You deserve it, baby.' She looked up and kissed my nose.

'No, I was thinking, I really have to change my life. I liked my job, I mean, I loved it at the time, but it really took it out of me. You know it did, I've told you, I've told you about what went on back there, the things I did, the things I said to people. I've got to take the stress out of things, try to do something more, try to get some meaning from something different. You know, I've been thinking about meditation. Maybe we could go on one of those silent retreats? I mean, have you seen the people who do yoga? It takes years off your face.'

'Oh I know, and those people always live so long. We'll juice every day and we'll learn to do headstands. It'll be really good for us, we can take some time out.'

'And you know what else I've heard about? There's this new thing called "mindlessness". Apparently it's massive in New York at the minute.'

'Yes, I read about that. Isn't the idea that you have to schedule in "unmindful" leisure time – right? So, you watch a dumb action film or throw a ball at a wall, count the ridges on your radiator – whatever. It's all about zoning out and letting your mind be free and easy. It makes so much sense. Because when you need your brain to kick in, it's had time to recharge. I read they even did a survey of some of America's top CEOs and nearly all of them had been practising it. Isn't it something to do with how your brain rests when you switch off? Isn't that right?'

'Yes, I think it's called the default network. It switches on when you're daydreaming. It's like a filing system.'

'So, daydreaming is actually good for you. I mean – wow. And this is science!'

'Incredible, isn't it? Well, I want to do all of that with you, sweetheart. Let's go forth and be mindless.' I pulled her closer, and we stopped talking then, just listened to the clicks and taps and bellows of the African birds around us. Maybe that is what attracted me here: all the paths still untrodden.

By the time we were battling out of Kenya, the tensions had surfaced. The days were mashing up into shapeless weeks. We had thick rings of brown beneath our eyes. All the journeys by car, bus, light aircraft, etc. The hours and hours of just sitting around or being squeezed next to livestock.

And the timekeeping of this godforsaken continent! It no longer seemed quaint. And the smiles on faces no longer looked genuine. There were just too many missed connections. Too many escorts who almost killed us in cars with broken windows and rusted metal. Like I needed another crash in my life. Like I needed that fear.

And, you know what, this trip hasn't even been cheap! I've kept it from Annabelle, but thousands and thousands of pounds have slipped right away. We are clearly stamped with the word 'tourist'. I really do think that hoteliers and servicemen simply hike up their prices and add up lucky stars.

But, anyway: I can't even remember much of this part, to be honest. There was a sulky air-balloon flight over some national park. We pointed out wildlife but that, like everything, lost lustre as it turned too familiar. We also spent a week on a treasure-island-style beach, where we lost ourselves in trashy books and forewent conversation. I wish I could remember more – but at least Annabelle was keeping track.

I'd always known she kept a diary, but I didn't realise it went any further than that. I found out more when we had a terrible falling out at the beach. She got out this sketchpad and dragged the pencil across the paper, her lips all bitten and her eyes all narrowed.

'You look very serious when you draw,' I said. It was the first thing I'd said to her in about a day.

'I take it very seriously,' she replied, not looking up from the paper.

'More seriously than you take me,' I said. She rolled her eyes – she did that a lot. That was one of the trip's discoveries. 'I don't remember you doing it at the base,' I continued. 'In Malawi.'

'That's what I was doing in my diary. I pretended to be writing, but usually I'd draw. It explains all my thoughts much better, I think. I really, really love it. That's why I take it seriously.' Finally, she looked up – met my eyes. 'I did tell you about the blog. And I'm getting these good comments, now. It's what I want to do for a living.' Pause. 'When I grow up.'

I snorted. 'When you're grown up?'

'Yes', she said; hurt. She obviously thought it would sound

cute and coquettish. 'I told you already, but you clearly weren't listening. I'm thinking of turning it into a career. I just really, really love it.'

'I've got a secret for you, Annabelle. There is no "grown up."'

'What do you mean?'

'It never happens.'

'Well, it's what I want to do for a career,' she huffed. 'I've loved drawing ever since I was tiny.'

As if that confirms it is ingrained in your soul! All that does is highlight the one positive experience you had as a kid. Maybe a teacher praised your crayon piece of shit. Maybe it was the only thing your parents ever hung on the wall. And now she will forever pursue this one ideal, this shadowy dream: unaware she is just a stodge of a sponge with the holes stuffed in. Oh, Annabelle. There is never any 'grown up'. There is only make-do, make-believe, make shit up...

The hostilities turned to proper arguments, then: head-swinging, arm-jabbing, fist-thumping arguments. It was sort of exhilarating: like the kind I used to have with Nancy. Annabelle had been so precious in the beginning. It was sort of wonderful and sexy to see her shell grow so mottled and spotted and worn down into fragments.

By Ethiopia, we were argued out. We dragged ourselves around the resting place of Haile Selassie in submissive silence. We pretended to be deep in awe at the cathedral around us – but, to be blunt, it was nothing much to look at. If you've been to Rome – as I have, many times – I reckon you'd leave unimpressed. If you've seen a large church, you've seen them all. Don't you think? Stained glass windows: check. Pews: check. Long aisle: check. I would rather be in Vatican City, looking up at the Basilica. You could get a nice bowl of carbonara afterwards.

Still, we hovered around those massive tombs of Selassie and his wife. We felt compelled to carry on the silence – now a feigned sign of respect. All I could think of was Bob Marley: on his knees to worship the King of Kings. A joint jutting out of his lips, his hair clotted with dreads.

It was then a two-day bus journey to the toy town of Lalibela, where ancient churches had been carved from solid rock. It looked like the earth had exploded and structures now grew organically out of matter, like mushrooms or cankers. Without the weariness of time, seeing sweat poured into decades of toil, it all looked so natural and effortless. Slicing through rock must be as easy as sliding a knife through butter.

It was here, however, that we had the biggest fight of them all. It had been brewing all this time – ever since Tanzania. And there was the ennui factor, too: town after town, tourist sight after tourist sight. I was starting to get bored with it all. I was having visions of London: its grey skies and skyscrapers and wrought-iron bridges.

I think she must have picked up on that, as she suddenly boiled over and accused me of being a philistine, a cultural amoeba (yes, I remember the words, as they seemed to have physical spikes). She questioned our relationship, said it had moved too fast, said I was incapable of love, maybe I was hollow at the centre – just like everyone at the Malawi camp had said to her. Nobody had liked me – nobody at all.

I felt ludicrous. Diminished. Like I was only left with my core and it was now as meagre as a grain of dirt. Hearing her holler these things – accusations I just would not take and could not stand. There was a very odd feeling in my body, and it took me a few hours to find the words in my head. It was this: a feeling that you are unknowable. That no-one will ever truly know you or get you or understand you accurately. It is very sad and thick, like grief.

All I could see that night were barriers; barriers everywhere I looked. Barriers between me, her, Nancy, Mum, Dad, Jackson and everyone. All these walls and divisions. I started to gasp and gulp a little bit, but luckily I did not wake her. Maybe it was a panic attack. Maybe my morbid thoughts had gone too far. At the point of the attack, I was – after all – feeling trapped in some concentration world, all my cells being gassed by the very air that I breathed.

At Addis Ababa airport, we sat and twiddled our thumbs, flicked through magazines, barely looked each other in the eyes. We were waiting for a plane that would not come for seven hours. (We didn't know it at the time.)

The next thing I knew, we were in some bazaar in Egypt, and I bought her a ring on an impulse, while a guy was hassling her about a disgusting carpet. I looked at that ring several times over the next few days, while we were bickering or giving each other the silent treatment or talking about insignificant details, like where to go for kofta.

There was no bit of my brain that could really rationalise this action. We'd spent a long time together and it wasn't working out. It had a been a spur of the moment, whirlwind thing, which had blown up into the sky majestically like a dandelion head, now covering everything in weeds. We weren't compatible. The lust was going. The love smacked of dependency. But I knew I couldn't be alone again. I didn't want to be alone. And if I'm going down, there isn't a sweeter person to drag down with me than Annabelle.

So that brings us back to Pizza Hut by the pyramids: me getting down on one knee, and the sand on the floor, and that smoky smell of roasted dough. It always turns me on now.

We tacked on to a guide, and Annabelle was holding my hand and staring up dreamily and I felt the glow of her love surge. I'm not sure what she was even thinking. I've no doubt she was transmuting me into something I wasn't, but I was more than happy to let her do that. Like I said, I've got no problem with lying if it gets you results. I don't tell the truth, but I tell my truth.

I remember very little from the tour except thinking that the pyramids – like so much I had seen – were a bit of an anti-climax. Sure, I was as trigger happy as anyone, and I'm pretty chuffed to have those photos now. But just because something has antiquity doesn't mean we should automatically revere it. Maybe I need to renew my poetic license – but there always seems to be too much paperwork.

I don't remember what the guide even said. I was too busy feeling claustrophobic and bored and strung down. Inside the pyramids were these cramped partitions with the same-old stone: bleached out and sandy. We saw Tutankhamen's tomb and some Egyptian stuff (can't remember what exactly). We weren't allowed to take photos for that bit, so I couldn't even tinker with the camera settings as distraction. I was dripping with sweat, and I watched that instead: drops of me splashing on to artefacts all these thousands of years old.

Later that night, Annabelle spoke to me all super-enthusiastic about the 'creation myth' that the guide had told us. My ears perked up at that: I always like a chance to laugh at people's ideas about God and the way that everything is. It's like hearing a child say the moon is made of cheese.

Anyway, Annabelle's eyes were glistening in the candlelight and her hands were swishing around and her voice tripped over itself as it pulled in different chatty directions.

It turns out that Ancient Egyptians were just as retarded as I reckoned.

'In the beginning of time,' began Annabelle. Here we go, I thought – here's the first contradiction. How can time just begin? Time, by definition, is circular, infinite. Otherwise, what was the time before time?

'Here's the first contradiction,' I answered – and I told her exactly what I just told you.

She rolled those limpid eyes of hers and shook her head. 'Just listen, will you? It's poetic.'

I told her the line about needing to renew my poetic license. She wasn't impressed.

She carried on instead. She told me how there was this complete and total darkness and swirling chaos. Everything amorphous and indeterminate. And that this was called Nu.

I shrugged. 'Good a name as any.'

'Shut up. Listen to me. I'm trying to tell you about this. It's really, really beautiful. Anyway – you were there. Weren't you listening?'

'There was a lot to take in,' I lied.

She nodded.

'Anyway, out of this nothingness came somethingness. Everythingness. There was light – the sun! The creator of everything.'

'This is very Earth-centric,' I countered. 'Obviously now we know that there isn't just one sun. There isn't just one galaxy. There is nothing unique about us at all.'

'Oh, apart from the fact that we're the only planet with life on.'

'That's debatable.'

'Why?'

'The odds are overwhelming. It's hugely likely that there is life elsewhere in the universe but for some reason we can't communicate with them. Perhaps we're not at the same stage of technological advancement. Perhaps there are time loops and worm holes involved. Perhaps they are not intelligent and sentient in a life form we would even recognise – even if they were standing right in front of us now.'

'But you said maybe you didn't believe in God anymore. And plenty of people say that the odds are overwhelming that there must a god – an originator – a creator, whatever. Everything just doesn't make sense otherwise.'

'I thought you didn't believe in God yourself! And there's absolutely no proof of that, anyway.'

'There is absolutely no proof of aliens.'

'Plenty of people say they've seen UFOs,' I said – and then instantly regretted going down that argumentative route.

'Plenty of people have seen Jesus Christ in toast.'

'Can we go back to the creation myth, please?' I said. 'It was interesting.' She didn't even notice the little smirk on the right-hand-side of my upper lip.

So they thought this sun was a god. He was given lots of different names, but the one that seemed to stick was Ra – as that was his name when the midday sun was giddy with power. When the sun set, it was more like an old man, and it was given a different name entirely. Annabelle couldn't remember that one. She was annoyed with herself for that.

'It was hot,' I said, trying to maker her feel better. 'And the acoustics were terrible.'

'Oh!' said Annabelle, remembering something. 'I keep saying "he", but apparently that's wrong. This sun god wasn't female or male. They weren't as sexist as all the other religions. This god was just an all-seeing power, a presence that was everything. Represented by this giant eye that was aware of everything. If you can picture that.'

'Omnipotent. Omniscient. Omnipresent.'

'Yes, Marcus,' she sighed. 'I know those big words too.'

But I bet she didn't.

And I thought the story was coming to an end – but it wasn't.

Apparently, having all the power and knowledge and mastery of the world isn't enough. You need companionship. You get lonely. But instead of logging on to a dating site or accepting a few more party invites, the sun god 'did the business' with his own shadow and had a son and daughter.

'A bit egocentric,' I commented. At least that was one depth I hadn't tried to sink to yet.

'And he gave birth to them in a funny way,' she said, screwing up the table napkin in her hand and looking agitated. 'Oh dammit. What was it? So – he spat out his son and he was the god of air. And – I think he just vomited her. His daughter. Yes, I think he vomited her and she was the god of water. Rain, I mean.'

'And did he shit out a third child – the god of earth?'

'Marcus.'

'Sorry.'

And she continued. Telling me how the son and daughter were straight away put to good use and told to do the chores. They had to put the chaos into order and pull out strands of light from the darkness. But somehow – maybe they were too young for the task, poor tikes – they got lost in Nu and all his mess.

The eye of the sun searched endlessly for the children, peering into all the corners of the universe, but seeing only entanglement and formlessness. Until eventually it found the children and returned them to the sun god.

He wept with joy and the tears tumbled to earth like little seeds – sowing human beings wherever they fell.

And there was more to that story (I think they had to make more gods – gods of this, gods of that) – but she decided to stop there.

'Isn't it lovely?' she purred.

'It's horrible. We're made out of tears.'

'Tears of joy,' she said. '*Joy*, Marcus. We are happiness turned solid.'

'You don't really believe that?'

'No,' she groaned. 'But it's fun to believe. Isn't it? Can't you just let your imagination drift a bit?'

'I'm sorry,' I said – remembering our engagement. 'And of course I can, I'm all for a good yarn. I just don't see what's so great about being made out of tears, that's all.' And then it struck me. 'No,' I said, reaching out for her hand and caressing her ring finger. 'You're right. You're totally right. It's perfect. It's beautiful.' And it was: it made perfect sense.

I leant over to kiss her. Even the lewd, sexual catcalls of a passerby couldn't put a dent in my enthusiasm.

So we left Egypt sky-high, with the clouds in our hair: taking off over the rocky sands of Libya, looking down at a Tunisian runway. While we were up in the air, shaking with turbulence, our conversation turned to marriage. And children. And the long inevitability that stretched before us.

'You do want children, don't you?' asked Annabelle. 'We should have discussed this sooner. Oh God. You do, don't you?'

I saw she looked worried – so I reached for her hand. 'Don't worry. I want children.'

'Really?'

'Really.'

She giggled. 'How many?'

'What?'

'How many?'

'Well, I don't know. Just a normal amount. I guess.'

'What's a normal amount?'

I shrugged. 'Two?'

'Two! Oh God. Jesus.'

'Why are you doing that?'

'What?'

'That groaning sound.'

'It's just it's – ugh.' She shuddered with revulsion. Like she was having to eat shit. 'It's just such a cliché. I'm sorry. But it is. Two children. A boy and a girl. La di da, la di da.'

'Well, how many do you want?'

She smiled in a daydreamy fashion. 'Me?'

'Yes.' It was obvious that she had actually wanted to answer her own question all along. 'Well, as many as possible, I guess.'

'Yes, but how many is that?'

She giggled again. 'Six?' She said it slowly: long and drawn out, with a mischievous giggle on her lips.

'Six?'

'It's a good number. I want six.'

'Fuck. We'd better hurry up then.'

She laughed like I was hilarious. I wasn't even joking.

'Annabelle...' I began – but it faded out.

'What?'

'Forget it.'

'No, what were you going to say?'

'Just – can we afford that many? Kids are pretty expensive. So I hear. And last time I heard, philanthropy didn't pay so good.'

Her lip jutted out. 'We'd manage. People manage.'

'People manage on two. People that have to "manage" don't tend to have six.'

'OK, you're right. I guess you're right.' She turned her shoulder to block me and stare miserably out of the window. It was obvious she was sulking and I cannot bear sulking. I reached over.

'Whatever you want, sweetheart. We'll have six. We'll manage.'

'No, you're right,' she said, with the sound of tears in her throat. 'We probably can't afford to have children at all. God knows how long it's going to take me to get my drawing thing up and running.'

I was glad she couldn't see my face. I was struggling to mask the incredulity. If that was her best career move, we were well and truly fucked.

'Maybe I could go back to my job,' I said – before I even knew what I was doing.

'What?' She shifted back round. 'But you hated that job. You said it was evil.'

'Evil's a strong word. Much too strong.'

'You said it made you a bad person.'

'I'd know what to look out for this time.'

'You said you hated it.'

'I didn't hate it.' I didn't tell her that I was missing it. That this – a lifetime of backpacking and sweet-talking – would send me straight on the next plane to Dignitas.

'But what about the recession?'

'These things come and go. It's going to recover.' And then get worse again, and then recover. Just a see-saw ride for suckers and succubi.

'You would do that? For me?'

'For us. For our kids.'

'Oh Marcus, that's so sweet.' She leant forward and our tongues mushed together a bit. I was thinking about taking my old job back. It felt right and good, like a made-for-measure suit. Of course, I'd be going back with a new perspective though, a different cloth.

She pulled away first, like she could hear my thoughts. 'I don't know if it's right, though. It doesn't sound very ethical.'

'I'd be careful this time. I'd go in with my eyes wide open.'

'Well, I suppose you wouldn't have to do it forever. Just until my drawing took off.'

'Precisely,' I said – pretending the laughter was for joy.

'We'd just do it for the money. Save some up and then you can walk right out of there. We'd be using them, if you think about it. I mean: it'd be like a gigantic "fuck you" to the entire industry.'

'I couldn't put it better.'

'Nobody could actually blame us for doing it. Not if we were doing it for our children.'

'We want our children to have a good education. To be healthy and bright and happy. Sometimes you gotta do what you gotta do.'

'And we can donate most of the money to charity, can't we?' she persisted. She was looking up into my face with an earnest expression, but I could see the truth in her eyes.

'Of course,' I lied back. It was fun playing this game with her. She was as good at it as me. It brought us even closer.

'We don't need a big house. We'll just get somewhere small but make sure the children are all right.'

'Of course.'

'We don't need very much.'

'No.'

'You'll just take the money and then – walk away.'

'Yes. Exactly.'

We told ourselves these things, over and over. It was a more a case of stabbing them in, rather than letting them sink in.

#

We landed to brilliant sunshine. Although the country is Muslim, the capital was studded with fairy lights, fake mistletoe and snow. It was Christmas time in Tunisia.

We headed east, to the tourist resort of Port el Kantaoui. Everything was white and glistening, from the sand to the yachts to the low-rise hotel complex. The first thing we did was order a cocktail and lie under the parasols, staring to the edge of the sea. Our inactivity felt luxurious and sensual. We let the sun warm our skin while we twiddled the drink umbrellas and the waves were whooshing us into womb-like sleep.

The plan was to stay a couple of weeks – see in Christmas, New Year, then travel to Morocco for a final fortnight. But one day we heard the hotelier shout something to a waiter, and the building buzzed with commotion and the switch-ons of radios.

It was mid-December and a man called Mohamed Bouazizi had set fire to himself somewhere called Sidi Bouzid.

We didn't do this very often (we liked to keep ourselves to ourselves), but we leant over to ask a couple beside us if they knew what was happening – and why everyone looked frantic.

The guy was foreignish. He turned out to be half-Tunisian, so he understood Arabic. His eyes were dark and sort of twitchy, which made us feel panicked. But he didn't tell us anything that we didn't already know. This guy in his twenties had set himself on fire. He was a fruit vendor. It was in Sidi Bouzid. Other than that, the information was thin on the ground, but people were still rushing around and looking alarmed and raising their voices – and Annabelle looked pale and anxious and I wanted to settle her.

I sat her by the bar with a large gin and tonic, then made my way to the hotel computer before any queues could form. I clicked to the BBC, but in typical form, they were vague and understated. Everything was a 'report' or 'alleged'. I logged out and joined Annabelle, feeling a little unnerved and put out. This was meant to be the most relaxing bit of the holiday – the bit before life had to go back to normal. And we couldn't even get served another drink. All the staff had gone from their stations. Some were gathered in corners, making loud, urgent whispers. They were oblivious to any finger clicks or shouts of 'Excuse me'. Our moods were deflating and I was extremely pissed off.

We returned to our bedroom and made nervy, rabbit-like love: the sort of sex with quick, repetitive thrusts and half your clothes still on. Then Annabelle read for a bit on the balcony and I flicked through music channels. We had our showers, got dressed – it was time for dinner.

We bumped into the couple from earlier in the foyer and I pushed him for more information. Yes, he said. The man had set himself on fire as a protest.

'Against what?'

'Oh, you know what youth are like. The injustices of the world.' He laughed crookedly and with his eyes like slits. 'Nothing to worry about. Just a few rumbles in his hometown, that's all. Have a lovely dinner.'

'Yes, where do you recommend?' I asked. 'We've been eating here most nights but we'd like to try somewhere new. The staff were terrible today.'

'Yes, they were. I agree. They should have been more professional. Well, there's a lovely restaurant by the harbour.'

'Oh yes, we know the one. Has it got the red tablecloths?'

'Yes, that's it. We ate there last night and the seafood was lovely.'

'Thank you very much. We'll definitely head over there. Good night.'

'Good night,' he said – his chic lady stayed talkless but her eyes flashed in parting.

I turned to Annabelle with a smile, but her arms were folded. 'I'm not hungry anymore,' she blurted.

'What?'

'How on earth can you eat after hearing that?'

'What?'

'Is that all you can say?'

'I don't get it. What's the problem?'

'Why would a man just set himself on fire? There must be more to the story.'

I was thinking of scallops and squid. My stomach was rumbling. 'Well, what would you like me to do about it?'

'There's the manager over there. Please just ask him for a bit more info. For me. Please.'

For dinner, I would do anything. I hurried over and asked him for any further updates on this shocking situation. I knew the adjective would please my Annabelle.

'It's nothing for our guests to worry about,' he smiled – with the same look as the last guy.

'Yes, but why did he set himself on fire?' Annabelle was paler than ever.

'I really can't say.' He shrugged. 'He was young and passionate. Who knows?' And he left abruptly.

'Something's not right,' said Annabelle. She marched over to the computer.

'I checked that earlier.'

'Well, I want to check again.'

Finally, the BBC had updated its webpage, and we read it together, in silence.

An impoverished fruit vendor, blah blah blah. He may or may not have been slapped in the face by a female police officer. They took away some of his fruit. He poured oil over himself and burned himself into a coma. He was now being called some kind of martyr in his hometown. I didn't get it at all.

'Ten dollars a day,' gasped Annabelle. 'That's how much he was earning.'

'That's going to be a lot where he lives. Remember it's all relative.'

'Thirty per cent,' she said after another minute. 'That's what the unemployment rate is here.'

'You'd think they'd find better staff, then.'

Another minute. 'Twenty-three years in power.'

'What?' I had long since grown bored and was staring out of the window, watching the sun sink into slumber. The juice of prawns on my tongue.

'How long the President's been in power. It's a dictatorship.'

'Sweetheart, this trip hasn't exactly been a democratic tour of the world. Have you only just realised?'

'I guess I wasn't thinking about it.' Tears sprung out of her eyeballs. 'It's terrible.' She turned to me, her face all wide and open and popping out of its apertures. 'This man has had to work since he was ten. He was having to bribe the police. Every day. More than he could earn in a day. It says so, right here. It says he just wanted to make a living. He was just trying to push a cart of fruit around. And they just kept demanding and demanding these bribes. It sounds like everything here is just so corrupt and horrible. The poor guy. I feel sick. And we're here on holiday, giving our money to a dictatorship?'

'Annabelle. The guy didn't have a permit. He should have had a permit. Shit happens like that.'

'It doesn't sound like you do need a permit. Not for a fruit cart. I'm sure that's what it said...'

'Well, we're not Tunisian legal experts, are we? We don't know the ins and outs of any of this. The facts are extremely confusing. And does it even matter to us? We don't live here. Come on, let's forget about it; let's go out, get some food...'

'Marcus. He stood in the middle of the traffic. Read this. Read it again. He shouted "How do you expect me to make a living?" Look. Read it. It says that he lit the match and his skin just melted right off his body.'

'It doesn't say that exactly, you're–'

'Marcus, his skin slithered off the bones. Can you imagine that? Can you imagine being so desperate that you would do something like that?'

'So you want to catch a bus, right? And go to this place and run out on the streets and join in the protests against all the unfairness and corruption and how terrible it all is? If you want to do that, we can do that. Just tell me and I'll pack the bags.'

She drew in a large gulp of breath. There was a long agonising pause when I thought my own bluff had been called. 'Don't be dramatic,' she said, finally. 'I'm only saying it's terrible. Isn't it?'

'Of course, it's terrible. It's bad, it's really bad. But we don't know the full story. And we have nothing to do with it, anyway. This isn't our country. Thank God. You wouldn't see people acting like animals on the streets back home. So let's not pay people like that any attention just because we're here.'

'Maybe you're right. I don't know.'

'Look, things will blow over. The riots will stop and life will go back to normal, like it always does. It doesn't mean anything.'

'Well, I hope so. It's a bit scary, thinking about it. All those people protesting.'

'And it's quite far away from us, sweetheart. There aren't any riots going on here, that's for sure. We're in paradise.'

'Yes. I know.'

'So can we go get some dinner in paradise, please?'

'OK. God, I'm starving.'

'Thank you! Me too.' And I dragged her by the hand and started to ramble about the wedding. I knew that would distract her – and it did. It kept her busy and whimsical for several more days. Even through the time that the TV was on, and that man, Mohammed, was served up on a hospital bed, rolled up in white sheets like one of the mummies in Cairo. Someone had placed a pretty patchwork quilt on his legs – like he might catch a chill. The only bit of him you could see were these two scorched-out lips.

'I want to go home now,' said Annabelle, as we sipped nightcaps one night.

'And miss Morocco?' I asked.

'Yes. What do you think?'

I thought of the pylons, the circuits, the networks, the motorways. 'Yes. I guess I'd like that too.'

'It just feels right, now. Don't you think?'

I smiled. I'd been drip-feeding her this suggestion ever since that guy burned out. I was tired of this lifestyle. The thought of returning to my old job had fired me up and everything else was just dull and clockwork.

Life is an orchestra and something conducts. But it is me who is playing. It is me holding the instrument with the power to play. I had seen the footage of protests spreading across Tunisia like rust or disease. I didn't want to be on this soil anymore. I was disappointed with this country, this continent. I had expected better. I had expected epiphany, and I'd had an epiphany, and it wasn't even all that.

You see: we might not grow all our own food, but back home we have supermarkets. Everywhere, anywhere. Giant warehouses packed with groceries at specific temperatures, like bodies in a morgue, but none of that matters because it is food, it is food, and none of us go hollow or have rickets. Look at the lattice of lorries, the crates full of produce, and this network of circuitry that pings and beeps and bleeps and dings. Chickens plucked bare under bright ribbons of light, with wax-sheen skin pumped with water and E numbers, genes tangled up into stodge. Bees fall to the ground. Prescription after prescription, pews of antibiotics, painkillers, statins and tranquilisers, disinfectant, shower wash, floss. The grids and the skids that keep everything moving, the flow charts still flowing, all of this turned up to the maximum, the light switch, plug socket, the reverberation of boilers. A flicker of neon, the hands held at the cinema, the laughter of restaurants, a wine glass knocked to the floor. I'll take all of it, all of it.

'I'd like to go home. Everything here just seems primitive and depraved.'

'Oh, don't start that again.'

'It's true.'

'Well, what about the children? They're innocent, aren't they?'

'They'll grow up the same way. I mean, you'd think they'd look around them, wouldn't you? Spain isn't that far away. We're right near mainland Europe. You'd think they'd look up there and see something to emulate, something civilised. Instead of all these protests and wars and failed progress. Why can't they just get their act together? We did. Europe pulled itself from the mire, didn't it?

'I mean, there is so much misdirected anger in the world. We're always fighting the authority figures and not the scum: the beggars, the drifters, the scroungers. You've got to have something at the top, holding everything together. And we can only make things better if we cut out the waste. But I guess it's the human condition. Humanity doesn't exist anymore: only humans.' I liked to end these speeches on a high note, even if I didn't exactly know what I was saying.

'I don't know anymore,' she sighed. 'I'm tired.'

'This place has worn you out.'

'I'm just tired of always being dragged back to such a dark place. Can't I just be happy about our wedding? And our children? And all the potential still in me? All the things left to do? Without feeling guilty all the time?'

'Of course you can. Of course.' Then our faces melted together and there was a momentousness to the moment: special, romantic, significant.

After all, we fit together comfortably. There have been no more arguments and I don't think there will be more to come. We have played out our game of chess – and I won.

And now we are sitting here in the airport, waiting for a flight to take us home. There are so many unironed, crumpled details. Like – what happened to Stephanie and Kondwani? And will the children in that Malawi school live long enough to become proper characters? And why was Philippa such a closed book? (Plot shock: her husband died on their honeymoon, but I couldn't be arsed with the details.)

I do wonder about these things, but then I forget them; they seem inscrutably small and unrelated to my life. My story.

Question: But where will Annabelle stay?

Answer: We will stay at a hotel for a day or two, as my house is still being rented, worse luck. Then we'll head over to her parents in Sussex while we sort ourselves out. She hasn't told them the news yet – about us getting married. She hasn't told anyone. Which makes me worry that it isn't real. Everything else feels fake and fanciful: I just want this one little thing to be real.

Question: Are you really going back to that job? The one that made you go all English Psychopath?

Answer: Of course; if they'll have me. But if it's not there, it will be somewhere else. Don't worry: I am returning with a renewed sense of purpose, a better sense of wonder. I feel like a new man. I can see the bigger picture. Which leads me to the next–

Question: Why did you come out here, anyway?

Answer: Well, I don't know, precisely. To try and conquer death? To try to be a good person? I think I've become one. (I love someone again, don't I?) I don't know what you think, and I don't really care. How am I so different to you, anyway? Your thoughts are as murderous; your deeds just as loaded. The only difference is you don't have the guts to write them all down, but I know that they're there, in your head. You live out your life, try to get through the day with the least bother possible. We're just the same, really.

Still, that's enough enquiring, for now. It's my turn for questions. What if I told you something shocking – like I murdered Nancy? Like – I put a nail in her tyre? You know that convention, the unreliable narrator. Everyone does. So do you believe me or not? Why do you hang on my words? Why do you look through my eyes?

We're all wired for belief. That's what Annabelle told me. But that's not the same thing as being wired for truth. That's what I said. We want a truth, but not necessarily a truthful one. I think that's what they call a paradox. But she just rolled her eyes.

It's been a funny old journey – and it all started with Nancy dead. But it could have started with me being fat. Or having a mother with depression. Or her talking shit to me as I wafted in the womb. It could have begun in a million different places, don't you think? But I began it with Nancy. And I still think that's right.

It's true that I lost myself for a while, around the time I came to Africa. I saw everything as if I were someone else, someone new. But I don't really like that person: he is weak and insufferable and that attitude doesn't benefit anyone. Plus, life isn't much fun when it's just him around.

So now's as good a point as any to end it, I think. With Annabelle's hand in mine, and her turning the magazine page, and the hum of conversations and air-conditioning units, and the shopping and eating and gentle wasting of time.

I'm going to forget Nancy. I'll forget Mum and Dad and the brother who got away. There'll be no more Malawi or bleeding my heart. I'm going to let go of blame. We just want to get married, have a really big family: at least six kids and very probably seven. I want a happy ending. I deserve a happy ending. I was born into that genre and I want all the conventions. Let's make this a comedy, not a tragedy. Come on – you're the same.

So, you see, that's why we're waiting for a plane, right now. We've got a chance to be ourselves and live for ourselves. We have good fortune and why should you begrudge that? And isn't this what we all do? Don't you think we're justified to do it? Pull the wool over your eyes and ignore the occasional itch. Everyone's a sheep. You live with things too, every day of your life. You pass the homeless person with your eyes on the ground, you switch over the TV when the sad news comes on. We all do what we can to get through it. That's OK.

Another Justified Sinner

And now the number for our boarding area is flashing up on the screen and Annabelle is squeaking and trying to gather our stuff, I'm patting my jacket for the feel of the passport and Annabelle is dragging the suitcase over a dropped magazine and I'm sucking a mint and tapping my jacket again, just to check the passport is still there, and it always is, but I always keep checking, and her hand's squeezing mine and I feel the heat spill from her palms and I'm walking slightly in front, moving us down the long corridor, where we will board the next chapter, and it's already written, it was written for people like us from the very first line.

About Dead Ink...

Dead Ink is a small, ambitious and experimental literary publisher based in Liverpool.

Supported by Arts Council England, we're focussed on developing the careers of new and emerging authors.

We believe that there are brilliant authors out there who may not yet be known or commercially viable. We see it as Dead Ink's job to bring the most challenging and experimental new writing out from the underground and present it to our audience in the most beautiful way possible.

Our readers form an integral part of our team. You don't simply buy a Dead Ink book, you invest in the authors and the books you love..

Publishing the Underground

Publishing the Underground is Dead Ink's project to develop the careers of new and emerging authors. Supported by Arts Council England, we use our own crowdfunding platform to ask readers to act as patrons and fund the first run print costs.

If you'd like to support new writing then visit our website and join our mailing list. This book was made possible by kind contributions from the following people...

Mediah Ahmed
Jane Alexander
Geoffrey Allen
Lulu Allison
Rj Barker
Alex Blott
Naomi Booth
Sarah Bradley
Julia Brich
Edward Burness
Ailsa Caine
Daniel Carpenter
Maria Carvalho
Sarah Cleave
Sarah Clough
Tracey Connolly
Nyle Connolly
Catriona Cox
Stuart Crewes
Steve Dearden
Vanessa Dodd

Jack Ecans
Su Edwards
Laura Elliott
Lee Farley
Naomi Frisby
Peter Gallon
Heidi Gardner
Sarah Garnham
Martin Geraghty
Tim Gomersall
Vince Haig
Graeme Hall
Paul Hancock
Harriet Hirshman
Darren Hopes
James Hopesmith
James Howard
Laura Hughes
Rob Jessup
Laura Jones
Alexa Kellow

Haroun Khan
Lewis King
Cassie Lawrence
Simon Lee
Duncan Lewis
Margaret McCormack
Heather McDaid
Chloe McLeod
Kiran Millwood Hargrave
Claire Moruzzi
Chris Naylor
Lydia Patterson
Emily Pearce
Ruth Pooley Ford
James Powell
Hannah Powley
Sarah Pybus
Mal Ramsay
Liam Riley
Matthew Shenton
Tamar Shlaim
Alex Shough
Yvonne Singh
Nicky Smalley
Vicky Smith
Julie Swain
Catherine Syson
Mia Tagg
Michael Thomson
Emma Tomlinson
Anna Tyler
Sally Vince
Cate Walker

Emily Whitaker
Sara White
Eley Williams
James Yeoman

Also from Dead Ink...

Every Fox is a Rabid Fox
Harry Gallon

'Every Fox is a Rabid Fox is a harrowing and brutal read. But I fell for its incredibly tender heart. I loved this book.'
- Claire Fuller, author of Swimming Lessons and Our Endless Numbered Days

'Beautifully executed tale of innocence, tragedy, and the family traumas we all carry with us and many times fail to leave behind.'
- Fernando Sdrigotti, author of Dysfunctional Males

Robert didn't mean to kill his brother. Now he's stuck between grief and guilt with only ex-girlfriend Willow and the ghost of his dead twin sister for company. Terrified of doing more harm, Robert's hysteria and anxiety grow while Willow and his sister's ghost fight over him: one trying to save him, the other digging his grave.

Every Fox Is A Rabid Fox is a brutal yet tender tale of family tragedy, mental illness and a young man searching for escape from his unravelling mind.

Guest
SJ Bradley

Samhain is a young, angry and bewildered squatter living in an abandoned hotel in the North of England. One day he receives a message: His father – a man he never knew – was an undercover policeman infiltrating the Green movement of the 80s. What's more, he finds out that he too is now a father.

As Sam leaves for Europe, he pursues freedom and flees from his responsibilities. Responsibility, however, is hard to escape. Guest is a story of disillusionment, protest and, eventually, redemption.

SJ Bradley is a writer from Leeds and one of the organisers behind Fictions of Every Kind. She won the Willesden Herald Short Story Prize and was shortlisted for the Gladstone Writers in Residency Award. Her debut novel, Brick Mother, was published by Dead Ink in 2014.

Sophie Hopesmith

Sophie Hopesmith is a 2012 Atty Awards finalist and her background is in feature writing. Born and bred in London, she works for a reading charity. She likes comedy, poetry, writing music, and Oxford commas. All of her favourite films were made in the 70s.